Christian White is an Australian author and screenwriter whose credits include feature film *Relic*, Netflix series *Clickbait* and numerous other projects in the pipeline. His debut novel, *The Nowhere Child* (2018), was one of Australia's bestselling debut novels ever, with rights sold in 17 international territories and a major screen deal. Christian's second book, *The Wife and the Widow* (2019), and third, *Wild Place* (2021), were instant bestsellers. *The Ledge* is his fourth novel.

PRAISE FOR CHRISTIAN WHITE'S
THE NOWHERE CHILD

'[White] is a born storyteller, one who seems to instinctively understand the weave of a proper yarn, and *The Nowhere Child* is tight, gripping and impressive in all the right places.'
The Saturday Paper

'Hugely entertaining … a multifaceted, unsettling debut.'
The Age

'*The Nowhere Child* has everything that comprises an excellent crime novel. It's taut, raw, emotional, intriguing. The tension becomes unbearable, the story gets creepier as it goes on and the puzzle keeps you reading beyond midnight. Possibilities lurk at the edge of the plot like shadows. Christian White – take a bow.'
Better Reading

'[White's] control of the structure of the novel is impressive throughout … He should be emboldened to undertake that notoriously hard task: the second novel.'
The Australian

'*The Nowhere Child* is a page-turning labyrinth of twists and turns that moves seamlessly between the past and the present, revealing the story in parts and successfully keeping the reader guessing until the final unexpected reveal … It's an exhilarating ride and a thrilling debut.'
Books+Publishing magazine

'An exciting new voice in crime fiction.'
Sunday Life

'*The Nowhere Child* is the personification of a high-concept thriller, brilliantly executed. Author White raises the bar on psychological suspense, telling Kim Leamy's tale in a stylish voice and with a heart-pounding pace. Read page one, and you won't stop. Guaranteed.'
Jeffery Deaver

'*The Nowhere Child* is pure dynamite ... You do not want to miss this book!'
Linda Castillo

'White skilfully builds an uncertain, noxious world of dysfunctional families and small-town secrets – *The Nowhere Child* is a gripping debut from an exceptional new talent.'
Mark Brandi

'How do any of us know that we are who we are told we are? This gripping read takes you to the very edge of reality.'
Jane Caro

PRAISE FOR CHRISTIAN WHITE'S
THE WIFE AND THE WIDOW

'White is a master of the art of misdirection ... he writes like a dream. *The Wife and the Widow* is one of the most original crime novels of the year and White is clearly a rising international star. Prepare to be dazzled.'
The Age

'[White] is the king of the twist, he's becoming famous for it. I loved it even more than *The Nowhere Child*.'
Angela Bishop, *Studio 10*

'Jaw-dropping ... one of the best twists I've ever read.'
Michael Rowland, *ABC News Breakfast*

'This is a flat-out excellent second book, riveting from the start, twisted and clever.'
Readings

'A meditation on grief and trauma as much as it is a gripping novel, *The Wife and the Widow* is to be especially recommended for its inventiveness and risk-taking in terms of plot. It is a risk that handsomely pays off for the attentive reader.'
Australian Book Review

'A gut-punch twist no one will see coming, a plot that hooks from the very first page, and a conclusion that will leave readers breathless. *The Wife and the Widow* cannot be missed.'
JP Pomare

'I read it in one sitting and didn't get much sleep. So be warned. This book will keep you up until the very last page. And it was worth it. Thrilling, brilliant storytelling, unputdownable ... Christian White has another hit on his hands.'
Better Reading

'Dark, atmospheric, and full of twists and turns. 4 stars.'
Who magazine

'*The Wife and the Widow* establishes [White] as one of our best new talents … his trademark style and energy will be enough to keep readers up all night. 4 ½ stars.'
The Big Issue

'An exciting page-turning thriller with mechanisms that are all but invisible, and pace that is perfectly calibrated.'
The Australian

PRAISE FOR CHRISTIAN WHITE'S
WILD PLACE

'With the release of *Wild Place*, White has hit his stride, taking his place as one of this country's most accomplished thriller writers.'
Better Reading

'He's owning the thriller genre right now … This is neatly, cleverly addictive writing … a cracking story that explores masculinity and grief and the affects of suburban claustrophobia.'
The Weekend Australian

'A compelling and suspenseful story that looks at the manifestation of hysteria in response to fearing what we don't understand.'
Good Reading

'Aside from being a fast-paced and engagingly written story, *Wild Place*'s strength lies with White's reflections on masculinity and violence.'
The Guardian

CHRISTIAN WHITE
THE LEDGE

First published by Affirm Press in 2024
Bunurong/Boon Wurrung Country
28 Thistlethwaite Street
South Melbourne VIC 3205
affirmpress.com.au

Affirm Press is located on the unceded land of the Bunurong/Boon Wurrung peoples of the Kulin Nation. Affirm Press pays respect to their Elders past and present.

10 9 8 7 6 5 4 3 2

Text copyright © Christian White, 2024
All rights reserved. No part of this publication may be reproduced without prior written permission from the publisher.

 A catalogue record for this book is available from the National Library of Australia

ISBN: 9781923022829 (paperback)

Cover design by Christa Moffitt/ Christabella Designs © Affirm Press
Typeset in Bembo and InterFace by J&M Typesetting
Printed and bound in China by C&C Offset Printing Co. Ltd.

For Zaleese

1

NOW

The headline – *HUMAN REMAINS FOUND IN WEST HAVEN* – grabbed me by the throat and squeezed.

There was a big colour photo underneath: uniformed police and forensics people in white jumpsuits picking through damp green bushland. A landscape of blue gums, winter sunlight spilling in through the canopy of branches overhead, casting long shadows over the investigators.

I felt sick.

The accompanying article explained that a team of surveyors had been updating boundary lines at the edge of the West Haven State Forest. A member of the group – I pictured a hefty man in a high-vis vest with stony, unmoving eyes, although there was nothing in the copy to suggest this – stumbled on the body while taking measurements. The corpse was severely decomposed so estimating a time of death was difficult, but the police were speculating it had likely been out there for years, probably decades.

A fresh wave of nausea hit. I thought I might throw up, but feared that if I ran for the toilet, my legs would give out beneath me and I'd crumple to the floor of my study like a popped balloon. Instead, I put my head between my legs and took long, deep breaths, a passenger in the brace position as their plane crashed into a mountain.

Because when I was sixteen, my best friend went missing.

After a while – it might have been thirty minutes, but it was probably closer to three – I got my nerves under control and put my computer to sleep. I listened to the drone of the TV in the next room. Steffi – my six-year-old – was re-watching *Dragon Riders* for the fiftieth time. I didn't want her to come in and find me wrecked and shivering like this, so I forced myself up, then slipped quietly out of my study and across the apartment.

The stealth was unnecessary. Steffi was kneeling inches from the television, totally engrossed, hands folded as if in prayer, a true believer listening to a sermon. I could have led a marching band through the living room and she wouldn't have noticed.

Our apartment was a two-bedroom in Elwood, a slightly posh suburb of Melbourne. The interior was open plan: tidy kitchen and simple living space. The place was small – we nearly murdered each other during the pandemic – but we were just two streets back from the beach, so you could smell the sea when the windows were open.

I stepped onto the balcony and closed the sliding door behind me. It was an icy, storm-lit Friday afternoon. The cool blast of wind reset my nervous system. Huddled against the wind in just a T-shirt and jeans, I found Chris Chen's number in my phone.

He answered on the first ring, as if he'd been waiting for me to call.

'Have you heard?' I asked.

'Yesterday,' he said. There was a strained, resigned tone to his voice. 'I was working up the nerve to call you. It feels like a punch in the nuts, doesn't it?'

Chen and I didn't talk much anymore. He'd call every few months, usually late at night after a few drinks, feeling nostalgic. Sometimes I'd answer, but mostly I let it go to voicemail. Not because I didn't like the guy – Chen and I were like brothers back in the nineties – but because sometimes it hurt to remember.

'Do you think it's him?' I asked.

'If not him, who else?'

'A hiker,' I said. 'Some poor idiot who went out into the forest underprepared and got turned around. You remember what those tracks were like.'

The West Haven State Forest was a vast stretch of wilderness packed with red stringybark and peppermint gums. There were high rocky ledges and deep valleys that turned every shade of green, depending on the season. The whole place was foaming with wildlife. We spent much of our childhood exploring it, memorising the trails that zigzagged through the woods like a maze. After staying up late to watch repeats of *Tour of Duty*, we'd pretend to be soldiers fighting in the hot jungles of Vietnam. Then, when *Jurassic Park* hit in '93, we'd be running from velociraptors and the T-rex. Later, when we were too old to play, we just walked and smoked stolen cigarettes, talking about girls and ghosts.

It wasn't just Chen and me. There were four members of our gang.

'If a hiker went missing out there, it would have been reported,' Chen said. 'There would have been a massive search and rescue operation, and it would have been all over the news.'

'I know,' I said. 'I think I'm just looking for a way to make it …'

'Not him.'

'Yeah.'

'Have you talked to Leeson?' I asked.

Geoffrey Leeson was the third member of our gang. He was in the police force now, a senior constable with the West Haven Crime Investigation Unit.

'He came over to my place last night,' Chen said. 'He was very stoic. He warned me not to jump to any conclusions. But I could smell the Scotch on his breath.' He hesitated. Then, 'He saw it.'

'Saw what?'

'The *remains*,' Chen said in a near whisper. 'He's part of the team investigating it. Can you imagine what it looks like after all those years?'

'I'd rather not.'

I held on to the balcony rails and looked down over the little strip of shops across the street. A bar, grocery store, coin laundry, and a Chinese medicine clinic. There were no people, no cars, no movement. As if the outside world had been temporarily emptied.

'The article I read said they hadn't identified him yet.'

'Leeson isn't sure they ever will,' Chen said. 'They might be able to scrape a little DNA off the bones, but what do they have to compare it to?'

'What about dental records?'

'It's been twenty-five years, mate. I just don't know.'

I pulled together a half-nutritious meal for Steffi's dinner that night: store-bought ravioli, garlic bread and mashed potato. An eclectic combo, I know, but it was all we had in the house, and I couldn't muster the energy required to walk across the street to FoodWorks.

As we ate, Steffi stared an accusation across the table. 'Why do you look like that?' she asked.

'Like what?'

'Your face is scrunchy, like this.' She made the face – an expression of deep, exaggerated concern. Over the last couple of years, Steffi had transformed from a short, round-faced little kid into a tall, gangly young lady. At just six, she already had more style than I would ever have, with short-cropped curly hair and a bright pink pair of glasses. Not that I could take any credit. Her mum had good taste.

'I'm fine, Steffi,' I said. 'I'm just – you know – working.'

I was allowed to say that because I was a novelist. If I stayed too long in the shower, muttered to myself in the supermarket or smiled blankly at a dinner party, there was a good chance I was working. Untangling a nagging plot point, inventing a tragic backstory for an underwritten character, stuff like that. In this case, it happened to be bullshit. Because how would I explain any of this to a six-year-old?

'That's not your working face,' Steffi said. My daughter, the human lie detector. '*This* is your working face.' She made the face.

'That looks more like my constipated face,' I said.

'What's *constipated* again?'

'When you can't poo.'

'Oh,' Steffi said. '*Oh.*'

That set her off into a giggling fit and, for now, she forgot all about my scrunchy face.

★

I put on my brave face for the rest of the evening and focused on our nightly schedule. After dinner, it was bath time, then half an hour of play followed by a book in bed. I leaned into the ritual, trying to put everything else – HUMAN REMAINS FOUND IN WEST HAVEN – out of my mind. It would all be waiting for me later, after dark. But then again, wasn't it always?

'When the three bears went upstairs, they discovered Goldilocks sleeping in the bed.' *The Three Bears* was too young for Steffi, but she liked the way I read it. 'Mummy Bear immediately called the police.'

Steffi giggled.

'There was a big trial, and despite her defence attorney's best efforts, Goldilocks was sentenced to six months in a state penitentiary for unlawful entry of a bear's house.'

'Wow, that's long,' Steffi said, with that earnest little crease in her brow. My face must have still been scrunchy because she sat up, fixed me with a dark, curious look, and asked, 'Are you sure you're okay, Daddy?'

'It's my job to worry about you,' I told her. 'Not the other way around.'

Later, after Steffi was asleep, I dug out an old baby monitor and set it up on the dresser in her room. It was an unnecessary precaution. Our apartment building was practically a stucco fortress. There were bars across all the ground-floor windows, and nobody could get in without being buzzed up by one of the tenants. Besides, I'd only be out for a couple of minutes. Still, I double-locked the door and dialled the volume on the baby monitor receiver all the way up.

I slipped out the front door, down the short walkway and into the stairwell. I jogged down two flights of concrete steps, then pressed out into the underground car park. It was a wide, dark space with a low ceiling. Once upon a time, the car park had been brightly lit with rows of fluorescents, but the body corporate had gone green in recent years, so the tubes were stripped out and replaced with motion-sensor eco-lights. Now, after every few steps, a square of light blinked on overhead with a heavy *click*, then faded to black behind you as you left each zone. It was creepy. What was good for the environment wasn't always good for the nerves.

Clicking lights followed me to the far wall, which housed a long row of storage cages. When I reached mine, I popped the padlock, swung open the chain-link gate, and gasped as something lunged at me. How long had it – *he?* – been waiting for me there in the dark?

The air rushed from my lungs. I drew my hands up quickly and madly to protect myself. The sudden rush of movement activated the sensor above my head. A fluorescent tube blinked on, and in the sick yellow strobing light, I saw rotting skeletal fingers reaching for my throat. The light settled. The imagined corpse disappeared. A tower of packing boxes lay tumbled at my feet.

I exhaled, long and slow.

Get a grip, honey.

That's what my wife would have said if she were there. Before the separation, it wasn't uncommon for Hannah to wander into my study while I was working, ask me if I wanted a cup of coffee, and have me respond by screaming in terror. When you wrote suspense novels, a certain level of jumpiness was expected. It was my job to picture terrible things hiding in the dark.

'Get a grip, honey,' she'd say.

As in, get a grip on reality. Easier said than done. It wasn't just jumpiness that was part of the job. I'd had to do my fair share of forensic research over the years, and now I knew a lot of things I wished I didn't. Take, for example, human remains. I'd looked at crime scene photos before and even visited a real-life body farm once, where scientists with strong stomachs study the decomposition of humans and animals. Now I could picture what the body would look like after all those years in West Haven forest. Leeson had seen it in real life. I could see it as crisply and vividly in my mind as if it were in 8K resolution. I could scrub back in time to when the corpse was still fresh, could imagine it on the damp forest floor, half swallowed up by ferns. A time lapse played out in the shadowy darkness behind my eyes …

… The sun rises and sets. Rises and sets. Troops of insects gather in their thousands. The body swells and stinks. Scavengers, mostly ravens, come to scrounge and pick. The body becomes parts. Chunks. Those chunks are spread across the forest floor. Skin turns a sickening shade of brown. Fat turns to grave wax. Toxins disintegrate whatever clothing the body was dressed in. Ten years pass. Then another ten.

Then—

Get a grip, honey.

'I'll try,' I whispered to the empty car park.

After restacking the fallen boxes, I waded into the storage cage. Inside was three square metres of *stuff*. Crates, boxes, three bikes and the cobwebbed remains of the treadmill I bought during the pandemic and used twice. Most of the boxes were filled with things Steffi had grown out of, which I couldn't bring myself to donate: time-damaged teddies and teeny onesies. The smallest box, right at the back, wedged between a stack of half-empty paint cans and a cracked plastic tub with old gardening supplies, contained the few objects left from my childhood.

I dragged the box out under the light, mindful not to hit my head on the low ceiling. It held the musty lunchbox smell of nostalgia. I set aside a pile of water-damaged school reports, a snow globe I got at the Fremantle Crocodile Farm as a kid, and my old beloved copy of Stephen King's *It*.

Then, there it was.

A floppy disk.

I'd tried to get rid of this thing at least a dozen times over the years, but it never made it further than the back of a closet or the bottom of a packing box marked *MISC*. It was a black 3.5-inch with a white label turning yellow. This artifact was standard when I was a teenager in the nineties. Now it's a collector's item.

I snatched it up, packed everything else away, and hurried towards the exit, eco-sensor lights switching off behind me, and more and more layers of darkness chasing me into the stairwell.

I spent the next hour dragging my old Pentium II out of the wardrobe and setting it up on the kitchen table.

I'd emotionally blackmailed my dad into buying it for me when I was a teenager, and I'd been lugging it from place to place ever since. Hannah had begged me to donate it when we'd bought our first home together. I'd convinced her to let me keep it for nostalgic purposes. I wrote my first novel on this dinosaur (I was nineteen, and it was never published). But the truth was, I couldn't bring myself to let go of what was on the floppy.

While I waited for the computer to boot up, I turned the disk over in my hands. On the label was the little alien I'd drawn twenty-five years ago, with big, almond-shaped eyes. It was flashing the peace sign. Above that, in neat block letters, it read *JUSTIN SMITH, 9F, COMPUTER STUDIES*. The *COMPUTER STUDIES* part was a cover to throw people off the scent if they stumbled upon it. In reality, this floppy disk was a recording of my sins.

A keeper of deadly secrets.

A chest of dark wonders.

The diary of a teenage boy.

2

From the diary of Justin Smith

THURSDAY 4 FEBRUARY 1999

It's hotter than the devil's butthole. The kind of heat where the bitumen road is too hot to walk on barefoot, and the air is so thick you could take a bite out of it. The insulation in this house isn't worth shit, so you feel every bit of it. Mum called the real estate to see if we could install an air conditioner, but our landlord would rather we burn to death than shell out on a split system.

At breakfast, Mum opened all the windows to take the edge off, but then the kitchen filled with fat blowflies, and we had to Mortein them to death. It bums me out watching flies die, the way they kick around on their backs. It has ever since Chen told me how flyspray works. It cuts off the chemical in the bug that tells them to stop moving, so they just run themselves to death. That's if Chen was telling the truth and, let's face it, he isn't the most honest person in the world. Example: there is *no way* in this world that Linda Shin let him feel her up at Matt Keplin's bonfire party.

But I digress ...

(Am I using that word right?)

We all sat around the cluttered dining table, fighting for the fan, me in my school uniform, Mum in her cornflower-blue West Haven Meats polo, my brother Scott in whatever you wear during your 'gap year'.

Does it count as a gap if there's nothing on the other side?

You'd never know Scott and I were brothers by looking at us. He has blue eyes, mine are brown. His hair is dark, mine's light. He got Dad's full, round nose. I got Mum's pointy one.

Mum told me about a weird dream she had last night. In the dream, she was standing on the roof, clinging to the chimney because she was afraid of slipping down the sloped tiles and going arse-over-tits into the garden bed below. A big storm was rolling in over the town, fat clouds scudding down from the mountains, full of rain and lightning.

'The wind was so strong that it started blowing chunks of my hair out,' she said. 'Look it up in your book, would you, Justin?'

The Dream Dictionary: An introduction to universal symbology and the psychology of sleep was already open in front of me. It's a big hardback filled with weird, brightly coloured drawings. I borrowed it from the library last week and haven't had my nose out of it since. Reading from the book, I told her, 'Dreaming about a storm means there's conflict in your life. The bigger the storm, the bigger the conflict.'

'Why would I be dreaming of conflict?' Mum asked. Then, 'Well, I am expecting a call from your father.'

'That'll do it,' I said.

'No offence, Mum,' Scott said, 'but listening to other people's dreams is the most boring thing in the world.' Then to me, he said, 'I'm going to wipe my arse with that book. How can you buy into all that horse shit, Justin? If I dream about a hamburger, all it means is that I want to eat it.'

I checked the dream book.

'If you dream about hamburgers, you may feel unsatisfied with your relationship or career,' I said. 'That can't be right. You don't have either of those things.'

Scott gave me the finger, but he was smiling while he did it. It didn't matter that I was giving him shit. A good one is a good one.

My brother thinks I'm weird because I'm into interpreting dreams, ghost-hunting, cryptids and anything paranormal. He also thinks I'm weird for writing this journal. He tells me – loudly and often – that it's a complete waste of time. I should be living my life instead of *writing* about it. But Stephen King says that to be a writer, you must read and write a lot. I have the reading part down (I have eighty-three paperbacks, mostly horror or sci-fi but also some smarty-guy stuff like Salinger and Hemingway), but I need practice with the writing part.

Hence, this diary.

Mental note: try to use the word *hence* more.

Mum asked, 'What about the part of the dream where I lost my hair? What does that symbolise?'

I leafed to H in the dream dictionary.

'Hair symbolises sexuality and vitality,' I said. 'It must be about your fear of getting older and ... you know ... uglier.'

'I should have had daughters,' Mum said.

After breakfast, I dragged my bike out of the carport. It was hot, but at least there was a bit of a breeze. After pedalling to the end of my street (Westlake Drive), I was already drenched in sweat. When I'd crossed the intersection of Miller Street and Castle Creek Hill Road and was halfway up the hill on the other side, I felt like I was riding in a sauna. There was a deep burn in my lungs and legs.

Chen and Leeson were waiting for me when I reached the corner of Castle Creek Hill Road and Elm Street, beside the big dark storm drain that gurgles like a mouth behind rusted steel bars. We meet at the drain every morning before school and part ways there at the end of each day. It's a little out of the way for everyone, but Aaron and I are big fans of Stephen King's *It,* and there's something funny and spooky about imagining a killer clown lurking in the shadows. The fact that the Elm Street culvert feeds right into this drain only adds to the appeal.

Leeson stood halfway off his chipped blue racer. I'd never say this to his face, but that bike of his is a real piece of shit. It's a hand-me-down from his older brother. The seat is torn, and the chain slips whenever he tries to change gears. But we don't give him any grief about it. Leeson's family doesn't have a lot of money. Neither does mine, but Leeson is next level. He lives in a little cottage machine-gunned with bird shit, set back from the street across a yellow yard with random piles of rusty car parts.

Chen, on the other hand, has an incredible ride. A cherry-red BMX with Rock Shox suspension and titanium dinking pegs. He unceremoniously dumped said bike on the nature strip and waved me in like an officer on an aircraft carrier. His bright yellow stackhat was a pop of colour against the grey morning.

'Hello, dickhead,' he said.

That's how he greets me most mornings.

I looked up Elm Street, expecting to see Aaron rolling down the hill towards us. He's usually the first one there. But there was no sign of him.

While we waited for him to arrive, Leeson and I leafed through the latest issue of *High Strangeness Monthly*. There was a photo of a flying saucer on the cover. Other highlights included articles about the Beast of Lake Benchley and a mysterious humanoid creature spotted in Antarctica. There was also a think piece about the Vela lights and a creepy story on the letters-to-the-editor page about a guy who got scratched up by a poltergeist. There were photos and everything.

Chen snatched the magazine from our hands and pointed at the UFO on the cover. 'First off, this is a frisbee. Second, you should be looking at pictures of tits and pussy instead of Bigfoot and Sasquatch.'

'Technically, Bigfoot and Sasquatch are the same creature,' Leeson said. 'Actually, *creature* might not be the most apt term. *Interdimensional entity* might be more apt.'

'Dude, no offence, but you need to stop using that word so much,' Chen said. 'Everything is *apt* this, *apt* that with you lately.'

I checked my watch — quarter to nine — and looked up Elm Street again. A blood-red Statesman was backing out of a driveway, and an old man in slippers and a wife-beater was shuffling quickly to the footpath, his arms like two old bits of rope dragging his bin behind him, hoping he didn't miss the truck. But there was still no sign of Aaron.

'Have either of you talked to Az?' I asked.

They hadn't.

'He's probably sick,' Leeson said.

Chen said, 'If I'm late for homeroom again, Mrs Reid-Howard will shit a brick. Come on, let's go.'

Leeson pulled his racer onto the footpath, and Chen mounted his BMX. They set off, and I hung back a second, still looking up Elm Street, still watching for Aaron. But the only thing that came rolling down the road was the wind.

When Chen, Leeson and I got to school, Dave Billers was kicking a footy back and forth with his mates. You'll remember Dave from my April entry when he stuck a load of ants into my Vegemite sandwich when I wasn't looking. Ha-ha, very funny. RIP the ants I accidentally ate. Anyway, when Dave spotted me riding past on my bike, he took a quick moment to line up, then kicked the footy right at me. I swerved to miss it, hit a puddle outside the bus shelter where the irrigation always leaks and soaked the crotch of my shorts.

Turning back, I saw Dave and those other guys laughing their heads off. I could have given him the finger or called him a fucking arsehole, but that would only have made him come after me later. Instead, I turned the other cheek and started riding away.

'Kick the ball back,' Dave shouted.

I hit the brakes. The Sherrin had rolled down the small hill on the other side of the footpath. I looked at it, considering my options. I could give the ball back and look like a pussy, like I was grateful he'd kicked it at me in the first place and was inviting him to kick it at me again. Or I could leave it where it was and ride away, which would risk angering Dave, who I have already established is unstable (again, the ants).

Chen and Leeson pulled up on either side of me.

Reading my thoughts, Chen said, 'Leave the ball. If you kick it back, you'll embarrass yourself.'

'I have to side with Chen here, Justin,' Leeson said. 'You have no hand–eye coordination. Also, people are watching.' He pointed. A small group of kids had gathered beneath the bus shelter.

'Kick it back!' Dave shouted.

His mates started shouting too, waving and gesturing for me to return the ball. Turning back to Chen and Leeson, I whispered, 'What if I do an amazing kick and everyone sees?'

'What if you fuck it up and fall on your arse?' Chen said. He pointed to my pants, now soaked with water. 'You already look like you pissed yourself. Don't be an idiot.'

'*Give us the fucking ball, Justin!*'

'Keep riding,' Leeson warned.

I wondered what Aaron might tell me if he was here and, all at once, I had the answer. Grinning like an idiot – because what I was about to do was *stupid* – I slid my kickstand down, got off my bike and strolled casually across the path. The legs of my shorts made wet sloshing sounds. I picked up the football, brushed the mud off, and faced Dave Billers. He and his mates were about six metres away. His friends had their hands up, ready to mark it. Dave had his arms crossed. He didn't think I could kick it that far.

After a quick check to see if everyone was still watching — they were — I swung suddenly to my left, dropped the ball and kicked hard. There was a roar of laughter at first because Dave's mates all thought I'd messed up. But Dave didn't laugh. He knew I wasn't aiming for him. I was aiming right where the ball landed with a loud, satisfying *thump* ... on the roof of one of the breezeways.

Then the bell rang.

Dave drew an invisible blade across his throat. The message was clear. I had lost his ball. Now he was going to murder me. I'd have to do my best to avoid him for the rest of the day, but what else is new? He'd make me take my medicine eventually, but right there and then, I enjoyed the feeling of sticking it to him. It felt, I'm guessing, like how it must feel to be a man.

I managed to get through the day without any more Dave-related catastrophes. Aaron never showed up, so I rode over to his house after school. I figured he probably had a cold, but he'd still be up for a few laps of *Mario Kart* or a round or two of *GoldenEye*. That was the reason I gave myself, anyway. But, thinking back on it now, I wonder if I already knew something was wrong. Leeson might call it a premonition. Most people called it a gut feeling.

Aaron lives halfway up Stricklin Avenue, on the mountain. It's not an easy ride. You have to watch for cars on the curves and hairpins. In some places, the roads are as steep as an isosceles triangle (my maths teacher, Miss Martin, would be impressed by that simile). Mum doesn't like me riding up there — she says it's too dangerous — but Aaron makes the same trip every day, and besides, I have a Mongoose 21-speed. What good is a mountain bike if you can't use it on a mountain?

When I got to his gate, I turned off the road and pedalled up his driveway, which opens into a teardrop-shaped clearing surrounded by trees. There's a big brick house in the middle. That's Aaron's place.

There was a police car parked outside. Seeing it, I felt heavy, like big hands had clamped down on my shoulders and were pushing me towards the ground, slowing me down. I leaned the Mongoose against the letterbox, then walked the rest of the way as if my feet were moving through dry sand. Somehow I made it up the front steps and onto the veranda. I hesitated at the front door, sensing a sick, frightening thing waiting for me on the other side.

'Justin.'

It was Benita, Aaron's older sister. She was rocking back and forth on the porch chair, hugging her knees. She was smoking a cigarette. Her hair danced around her face in the breeze. Benita is seventeen, one year ahead of us at West Haven Secondary. She has sunken cheekbones and always looks like she hasn't slept enough. I think they call that look *heroin chic*. She and Aaron have the same dusty blond hair and matching eyes, light brown like autumn.

Gesturing to the car, I said, 'What's going on?'

She jabbed the cigarette out on the bottom of her Doc Martens and flicked it over the rails into the garden. 'Aaron's gone.'

'What do you mean?'

'Nobody's seen him since last night,' she said. 'Have you talked to him?'

'Not since yesterday at school,' I said.

The wind picked up, but I hardly felt it. I was turning numb.

'Mum and Devin think he ran away again,' Benita said.

I shook my head. 'He wouldn't leave without telling me.' Then, when I noticed the hurt little look on her face, I took another swing at it. 'He wouldn't leave without telling *us*, I mean.'

I looked out over the rails of the veranda, over at all that green foaming at the edges of their land, feeling like Aaron could be anywhere. Benita rolled her thumb against a little yellow Bic lighter, sparking a flame and then letting it out. There was something compulsive and unsettling about it.

'I think I might know where he is, Justin,' she said.

'What do you mean?'

'If I show you something,' she said, 'do you promise to keep it a secret?'

I told her I would.

Benita swung open the front door to lead me inside. A rush of cool air hit me like a beautiful punch. The air conditioner in the living room was cranked up. With glorious goosebumps on my bare arms and legs, I followed Benita into the hall.

I paused to look inside as we passed the arched doorway that opened into the kitchen. Aaron's mum, Lucy, was pacing in there, panicked. Her big meaty arms were up, hands clamped behind her head. Her cheeks were fire-truck red, her eyes as wide as dinner plates. Devin was sitting on one side of the cramped dining table, his expression dark and still. Across from them, with her back to me, was a uniformed policewoman with a mushroom-shaped hairdo, like she'd walked to the salon with a picture of Dana Scully and got butchered. Nobody noticed me hovering in the darkened hallway.

'When was the last time Aaron spoke with his father?' the policewoman asked. Then, to Devin, she added, 'His *biological* father.'

In Devin's case, the 'step' in stepdad is purely a technicality. Devin loves Aaron and Benita like they are his own.

Lucy shrank a little, then looked down at her hands. 'My ex is not a nice man, Sergeant, but he wouldn't hurt his own son.'

Benita grabbed me and tugged me down the hall. For the next few steps, she held my hand. It was, despite everything, wonderful. She led me to Aaron's bedroom, then opened the door to let me through first.

I'd been in Aaron's room hundreds of times but had never seen it like this. Aaron likes a made bed and a clean desk, but today it looked like a crime scene. Clothes were spilling from his wardrobe like entrails, and a pile of comic books were strewn across the floor out of their protective, guaranteed grease-proof plastic sleeves. A shoebox was toppled to one side on the floor. Tipped next to it was a porno mag. There was a bare-chested woman on the cover with big hair and bigger breasts. I felt myself go red.

'Aaron wouldn't have left it like this,' I said. 'He's a total neat freak. Has that cop looked in here? Because these are, like, signs of a struggle.'

'Aaron didn't trash the room,' Benita said. 'I did.'

'Why?'

'I thought it might help me figure out where he is. I guess I was looking for a clue.'

'Did you find one?'

Benita glanced back down the hallway, stepped into the room and closed the door behind her. She moved quickly to the dresser and dug something out from beneath the socks in the top drawer. 'I found this between the bed and his mattress. I haven't told Mum and Devin about it.'

She handed me a Nokia 5110.

'Whoa,' I said. 'I didn't know Aaron had a mobile phone.'

Benita looked surprised by that. 'Joseph sent us one each for Christmas. His way of buying our love. I would have preferred cash. Mobile phones are practically useless in West Haven. The only place to get reception is in the toilet.'

Joseph is Aaron and Benita's biological father. I've never met him. Aaron hardly ever mentions him. All I know is that he makes good money working with computers in Sydney.

'It's weird he didn't tell me he had a phone,' I said.

'Maybe he doesn't want to show off,' Benita said. 'Or maybe it's just one more secret he's been keeping.'

'What do you mean, one more secret?'

She moved to the wall and put her palm against a Nirvana poster. 'These walls are paper thin. My bedroom is right on the other side. You can't let a fart rip without the other one hearing it.' Tears came to her eyes, soft and full and real. 'Sometimes, late at night, I'd hear him crying.'

If I were a different person, I might have hugged her. But I'm me. So I just stood there, hands still and useless by my side.

'What was he crying about?' I asked.

'I don't know.'

'You didn't ask?'

'That's not how we do things in this family,' Benita said. 'We talk about nice things. We put the bad stuff — the real stuff — in a box and hope it goes away.' She shot an accusation at me. 'What's your excuse?'

'For what?'

'You're Aaron's best friend, Justin. He loves Chen and Leeson, but you're the one who fills his cup. You must have noticed the way he's changed lately. The way he's ...'

'Darkened,' I offered.

Benita nodded. 'We both ignored it.'

I sat down on the bed.

'Everyone gets the blues sometimes,' I said. 'I thought it would pass.'

'This isn't the blues, Justin.' She sat down next to me on the bed. Our legs touched briefly. The cigarette smell drifting off her denim jacket was intoxicating. 'Turn on the phone. There, it's the button on the side.'

I did what she asked. The Nokia glowed to life. A grey animation showed two hands reaching for one another, followed by the Nokia logo. It must have been obvious that I had no idea how to work the thing because Benita took it back.

'Do you know what an SMS message is?' she asked.

I didn't, but I do now. Benita explained it to me. SMS stands for Short Message Service. It's like an email you send from one phone to another.

Benita used the little arrow keys to navigate to a list of written messages.

'These are all the ones from Joseph,' she said. 'He sends us a goodnight message every night. But these ones here are from an unknown number. It isn't linked to a name, and I don't recognise the number.'

'Did you try calling it?'

'Three times,' she said. 'It rang but nobody picked up. No answering machine either.'

She showed me the stranger's text messages. My hands trembled. My eyes began to sting, blurring the letters on the screen.

'Who would write something like this?' I asked.

'I don't know,' Benita said. 'But whoever it is wants my brother dead.'

3

NOW

I sat staring at the screen of the Pentium II, getting drunk on a dusty bottle of red wine I found in the back of the pantry and working up the nerve to continue on this reluctant trip down memory lane. I didn't like to *think* about my childhood, much less read about it. But tonight, it didn't feel like I had a choice. It was as if I were strapped to a rickety carriage creeping towards the apex of a roller-coaster.

So I spent the rest of the night drinking and reading. I read the whole thing, from the first entry to the last. Then I cried for a while. I'd hoped the alcohol would numb the guilt. It had the opposite effect.

The next day, I dropped Steffi off at my wife's house.

Was Hannah my *wife*? The question wasn't as easy to answer as you'd think. We were separated, which wasn't — I repeat, *wasn't!* — divorced. But *wife* was supposed to mean life partner, and that ship had sailed. Well, not so much *sailed* as chugged away while I stood dumbly on the pier watching, wanting to jump into the water and go after her but entirely unsure if I knew how to swim.

I was thirty-one when we met, living in a share house in Carlton. I worked nights as a bottle shop casual, which meant my days were free. I spent them writing. I had attempted four novels and abandoned all but one. I had given up on ever being published. That might sound bleak, but it wasn't. Somewhere along the way, I stopped writing to be a writer and started writing just to write. For me, writing was a necessary part of life. I couldn't have stopped if I'd tried. It kept the demons at bay, and there were plenty of those.

(*Enter Hannah.*)

She was twenty-nine, studying law: lots of late-night study sessions fuelled by red wine. That's how I met her. She'd buy a bottle or two weekly from the Happy Drinker, always on one of the nights I was working. I'd find out later this was no accident. She had a boyfriend at the time, but we connected on social media and, when that relationship ended, she invited me for a drink at a bar. It was her first time seeing me out of my bottle shop polo.

To say we clicked was an understatement. The spark between Hannah and me was explosive. It wasn't driven by lust or brain chemicals. This was something different. It was grown-up love, mature and thoughtful and considered. I fell in love with her brain. We got married while I was still poor. She gave me notes on my manuscripts and encouraged me to show my work to publishers. She made me work harder and held me accountable when I didn't. A direct line can be drawn between Hannah and the publication of my first novel, *The Carnivores*.

When I left West Haven, I had planned to reinvent myself – a complete Count of Monte Cristo. But the truth was I was lost before I met Hannah. She found me, gave me a life, then gave me Steffi.

Then I blew it.

We pulled up outside her white terrace house in Carlton North. Steffi wrestled her way out of her car seat, slung her too-big backpack over her arms, and hurried towards her *primary residence*. I was a few beats behind her, moving slower than usual, my focus distant and dreamlike.

The front door opened as Steffi reached it. Hannah drifted out, taking care not to get rained on. She was dressed in a soft pink robe and matching slippers. Her hair was slept on, tucked behind one perfect little ear, to reveal her dark angular face. Nobody should look that good first thing in the morning.

She gave me a nod as I slipped through the front gate. Steffi gave me a perfunctory little hug and said, 'Love you, Daddy.'

'Love you too, Little Bean.'

Then she disappeared into the house. Watching her go filled me with a deep familiar sadness. Something like homesickness. That was what being a part-time parent was like. Your kid was your home. When they weren't with you, you ached for them.

'See ya,' Hannah said. She was already halfway in the door.

'Hey, Hannah,' I said. She turned and crossed her arms, waiting. 'Do you have a couple of minutes to talk?'

It shouldn't have been a difficult question, but she seemed to labour over it. She looked into the house, nodded, and came down the steps to join me, pulling her robe tight against the morning chill.

'You don't want to go inside?' I asked.

'Tim's here,' she said.

'Oh.'

Tim. The boyfriend.

Hannah was an exceptional and accomplished woman: a family lawyer who dedicated her life to helping children in need. She was hilarious and beautiful, with rich dark eyes and hair the colour of cinnamon. She was miles out of my league. We may as well have been characters from Greek mythology: the goddess of kindness and purity and the flawed, petty mortal she fell in love with. All that, and I was the one to blow up the marriage. Go figure.

'What did you want to talk to me about?' she asked.

I hesitated. 'I told Steffi that Santa Claus won't give her anything at Christmas if she doesn't remember to wipe after she pees. So keep that one going.'

'You lied to her, in other words.'

'Han, I once heard you tell her if she didn't clean her teeth before bed, the tooth fairy would bite her toes while she slept.'

'That's different.'

'That's *sadistic*.'

She smirked, and my heart filled. It was like Chen's yellow stackhat – a pop of colour against the grey morning. Hannah and I used to laugh all the time. Now, on the rare occasion she cracked a smile, I felt like shouting, *Eureka!* But then the smile was gone, so swift and sudden that I wondered if it had been there in the first place.

'Is that it?' she asked.

'No.'

'Okay.'

'Hannah …'

'Yeah?' Long pause. 'What is it?' she said. Her icy tone gave way to concern. 'Is it Steffi?'

'No,' I said. 'It's nothing like that.' Hannah and I had been separated for nine months – the same amount of time required to grow a baby – yet she was still the first person I thought of when I got news. Good or bad. I took a deep breath. Then, 'They found a body, Han.'

'What?'

'In West Haven.'

She drew in a tight, unsettled breath. 'My God. Is it ...'

'They don't know yet.'

'Jesus.'

'Yeah.'

'But by now, wouldn't he be ...'

'Bones,' I said.

'*Bones*,' she repeated, her voice shuddering. 'Come inside. I've just made a pot of coffee.'

'What about Tim?'

'You shouldn't be by yourself right now.'

I wanted to take her up on her invitation. God, I wanted to. But this was not her problem to solve, nor a problem that *could* be solved. Not over coffee with Tim, anyway.

'Maybe next time,' I said.

'You sure?'

No.

'Yes.'

Without warning, Hannah put her arms around me.

When the hug ended, she held on to my shoulders for a moment, looking deep into my eyes in that old-soul way of hers, as if she knew more about the universe than most of us, like she had some secret pipeline to the gods and already understood what I was only just now figuring out: *change was coming*.

'Despite everything,' Hannah said, 'I'm still here for you.'

'Thanks, Han,' I told her.

On the walk back to the car, I thought I felt her eyes on me, but when I turned around, the front door was closed and she was already gone.

When I got back to Elwood, the apartment felt empty without Steffi. The weather was miserable. Drenching sheets of rain lashed the glass. The shops across the street were rain-streaked and gloomy. The old woman who ran the Chinese medicine place was peering out from behind the glass with a fearful look. Usually, lousy weather meant good writing, but not today.

Instead, I sat down at my desk and went online. Returning to the iMac after a night on the Pentium II felt like slipping into a comfortable pair of jeans. My first stop was the *West Haven Journal*, my old local newspaper. News of the body was splashed all over their homepage. No surprises there. The *Journal* usually had articles about Rotary club fundraisers and the fight to keep an old tree from being felled by the council. This was quite literally headline news.

GRISLY DISCOVERY IN WEST HAVEN BUSHLAND.

I took my time reading the accompanying article, but there was no new information here. Human remains were found. Identity and cause of death were still unknown.

My computer pinged. I had Facebook open on another tab. I

clicked over and saw a friend request waiting for me from Faye Miller. It had been years since I'd thought about her. I clicked on her profile.

There was a picture of her in an art gallery, smiling thoughtfully. She looked good: a greying brunette in her early forties. But there was something different about her. It took me a second, and then I saw it. She'd had a nose job. Faye had had a robust and angular nose when I'd known her as a kid. I thought it was striking, but she'd always hated it. She called it a ski slope.

Faye Miller. Wow. Believe it or not, I once asked her to marry me. I was seventeen and drunk on peach schnapps, but I meant it. Faye was sober enough to decline the offer. Still, we were a big thing for a while there. She was my first. I was her second.

Man, technology. Facebook was as outdated as skinny jeans, but it still amazed me. With a few clicks of the mouse, the past and present connected, like time and space folding in on itself. That Faye was reaching out now wasn't a coincidence. She had been with me in the trenches when it all went down. She didn't know the whole story, but she knew enough.

I accepted her request and closed the tab.

That evening, I'd been invited to a Melbourne bookshop to sign some books and perform a reading. The place was roughly the same shape and size as a shoebox, crammed so tight with shelves that it was hard to move without side-stepping. If you looked hard enough, you might have found one or two new releases, maybe even a work of great literary fiction, but Beyond Books specialised in genre: fantasy, sci-fi, horror and crime. My most recent novel,

Lured, fitted loosely into the latter two categories.

The turnout tonight could have been better. Just ten people had braved the stormy weather to be here. Eleven, if you counted the pregnant woman as two (which I did). Still, the cramped confines of the shop made the place feel packed, and what this group lacked in numbers, they made up for in enthusiasm.

After the reading, I took a handful of questions from the audience. A woman with a nose ring and an oversized military jacket asked, 'Would you consider this book a warning against the dangers of social media?'

The protagonist in *Lured* was a twenty-three-year-old woman called Cate, a serial dieter obsessed with the wellness and fitness industry. Looking for a mental reset, she'd drained her savings to attend a silent retreat run by her favourite influencer. There, she ingested an untested, 'all natural' cure-all weight-loss drug, which gave her frightening hallucinations and sent the other guests mad. It was part kidnap story, part zombie horror. Some authors wrote great works of literary fiction. I skewed another way.

'Well, yes and no,' I told the woman with the nose ring. 'I'm no fan of social media, but I didn't set out to take it down. Writing is a form of exposure therapy – a way to explore and come to terms with the most messed-up what-if scenarios you can think of. The idea for *Lured* came to me while watching my daughter stare at her iPad. She looked caught in a spell, drunk on those little pleasure pangs screens give us. I looked at that and thought, *what if?* I guess this book is about the fear of being a dad.'

The next question came from a big guy with a little pen and notepad. He leaned back and chewed his pen thoughtfully as he asked it, revealing a faded old *X-Files* T-shirt beneath his trench coat.

'Where do you get your ideas from?' he asked.

Every time.

But that was okay. That was *good*. I'd done a million events like this and had a soundbite for every occasion.

'Authors have been looking for a clever answer to that one for centuries,' I said, pausing for laughter. 'Imagine your life is a big bucket of sand. Finding an idea is a little like sifting through it, looking for flecks of colour. Personal experiences, fears, trauma. The trick is turning them into something positive.'

The big guy nodded and jotted something down in his notepad, seemingly satisfied. Another hand went up somewhere in the back. I checked my watch. There was time for one more. I gestured to the woman. She'd been eclipsed by the big guy in the *X-Files* T-shirt so I couldn't see her face.

'What's your question?' I asked.

'On a scale of one to ten,' she asked, 'how much of what you just said is bullshit?'

There was a collective gasp from the audience. Heads turned. The crowd parted to reveal a woman with short-cropped black hair and a trendy little pair of red glasses.

'… Benita?'

We moved to a hipster bar around the corner, with ambient lighting and indie music. It was busy with weekend drinkers, but we managed to nab a table by a big rain-streaked window. We sat across from each other behind pints of IPA.

'I should have warned you instead of just turning up like that,' Benita said as she fiddled with a coaster. 'I was going to call, but then I saw an ad for this on Instagram and thought: why not just show up out of the blue and try to give you a heart attack?'

'It's good to see you, Benita,' I said. 'How are the boys?'

'Josh is an angel, as per. Adam's deep in the throes of puberty. I'm still figuring out how to navigate that whole space. They're with their dad. How's Steffi?'

'Steffi's great. The best.'

'What about Hannah?'

'What *about* Hannah?'

'Has she taken you back yet?'

I raised a sad little smile. 'She has a new boyfriend.'

'Oh shit,' she said. 'Sorry.'

'That's life.' I shrugged and sipped my beer. There was a 7-Eleven across the street, throwing bright green and yellow light through the wet glass.

'So,' Benita said. 'When should we talk about the elephant in the room?'

'I've been stalling,' I admitted.

'Me too.' Her expression darkened. 'It's him.'

'Has there been a formal ID?'

'Not yet,' Benita said. 'But it's him. I feel it. I know it. In here.' She touched her chest. I knew what she meant. I could feel it too. But I said nothing. 'Are you going to come home?' she asked.

'To West Haven?' I shook my head. 'Why would I do that?'

'There are people who'd be glad to see you,' she said.

'There's nothing I can do there.'

'I know.' She frowned. 'But being helpless together is easier than feeling helpless alone. That's why families gather in hospital waiting rooms.'

'I haven't been back since the funeral.'

'Just think about it,' she said. 'If not for who we *are*, then for who we *were*.' She surprised me by taking my hand.

'Did you come all the way to Melbourne just to tell me to come home?' I asked.

She pulled her hand away. 'Actually, I came to give you something.' She reached into her handbag, which she'd slung over the back of her chair when she sat down. She shoved two objects into my hand. The first was a charger. The second was a Nokia 5110.

'You kept it,' I whispered.

'I could never bring myself to throw it away.'

Like the floppy disk, I thought.

'What am I supposed to do with this, Benita?'

'Throw it in the ocean. I don't care. I just can't carry it with me anymore.'

I gulped my beer and looked at the Nokia, a relic from another era. 'Does it still work?' I asked.

'Only one way to find out.'

When I got home, I plugged it in to charge at the outlet beside the microwave. Between the Nokia and the Pentium II, my apartment was beginning to feel like a museum.

I stared at the phone, hands folded beneath my chin. I had zero expectations. The device was at least twenty-five years old.

Then again, this was a *Nokia* we were talking about, undeniably the toughest phone brand of the late nineties.

A little light – long dormant – blinked. I tried switching it on, but nothing happened. I'd have to wait for it to charge. And it *was* charging. Perhaps it would hold its charge long enough to boot up. Maybe the Nokia would return from the dead and drag me back into the past. Maybe not.

While waiting, I sat on the living room sofa and thought about what Benita had said about families gathering in hospital waiting rooms. *Helpless together.* Was it time for me to go back to West Haven? What I'd told Benita was true. There was nothing I could do there to help. Then why did I feel as if I were being called home, as if a homing beacon had been activated?

I was exhausted. I closed my eyes and …

Thunk.

… opened them.

Had I really heard the noise or had I dreamt it?

Had I been asleep?

I was a sufferer of exploding head syndrome. Don't laugh. That was the actual name of the disorder. I was not making this up. It was a form of parasomnia characterised by a loud noise – wholly imagined – right before you woke up. It wasn't uncommon for me to wake suddenly in the middle of the night, convinced I'd just heard a door slam or a child scream, only to realise the sound had come from inside my head.

I wasn't sure when it started, and I tried not to draw connections that weren't there. But I couldn't remember it happening before the summer of '99.

This time, though, I wasn't even sure I'd fallen asleep.

I sat bolt upright and listened.

If the sound had come from my left, I'd have assumed it was someone in the adjoining apartment. But the sound – if there had been a sound – had come from my right. Near Steffi's room, empty now.

Thunk.

There it was again.

Real.

This time, the *thunk* was followed by another sound, like something heavy being dragged across the floorboards. It was coming from Steffi's room. I was sure of it.

I sprang off the sofa and started into the hall, flicking on every light switch I passed, like a kid tiptoeing from his bedroom to the toilet in the middle of the night, scared that the bogeyman was hiding in the dark.

When I reached Steffi's room, I swung open the door and reached in, groping for the switch. Before I found it, the furniture inside loomed in the darkness. The antique dress-up box was ajar, spewing jumpsuits, tutus and fairy wings onto the carpet like the gnarled tentacles of a Lovecraftian monster. The wardrobe was a towering, wide-mouthed silhouette. Steffi's bathrobe, which lived on a hook against the far wall, hung like some sinister winged creature.

Get a grip, honey.

I turned on the light. The monsters vanished.

Then, feeling rattled and a little dreamy, I turned to leave.

Thunk.

Pause.

Drag.

It was coming from under the bed. That wicked place where children's nightmares are born. Something was under there. Too big to be a rat or a mouse or a possum.

Thunk.

I cautiously entered the room and went down on my hands and knees. The overhead light barely penetrated the darkness under the bed. But I could see *something* down there. Something bigger than a cat or a possum. I moved closer to get a better look. I slid down onto my belly, my heart beating faster than it should have been.

Closer now, I could make out what it was.

Thunk.

Drag.

I gasped – an exaggerated, courtroom gasp – and a scream filled my throat.

It was the *thing* that had been waiting for me in the storage cage downstairs – a rotting, skeletal corpse. The *thunk* came from the thing banging its head against the underside of Steffi's bunk. The *drag* came as it pulled itself along the floor, closer and closer to the light. Closer and closer to me. Strips of flesh fell from its terrible hands, groping like talons.

I froze, gaping and shivering, knowing the corpse wasn't real – *couldn't* be real – but at the same time knowing that if it reached me, if it seized me around the neck with those long, rotting fingers, it would drag me under the bed and consume me. But I couldn't move. And the thing *did* reach me. I felt cold bones around my neck and …

… woke.

I was back on the living room sofa, drenched in cold sweat and wondering where I was.

It was just a dream, I thought.

It can't get you now.

He *can't get you now.*

Still feeling groggy, I looked into the kitchen. There was a dull green glow coming from the counter. The Nokia had sprung to life. I crossed the room and checked the screen in time to see the grey animation appear – two hands reaching for each other – before dissolving into the Nokia logo.

Without conscious thought, I navigated to the message I'd first looked at twenty-five years earlier. Here it was, still labelled as an unknown number.

The last time I read it, horrors followed.

Now I read it again.

follow the train tracks nth from the station until u c the stone with the cross on it. take the trail up the mountain. when u reach the ledge jump. gravity will take care of the rest

4

FRIDAY 5 FEBRUARY 1999

The three of us stood on the corner of Castle Creek Hill Road and Elm Street, looking at each other with grim faces. Each of us took a turn reading the message. The Nokia passed from Leeson's hands to Chen's, then back to mine.

'Is this real?' Chen asked. 'Is this happening?'

'It's real,' I assured him. 'Aaron's gone.'

'Don't say *gone*,' Leeson said. 'He's missing. *Missing* implies he'll come home. *Gone* implies, well, the other thing.'

Dead, I thought. *Gone* implied dead.

Leeson moved to run his hands through his hair — a nervous habit — but he was still wearing his bike helmet. He spread his hands instead and said, 'Who would send him a message like that?'

I told him I didn't know.

'Maybe the cops can trace the number,' he said.

'The cops don't know about this.'

Chen and Leeson exchanged a glance. Then Chen asked, 'Why?'

'Because if this is real, if Aaron—' It took a second to get the rest out. 'If Aaron killed himself, we should be the ones who find him.' I tried to make my voice sound sure and confident, more like Aaron's. 'I'm going to wag school today and follow the directions on this phone. I understand if you don't want to come with me, but if you don't, you'll be forever remembered as pussies.'

Chen raised a sad little smile. He and Leeson exchanged another look. The four of us were a family, but those two were closer with each other, just like me and Aaron. I looked up at the sky while I waited for their telepathic conversation to end. It was an icy shade of arctic blue.

'We're in,' Chen said.

I nodded. 'The message says to follow the train tracks north from the station, so we'll start there.' Then, as the other guys went to get their bikes, I added, 'Hold up a second. We're waiting for someone.'

'Who?' Leeson asked.

On cue, Benita rolled down Elm Street, astride her missing brother's ten-speed.

There was more to our mission than being the first to find Aaron. Benita was right: Aaron had changed, and we'd both ignored it. *I'd* ignored it. And hadn't Aaron given me an opening late last year, at the West Haven public swimming pool?

It was a warm day in December, somewhere between Christmas and New Year's. The place was heaving. The whole town had come down to cool off in the water or sunbake on the stretch of grass beside the pool. The guys were there, all of us sitting on the edge with our legs dangling in the water. The night before, we'd rented *Dawn of the Dead* from West Haven Video Hire and were now discussing what we'd do in a zombie apocalypse.

'The first place I'd go is West Haven Hardware,' Leeson said. 'I'd grab something big and meaty like an axe or a chainsaw for my primary weapon, then something smaller as my secondary weapon, like a tomahawk.'

'Do you even know how to use a chainsaw?' Chen asked.

'Of course,' Leeson said.

'How?'

'You just pull the little thing.' Leeson mimed starting a chainsaw. 'I genuinely think I'd be good at chopping up zombies. I wouldn't hesitate. Even if it was someone I knew.'

'Oh, please,' Chen said. 'You wouldn't kill a single one. You'd roll up into a little ball and cry. Then you'd get bitten, and I'd have to give you one in the head.'

Chen put an imaginary bullet in Leeson's temple. Leeson swatted his hand away and dragged Chen into the water. Laughing, I egged them on. Aaron just watched them with a tight, distant little frown. He was quiet for a moment, then said, 'Do you ever think about dying?'

'Like becoming a zombie?' I asked.

'No. I mean, dying. In the real world.'

I thought about it. 'Sometimes. Like, I wonder who would come to my funeral. Who would cry the hardest, and which of my relatives would be first to leave.'

'That's your funeral,' Aaron said. 'I'm talking about death. Don't you ever feel like just getting it over with?'

I didn't know what he wanted from me, and if I did, I wasn't sure I could give it to him. So I just shrugged, like a useless little turd, and said, 'I try not to think about stuff like that.'

He nodded regretfully, brushed invisible dust from the legs of his boardshorts, and slipped under the water. I sat on the edge of the pool, the hot sun on the back of my neck, and watched him sink to the bottom.

I might never have thought about that moment again if not for everything happening now.

The West Haven railway station is a small, two-platform yard that smells vaguely of dog pee. At least, I choose to believe it's *dog* pee. A covered ticket counter stands at the top of a concrete slope by the entrance. There used to be a kiosk attended by a bitter old woman called Gladys. When she died, they replaced her with a vending machine.

We locked our bikes to the chain-link fence across the street — Benita didn't bring a bike lock, so she doubled with mine — and got our story straight. We'd each have to buy a ticket to get us onto the platform, then wait for the perfect moment to sneak onto the tracks.

Benita bought four two-hour concessions while Chen and I fed change into the vending machine, getting supplies for our hike: two packets of Smith's chips, three Mars bars and four Cokes. Leeson stuffed it all into his backpack.

The four of us waited on the platform for the 9.33 train. We were alone, aside from an old couple huddled in the storm shelter, dressed as if they were off to a funeral, like it wasn't thirty degrees in the shade.

'As soon as the train leaves, we move,' Leeson said. 'The next one won't be for another fifty minutes. Hopefully that'll give us enough time to find the trail.'

'Hopefully,' Chen said. 'Otherwise, *splat.*' He shifted from one foot to the other. 'You know, there's a chance this is all a wild goose chase. When Kurt Cobain ate his gun, Aaron called him a pussy, and now you're saying he turned around and did the same thing?'

'So where do you think he is?' Benita asked.

'Occam's razor, Aaron ran away.'

'Then how do you explain the text message?' Leeson asked.

'I can't,' Chen admitted. 'But if Aaron offed himself — and that's a big old *if* — then he would have left a note.'

Leeson checked his watch. 'Train's one minute out. Get ready.' He tightened the straps of his backpack and cracked his knuckles, then his neck. Then he turned to Benita and said, 'I don't think your brother ran away.'

'Why not?' she asked.

'Because I've thought about it,' he said. 'Running away, I mean. When things are bad at home, sometimes I think about getting on my bike and just riding. Riding and not looking back. And you know where I'd go?'

We waited. Leeson looked to Chen, then me.

'I'd come straight to one of you guys,' he said. 'If Aaron ran away, we'd be the three people in town who'd know about it.'

He said something else then, but the words were lost in the roar of the approaching train. We walked up to the end of the platform as if we were making for the front carriage, but then we held back. I glanced back to the ticket counter and locked eyes with the attendant. He looked back lazily, then turned away.

When the 9.33 train pulled away from the station, we slipped quickly and quietly after it down onto the tracks. Leeson and Chen were first: Leeson crouched like a marine entering enemy territory, and Chen smiled a little at the adventure of it all. When I found my footing, I turned back to help Benita, but she was already on the tracks beside me. 'Move your arse, Justin,' she said.

I moved my arse. We all did. Swiftly but carefully, we all took off along the tracks, following them into the forest, into a brilliant tunnel of green. The tracks were raised. To either side was a shallow embankment littered with rubbish people had tossed from the trains. The air was cool. The light faded as the canopy of trees overhead grew thicker. It was creepy. Had Aaron made this journey on his own?

When I found my rhythm walking plank to plank, I powered up Aaron's Nokia. There was no reception, which wasn't a surprise. I brought up the text message even though I knew it by heart by now. Reading, I said, '*Follow the train tracks north until you see the stone with the cross on it.* Everyone keep their eyes peeled.'

Chen called back to me, 'Duh.'

He turned to look at Benita. She'd taken out a cigarette but hadn't lit it yet. She held it up and said, 'If a train barrels up behind us, I want one last smoke before I go out.'

'I've been thinking about who could have sent that message to Aaron,' Chen said. 'Tony Darnell. Do you know him?'

She shook her head.

'He goes to school with us,' I said.

Chen said, 'He's goth. He doesn't whiten his face or anything, but he has long black hair and black fingernails and wears a trench coat no matter what the weather is. There's a rumour about him that he breeds rabbits to drink their blood.'

Benita gave him a crinkled, sceptical look. 'Why do you think this kid sent Aaron the message?'

'Didn't you hear the part about the rabbit blood?' Chen said.

Leeson called back, 'It's not the most fleshed-out theory.'

'Who do you think it was, then, genius?' Chen asked.

'Look, if Aaron wanted to ...' Leeson threw a reluctant look back at Benita, then shifted gears. 'Well, if I wanted to kill myself, I'd probably want to do it in a way that didn't hurt, and if I wanted, like, advice about it, I'd go on the internet.'

'Where on the internet?' Benita asked.

Leeson shrugged and said, 'There's probably hundreds of chat rooms and websites dedicated to that stuff. Ever heard of exit guides?'

Benita shook her head.

'Exit guides are people — nurses mostly — who secretly help old people kill themselves when they're sick or losing their mind. Maybe it's something like that.'

'Maybe,' Benita said, less convinced by Leeson's theory than she was by Chen's. She turned to me and said, 'What about you, Justin? Any ideas?'

'Not really,' I said. 'But I don't think it was someone he met on the internet. It had to be a local. They know this area better than we do.'

'Unless this is a wild goose chase and we're on our way to nowhere,' Chen said.

The branches opened overhead, letting in a splash of light. I turned to look back the way we came. The train tracks arched around, disappearing back into a forest. I wondered how much warning we'd have if a train came up behind us.

'There,' Leeson called.

He broke into a jog up the tracks, his backpack of supplies making swishing sounds as it jostled up and down. The rest of us caught up. He stood beside a stone around the same shape and size as a boogie board. On its face, spray-painted in black, was a large X. Behind it was a narrow opening in the trees: the mouth of a trail plunging into darkness.

'*Take the trail up the mountain,*' I said, reciting the instructions on the Nokia. 'I guess we go this way.'

The others waited for me to go first. I might have argued about taking the lead if Benita wasn't there. Instead, I stepped off the tracks and into the trail.

'Look out for spiders,' Chen called up behind me, talking to nobody in particular. 'And leeches. And snakes. Just look out for everything.'

We fell into single file and followed the path up the mountain. It was steep and treacherous in places, but once we were inside, it was wider than expected and surprisingly well trodden. The air was moist, and the smell of damp soil was everywhere.

After a handful of twists and turns and a climb over the limb of a fallen gum tree, we arrived at the base of an old stone embankment. Wordlessly, one by one, we each went down on our hands and knees, looking for footholds. I was the second one up the wall, after Leeson. Halfway, I paused to read some graffiti on the rock. In black paint, someone had written, *NO FEELING IS FINAL*. Right next to that, in red, someone had written, *DON'T BE SCARED OF THE DARK — MAKE IT YOUR BITCH*. Next to that one was, *WHOEVER SAID LIFE IS TOO SHORT CAN EAT A DICK*.

I kept climbing.

At the top of the embankment, the forest wall opened into a clearing. The view was something else. We were halfway up the mountain, high over West Haven. Far below was a big blanket of green. The forest rolled on and on, lapping at the edges of a distant mountain.

Between the tree line and a sharp drop-off was an expansive rocky clearing littered with empty bottles, homemade bongs and a burnt-out campfire. Just ahead of me were two used condoms stashed in a crevice. The well-trodden path, the graffiti on the wall and now this. The spot was remote but well known and well used by ... someone.

Benita sidled up beside me and said, '*When you see the ledge, jump.*' She pointed to a narrow, horizontal stone ledge that jutted out from the side of the mountain, like a diving board over a fatal drop. '*Gravity will take care of the rest.*'

She started towards it. I surprised myself when I grabbed her arm and held her firmly in place.

'I'll go,' I said.

I took a deep breath and crossed the clearing to the ledge. The wind had been a cool whisper in the trees. Out here, it was a loud, guttural shout. Taking small, cautious steps, I eased closer and closer to the edge.

Once again, I wondered if Aaron had walked this way. I pictured my body superimposed over his, both of us edging towards the cliff.

I paused at the base of the platform but, in my mind, Aaron kept walking out to the tip of the ledge, arms outstretched, hair slicked back by the wind. I saw him stepping off like it was nothing, sailing into the valley below, crashing through the trees with a series of sharp, frightening snaps. I saw his body dangling for one long, sick second — snagged on the branch of a mountain ash — then slipping into the greenery below, a barely there thump against damp earth as ferns swallowed him up.

I don't know how long I was standing there like that, but it must have been a while because Chen called out, 'Piss or get off the pot, dude.'

Chen and Leeson were watching me with worried, supportive looks. Benita had her eyes shut. Turning back to the ledge, I went down onto my hands and knees, crawling at first. Then I slipped onto my stomach and began a slow, inch-by-inch shimmy. The stone platform was flat and cold beneath me. It was damp too, which made it slippery. Spreading my hands flat against the rock, I looked over the edge and down into the valley below.

Thirty metres below me, a sweeping field of green came into view. My stomach lurched. I suddenly didn't trust my hands to hold on to the ledge.

'Do you see anything?' Benita called.

'Not yet.'

Now that I was up here, that didn't seem so surprising. The canopy of trees was too thick. A body dropping into that would be like a stone in the ocean. It might not even make a sound.

I felt like I could puke.

Moving carefully, I crawled backwards on my belly towards the mountain. When I was close enough, I rolled onto my back and slid the rest of the way on my arse like a dog with swollen anal glands.

'It's too high up,' I said, shaking my head.

'So what now?' Chen asked.

It was close to a forty-minute hike down the mountain. It would have been safer — and longer — to return to our bikes, ride down the hill to Lake Stanton, and look for a way into the forest via one of the walking trails on the far side of the water. But now that we were up here, our mission seemed more important. Instead, we followed the steep path that dived into the valley.

The mouth of the trail — come to think of it, it's less a *trail* than a thin strip of dirt — starts at the far edge of the clearing. Without much thought of how we would get back up, we moved down a series of steep slopes and paths that hugged the mountain.

It hadn't rained in weeks, but the stone pathway was still slick and slippery. Still, that felt right, somehow. If we were climbing down to our best friend's body, none of this should be easy. None of us said that out loud, but I think the guys felt the same way. As for Benita, I have no idea what she was thinking. She didn't speak much on the way down. When we were close to the bottom, she sat on a rock and lit the cigarette she'd been carrying.

I hovered and asked, 'Can I have a drag?'

Benita raised her eyebrows. 'I didn't know you smoked.'

'I don't,' I admitted. 'But this seems like a pretty good time to start.'

Nodding, she passed me the cigarette. It was shiny from Benita's lip gloss. I took a drag and practically hacked up my lungs. Chen and Leeson stopped on the path ahead to look back. Chen shook his head at me, smiling in disbelief. Leeson just glared, like he was disappointed in me.

Handing the cigarette back, I said, 'That's good shit.'

Benita shook her head. 'If you say so.' Then, looking down at the valley of trees, 'We're gonna walk out different.'

'What do you mean?'

'If Aaron is in there,' she said, 'nothing will ever be the same again. Us included.' She stubbed out her cigarette and shoved it into a crevice on the rock. 'Let's get it over with.' She continued down the path.

The trail ended at the valley floor. Beyond a small mossy clearing stood a yellow wall of bushland. Mountain ash and stringybarks towered around and above us in all directions. For a moment, we all just stood there.

'Do you hear that?' Leeson asked.

'Hear what?' I asked.

'Exactly.'

'Why do you have to say it like that?' Chen moaned. 'That's like, such a cliché, dude. If it's quiet, say it's quiet.'

'Fine,' Leeson said. 'It's quiet. It's really fucking quiet.'

It was. We'd climbed down here to a soundtrack of wind, birds, insects and far-off streams. But here in the valley, it was silent, as if we'd just crossed an invisible barrier into some noiseless bubble.

'It's eerie,' Leeson said.

Benita shrugged. 'It's probably just the shape of the valley. The trees and hills must, I don't know, catch the wind or something.'

'It's the Oz Factor,' Leeson said.

'What's that?' Benita asked.

'It's a weird sensation, like being isolated, like you've just stepped into another reality, another world. The silence is unnatural.' Leeson craned his head to look at the valley walls. 'It's named after the Land of Oz, I think. Ufologists use the term a lot.'

'What's a ufologist?' Benita asked.

'*UFO*-ologist.'

Chen said, 'Jesus, dude. It's always aliens with you.'

'A lot of alien abductees describe feeling the Oz Factor right before they were taken. Some people say it's a warning before a life-changing event.'

I looked at Benita. Then I looked into the forest.

With no clear idea of where to start, we split up. Benita went with Chen while Leeson and I pressed through the wall of ferns and started across the valley floor, navigating creeks, dirt slopes and fallen branches, watching for leeches and snakes. We hadn't dressed for the occasion. I was wearing Converse All Stars. Leeson was in boots, but they were op-shop jobs, full of holes. Soon, we were both soaked and shivering.

At one point, Leeson said, 'There's a place in Japan called the Sea of Trees. It's supposed to be haunted because, like, hundreds of people kill themselves there each year.'

'Why?' I asked.

'I don't know,' Leeson said. 'It's a suicide hot spot. People who want to end their lives are drawn to it. It's like it's putting out a message at a frequency only they can hear. The way it works there is people will walk deep into the forest, find a quiet place, and then hang themselves or slit their wrists or, I don't know, take pills or whatever. Most of them run a string or rope from where they are to the nearest trail to make it easier to find their body.'

For a while after that, we were silent.

Then, when the quiet turned heavy and the horror of what we were looking for got too much, I said, 'Hey, that stuff you were talking about earlier, about wanting to run away ...'

'What about it?'

'Do you want to talk about it?' I asked.

'Nope.'

'Are you sure?'

'What's going on with you, Justin?'

I stopped walking. 'I think Aaron tried to talk to me about whatever he's been going through,' I said. 'I didn't listen. Actually, it's worse than that. I think I did listen. I just didn't want to *hear*. Does that make sense?'

'Not really.'

'Look, all I'm trying to say is that if you ever need to talk, I'm here.'

We started walking again.

'Hey, Justin,' Leeson said.

'Yeah.'

'This isn't your fault.'

I felt like crying.

Leeson looked up at the canopy, made a sour face, and said, 'Well, that's creepy.'

A plastic severed head dangled above us. The doll's hair, which was the colour of sweetcorn, had caught in a high branch. Its face had an eerie smile like it knew something we didn't. Its eyes were bright blue and seemed to be staring at us.

'Maybe someone threw it off the ledge,' I said.

'Or tied it up there as a warning,' Leeson said. He scanned the bushes. 'Maybe people do, like, rituals and stuff down here. Satanic stuff.'

Something crashed through the trees towards us. We heard branches snapping off and heavy footsteps. We both turned as Chen and Benita burst out of the tree line. I was relieved it wasn't a Satan-worshipper until I saw the look on her face.

'What is it?' I asked.

'We found something,' she said. 'Come on.'

It was a cave. The mouth was roughly the same size and shape as an ironing board, more like a crack than a door. All we could see from the outside — and let's face it, none of us were in a rush to get any closer — was a thick wall of darkness.

Chen led us to a spot on the dirt outside the entrance and pointed. 'Look,' he said. 'Doesn't this look like a footprint to you?'

It did, a little. It also looked like a formless little scuff in the dirt.

'Maybe it's Aaron's,' Chen said.

'Why would he go in there?' Leeson asked.

'He probably didn't,' I said. 'But it's the only place we haven't looked.'

I looked up through the trees. From down here, the ledge was a small black triangle silhouetted against a cold blue sky. It was nearly directly above us. If Aaron had jumped, he would have landed right where we stood. There was no sign of him. My first thought was he didn't jump after all. My second thought was darker. He jumped, but the fall didn't kill him. It broke his legs and spine and left him in a helpless heap at the foot of the mountain. Then, in a fit of desperation, he crawled into the cave to die. But if that were the case, wouldn't there be blood on the ground and some evidence he'd been here?

My third thought was darker and much, much stranger. I imagined a large black creature who lived inside the cave — something out of a Stephen King book. This entity calls to people telepathically and makes them kill themselves. When their bodies fall to the ground, he emerges from the cave, drags them back inside and eats them.

A good imagination isn't all it's cracked up to be.

Leeson was the first to step forward and look inside. With his head fully inside the mouth of the cave, he said, 'It's super deep. I can't see where it ends. It just keeps going on and on.'

Chen stepped up next and shouted, '*Echoooo!*'

It worked. His voice echoed around and returned to us, sounding distant and ghostly.

'Did anyone bring a torch?' I asked.

Leeson flipped off his backpack and handed me a heavy-duty Dolphin, one of the ones with the enormous batteries. I clicked it on and went to the mouth. I shone the light inside. It barely penetrated the darkness.

The morning had taken the wind out of me — out of all of us — but, somehow, I had enough fuel in the tank to step through the mouth of the cave and into the thick wet blackness on the other side. It felt less like stepping into a place than being swallowed up by it.

I turned back. Chen, Leeson and Benita crowded the entrance. They were backlit by daylight, so their faces were dark.

'Are you sure this a good idea, Justin?' Leeson asked.

'I'm pretty sure it's a terrible idea,' I told him. Then, I went deeper into the cave. It opened inside and twisted left into a long, apparently endless passage. When I turned the corner, I felt a rush of cold air. I looked back and couldn't see daylight anymore. My foot came down deep in a puddle of putrid water, and a low-hanging rock shelf nearly took my eye out, but I got the sense that I should keep going. I also knew that if I stopped — if I slowed down, even — the reality of what I was doing would be too much to handle.

It sounds like bravery, but it wasn't. I'm not brave. I just kept thinking Aaron needed my help. I wasn't there for him before, but I could be there for him now.

'Hello,' I called.

My ghost voice came back to me.

Hellooooooooooo.

'Aaron?'

Aarooooooooon?

I tried not to think about the creature I'd conjured in my mind. That black telepathic thing that fed on the minds of innocent people before feeding on their flesh.

I pressed on.

Ahead, the passage narrowed before opening up again. There was something in the middle of the path. A single discarded Chuck Taylor. I recognised it right away. It was Aaron's shoe.

'Aaron?' I called again.

My voice was the only thing that answered.

Aarooooooooon...?

Then I heard something else. The soft, sticky sound of dry lips when you open your mouth. I heard someone breathing.

Fear grabbed hold.

I wanted to run but couldn't turn my back on the sound.

Feeling terrified, I aimed Leeson's torch into the passage and moved the beam in a big slow arc. My hands were shaking, which made the light shake too. Then the light fell on a scared, pale face.

'Aaron?'

'How'd you find me?' he asked.

5

NOW

I threw some stuff in an overnight bag without thinking. I didn't know how long I'd be gone – I had no commitments until Steffi was due to return next weekend – but I didn't think it would be more than a few days.

It was time to go back; I got that now. Since seeing Benita and the Nokia's resurrection, the homing beacon in my head had grown louder. I could stay in Elwood, sitting on my hands and jumping at corpses, or be a man. I didn't particularly like that phrase. *Be a man.* But it got the job done.

A man returns to his home town to face his dark past.

It sounded like the plot from one of my books. But most clichés exist for a reason. Returning home would trigger a flood of memories. I hoped it wouldn't be strong enough to wash me away.

It was another overcast day. I tossed my bag on the passenger seat of the Prius. Before I pulled into the mid-morning traffic, I looked at my apartment building, wondering if I'd ever be back.

I followed the Hume, further away from the city and deeper into the mountains. I put on a podcast, but couldn't concentrate. I flicked on the radio but wasn't in the mood for pop songs, soft rock love-song dedications, or — God forbid — golden oldies. I ended up driving most of the way in silence. The road grew narrow, winding in big loops and arches like a snake. Prehistoric trees flanked me and my little car, closing in on all sides, rich and wet and just about every shade of green you could imagine.

The more time I spent away from West Haven, the foggier it became in my mind, like some long-abandoned Mayan temple shrouded with vines and decay, the jungle closing in on all sides. I was nineteen years old when I left. I drove away with my foot planted on the accelerator of a second-hand Datsun and didn't look in the rear-view mirror once. I went back for the occasional Christmas, but after Mum died, I couldn't see much point. The last time I went back was for her funeral. Chen and Leeson were there. Scott, too. He stood at the back and slipped away unseen at the end of the service.

When I reached the big WELCOME TO WEST HAVEN sign and crept over the crest of Main Road (which led directly into the town centre), I was reminded of how little things had changed. Sure, West Haven Video Hire was a trendy cafe now, and the music shop that used to be on the corner of Main and Mills was *another* trendy cafe. But the general store looked completely untouched, as did the big brick CFA building, the ugly brown Scout hall, and the West

Haven public swimming pool, where I saw my very first female nipple in real life (1993, Cindy Kites, faulty bikini top).

I drove the short distance up Main Road to the Golden Fern Motor Inn, another West Haven institution untouched by time. The same brown and yellow colour scheme was splashed over the same brick building, with rooms arranged around the car park in a loose horseshoe shape. I had booked ahead, but I needn't have bothered. My lonely Prius was the only car there.

A tall skinny kid with bright blue hair was working reception. It was a homemade dye job and a recent one, too. I could tell by the fading purple stains on his ears and neck. It made me smile, as some old men who know better do. I remembered what it was like growing up here in the mountains. Time moved slowly. Sometimes, you needed to give yourself something to stand out from the crowd, to bring a little colour to all that grey.

While he scribbled my name on some paperwork, he said, 'Did you hear about the body they found in the bush?'

'Yeah,' I said, keeping my voice steady. 'What do you think happened?'

We were alone at the reception desk, but he looked around to make sure, then lowered his voice to a conspiratorial whisper.

'It's gotta be a serial killer, dude.'

'A serial killer?'

'Yeah, check it out. The cops have only found one body so far, but there'll be more. It's a dumping ground, man. There could be dozens of people buried out there, maybe hundreds. Do you have any idea how big that forest is? And think about it, a serial killer would be, like, on brand for this town.'

'What makes you say that?'

'West Haven is quiet, but it's not the peaceful kind of quiet.'

I looked at him. 'What kind of quiet is it?'

He thought about that for a beat. Then, 'You know when someone's about to give you really bad news – *you've got cancer, I've been cheating on you with the pool boy*, whatever – and they take a long pause and, even before they say it, you know something bad is coming?'

'Yeah.'

'That's the kind of quiet West Haven is,' he said. 'The kind that makes people do crazy things.' He handed me a key – not a key *card*, but an actual key – attached to a bulky wooden paddle with *ROOM 6* engraved on it. 'Anyway, enjoy your stay, dude.'

My room was a twin-bed suite with drab yellow walls. I'd arranged to meet Chris Chen and Geoffrey Leeson for dinner, which meant I had some time to kill.

I spread out the contents of my overnight bag on one of the beds. Next, I set up a small workspace on the desk and answered some emails, wanting to distract myself. My inbox didn't cut it. I stood up and sat down. I checked the minibar, but there was nothing besides a plastic cup of long-life milk and some bottled water with a cracked seal. I pulled back the curtain. The streets were quiet. This end of Main Road was practically empty.

In recent years, I'd occasionally been struck with a sort of hyper-loneliness. It started on my first book tour – something about intense moments of social interaction followed by long hours alone in a hotel room. I'd had the blues before and had experienced long stints of homesickness when I travelled in my twenties. But this was something new: a thick, almost tangible sensation that settled over my body like an itchy wool blanket. It grew stronger when we had Steffi. There was more waiting for me at home, more to be away from.

More to lose.

In moments like these, I'd often be visited by the events of 1999. The memories would creep in, only they didn't feel like memories. They felt like a movie I couldn't turn off, an immersive theatre experience I was trapped in. The only thing that stopped me from spiralling was going for long walks, usually around unfamiliar towns and cities. Getting my body moving, my blood pumping, was a sort of control-alt-delete for the soul.

So, when I found myself sitting on the bed at the Golden Fern and could just about hear my past scratching in the corner like a rat, I grabbed my parka and got out of there.

I almost didn't see the man in the car. If I had glanced left instead of right as I stepped out of the car park and into the street, I would have missed him entirely. The car was a dark blue Subaru Forester, parked directly across from the motel in the shadow of the Uniting Church. There was an op shop attached to the church with a hand-drawn sign out front that said, *NO MORE BOOKS PLZ.*

The man was sitting behind the wheel, a black silhouette behind tinted glass. I couldn't see his face, so why did it feel like he was watching me?

Halfway down Main Road, I heard a lone pair of footsteps behind me, echoing against the street. I turned to see who it was. The man was out of his car, three blocks back, passing an empty shopfront with a *FOR LET* sign in the window. He was dressed in cargo pants and a black hoodie. I still couldn't see his face, but something about how he moved was familiar: his sizeable upper body lurched forward slightly while his skinny legs moved quickly to catch up.

When I turned back, he looked away through the empty shop window. Then, casually but not casually, he turned around and headed back the other way. As I watched him leave, I realised I couldn't be sure that he was the same guy who had been in the Forester. But it felt that way.

I got breakfast at the cafe where West Haven Video Hire had been. Once a dimly lit paradise with wall-to-wall video tapes, now it was stark white, with long pale wooden tables and wait staff who were far too good-looking for West Haven. But the eggs were good, the coffee even better.

Next, I strolled to Hidden Books, my old local. It was set back from Main Road, at the end of a narrow cobblestone laneway, between an Italian restaurant and an H&R Block. My headshot was posted in the window, above three small stacks of my books. Printed on a starburst was *LOCAL AUTHOR*. The photographer had captured me perfectly: a dumpy, middle-aged, perfectly average writer trying his best to look intense, dull brown eyes full of faux fire. My hair had been greying when the picture was taken. Now it was *greyed*.

Beyond the display, I could see that the shop hadn't changed much: wraparound shelving, a long sale table at the front, and a children's corner with dangling fake vines and a tunnel made from papier-mache.

I was about to leave when a familiar face appeared in the glass. It was Lisa Wu, the owner. She waved me inside without smiling.

My memories of Lisa were complicated. On the one hand, she was at one stage in my life – *how do I put this?* – a masturbatory staple. When I was fourteen, she was thirty. She wore black-frame glasses and Converse All Stars. Her jet-black hair had been streaked with green and purple, and her lip was pierced in two places. She was a nineties dream girl. On the other hand, she was mean. *Really* mean. If you spent too long browsing instead of buying, she'd call you on it. Then, when you chose a book, she'd read the title aloud in a mocking tone and scoff as if to say, *wow, your tastes are so pedestrian.* In those days, she had the uncanny ability to make you feel both shameful and aroused at the same time. Like I said, complicated.

It was warm in the shop, mostly empty aside from an old couple in the *New Release* section. A Smiths song was playing. Lisa was in her fifties now. The highlights and piercings were gone, and there were a few more lines on her face, but she was just as radiant.

'Did I seriously just catch you staring at your own books?' Lisa asked.

I turned red. 'No,' I stammered. 'I mean, yes, I was looking at my books, but it was an accident—'

'Relax,' Lisa said. 'I'm teasing.' She pulled her hair into a ponytail and let it loose again. Not once did she smile. 'What are you doing here?'

It was a good question.

'Visiting family,' I said. A pre-prepared lie.

'How long are you staying?'

'Just a few days,' I told her. 'How's business?'

'Good enough to keep the wolves from my door.' She frowned. 'You know what would help, though?'

'What?'

'An in-store event with a certain famous author.'

'Oh.'

'An in-conversation with a reading, sign some books …'

'Oh, I'd love to, but I'm not in town long, and my schedule's pretty tight.'

'Ah, I see,' Lisa said. 'You're too big for West Haven now.'

'That's not it at all—'

'Relax,' she said again. 'I'm teasing.' She looked off, then removed her glasses and polished them on the sleeve of her shirt. 'I'm guessing you've heard about the body.'

It was the second time I'd been asked that today. That made sense in a small town, I supposed. I nodded.

With a solemn look, Lisa asked, 'Do you think we're finally going to get some answers?'

'I hope so,' I said.

She looked at me sceptically, like I'd been browsing too long without buying. 'You know, there's something I've always wanted to ask. Back when it happened, people said a lot of things about you.'

'Yes,' I said. 'They did.'

For a moment, Lisa's cooler-than-you mask slipped. Beneath it was a cautious face, curious, nervous … maybe even a little scared.

When the mask was secure again, she asked, 'Was any of it true?'

A rush of anger gripped me. I pushed it aside and smiled instead. 'Trust me, Lisa, I'm not as interesting as people seem to think.'

'Well, I never believed any of it,' she said. That was code for: *I believed every damn word of gossip that came my way.* 'Let me know if you change your mind about the book signing.'

I told her I would and headed out.

I couldn't blame Lisa for believing the rumours. There were a lot of them back in the day. Most were wild and unfounded.

Some were right on the money.

6

FRIDAY 5 FEBRUARY 1999

After dragging Aaron out of the cave, he just stood there, blinking up at the sky as his eyes adjusted. Chen and Leeson stared at him. I wanted to hug him and never let go. I wanted to kill him.

'Where have you been, Az?' Leeson asked.

'You shouldn't have come here,' he said, shaking his head.

'That's not an answer, dude,' I told him. 'Why the hell were you creeping around in a cave? Have you gone mental?'

Benita moved between him and me and said, 'Take it down a notch, Justin.'

'I wasn't creeping around,' Aaron said. 'I was hiding.'

'From who?'

'You.' He glanced at the guys, then at Benita, who was standing away from us with her elbows cupped in her hands. 'I heard your voices in the bush, so I hid in there.' He pointed to the crack in the cliff face.

'Why?' I asked.

'Because I didn't want to be found.'

'Are you fucked in the head?' I shouted.

'Justin!' Benita snapped.

'*What?* I snapped right back at her. 'Why aren't any of you as pissed off as I am?' To Aaron, I said, 'When we found the message on your phone, we thought you were dead. We came down here looking for your body.' I felt tears coming but held them back. 'You scared the shit out of us, Aaron.'

But I don't think he'd heard anything I said after mentioning the Nokia.

'You went through my phone?' He glared at me, then swung to cast the same glare at Benita. 'That was private.'

Benita put a hand on her brother's arm. 'We were worried about you, Aaron,' she said.

He shrugged away her hand. He clenched his fists. The muscles in his forearms tensed. 'You should have let it be. You should have left me alone.'

'It's too late for that now, Aaron,' Benita said. 'But you can talk to us. We're here to help. We *want* to help.'

He put his hands in his pockets and looked down at his feet, shaking his head. He still hadn't put his shoe back on. The Explorer sock on his left foot was soaked with something.

'Are you in danger?' Leeson asked. 'Is someone after you?'

'Is it Tony Darnell?' Chen asked.

Aaron just shook his head. 'I can't tell you,' he said.

'Fuck that,' I told him.

Benita stepped between Aaron and the rest of us again. She said, 'You guys should go back.' She held my gaze. Her expression was like stone. 'Aaron needs some space. I'll bring him home when he's ready.'

That pissed me off. Benita wanted to shut me out of the conversation. If anyone should have stayed with him, it was me. In the social hierarchy of teenage boys, isn't best friend higher than sister?

'I'm not going anywhere,' I said. But my voice had turned weak and trembly, like the man inside my head had gone to take a leak and left the little kid in charge.

Aaron looked at me through cool, hooded eyes. 'What do you want from me, man?'

'I want to know why you ran away. I deserve to know. We all do.'

'This isn't about you,' he said.

I started towards him. I'm not sure why, not sure what I intended to do. If Benita hadn't blocked my path, I might have hit him.

'Justin,' she said, cold and sharp. 'Take a breath.'

'Why are you talking for him?' I asked her.

'Because I'm his family,' she said. 'And this is a family issue.'

'*We're* his family.'

With her eyes still on me, Benita said, 'No, you're not. Leave it alone. I appreciate you helping to find my brother, Justin, but I've got it from here.'

I took another step forward, then felt two sets of hands on me, pulling me gently back by the shoulders. Chen and Leeson.

'Get off me,' I hissed.

'Dude,' Chen said. 'Relax. Aaron's alive. He wasn't kidnapped by a sex predator or abducted by aliens, and he didn't throw himself off that thing.' He pointed up to the ledge. 'Don't make me hand you an invisible chill pill.'

'I know, I just—' The tears had reached my eyes now. I shook my head. I *breathed*. Because Chen was right. Aaron was okay.

I started back through the forest, towards the trail that would take us back up and over the mountain. Chen and Leeson fell in behind me. Aaron and Benita stayed behind.

We hardly talked on our way back up the trail. When we reached the ledge, we were sweating and red-faced. I glanced over the cliff edge and into the valley below, but I couldn't see Aaron and Benita through the trees. I couldn't see the cave, either. It was like I'd imagined the whole thing.

When we reached the train tracks, Leeson said, 'We should wait for the 11.40 train to pass before walking back.'

I checked my watch. We waited.

'Are we going to talk about it?' Chen asked. 'Or are we just going to keep on pretending nothing happened, like when my mum drops a silent but monstrous fart while we're watching TV?'

On reflection, Chen's joke was pretty funny. But at the time, I didn't think so. That guy needs to learn how to pick his moments.

'I guess it's personal,' Leeson said.

He was ready to let it go.

'Fuck him,' I said.

Chen and Leeson both stared at me, shocked. I was as surprised as they were. The words had come up without warning, from someplace deep.

'Justin?' Leeson said.

'If he doesn't want to tell us what's wrong, he shouldn't get our sympathy. He probably just ran away because he wasn't getting enough attention.' I paused. Then added, 'So, fuck him.'

Chen and Leeson stared back at me as if I were speaking another language. They exchanged a glance. I was getting sick of how they looked at each other like that, like grown-ups when their kid said something adorable and stupid. Then Leeson touched my shoulder and said, 'He'll tell us when he's ready, Justin.'

'When will that be?' I asked.

He shrugged.

'What are we supposed to do until then?'

'We wait, mate,' Chen said. Then he sighed and checked his watch.

A train whistled in the distance, the engine getting closer and louder until a great silver snake whooshed past, screaming along the tracks, blasting wind in our faces. There were blurred passengers in the windows. I wondered what they might think if they saw us, but they didn't seem to notice us at all.

After walking down the tracks at a pace, slipping back onto the platform and reaching our bikes, Chen said, 'My parents are at work all day. Do you guys want to come back to mine?'

Leeson said he would.

'What about you, Justin?' Chen asked.

'Nah,' I told them. 'I'm not really in the mood.'

They unlocked their bikes, and I waved them off. Watching after them, I thought about what Chen had said.

Wait.

But wasn't waiting what got us into all this? I'd waited for Aaron to talk to me and had ignored him when he tried. I had no intention of doing that again. So, when the guys had disappeared around the corner of Station Street, I dug Aaron's Nokia out of my pocket.

But finding phone reception at my house is a bitch. I spent an hour wandering around the house from room to room, holding the phone up, moving from corner to corner like an exterminator spraying for ants. I dragged a little stool behind me, thinking that the higher I could get, the higher the chances of getting a signal. If I could find reception, I could call the number that had sent Aaron that SMS message. Maybe I'd have more luck than Benita did when she tried.

The house was quiet. It was the middle of a school day, so Mum was at work. Scott was still in bed. He usually got up around two.

I made my way into the room at the end of the hall. Mum called this room *the spillover* because it acted as a catch-all to everything that didn't belong anywhere else. It was packed wall-to-wall with miscellaneous objects: Christmas decorations, an inflatable raft, a sewing machine Mum had found in a pile of hard rubbish and never got around to getting fixed. I swept the room, staring hard at the Nokia's little green screen, but all I found in the corners were cobwebs.

'Where'd you get that?'

I nearly jumped out of my skin. It was Scott. He'd come shuffling out of his bedroom, dressed in boxer shorts and a Billabong T-shirt, scratching his balls.

'Don't worry about it,' I said. I put the phone in my pocket.

'Why aren't you at school?' Scott asked.

'I wagged,' I admitted. 'There's just a lot going on. Are you going to tell Mum?'

He shook his head. His face looked distant, like he was watching a mildly interesting TV show. He pointed to my pocket. 'You won't find mobile phone reception in the house,' he said. 'I doubt you'll find it anywhere in West Haven. But there's a tower in Flockhart.'

Flockhart is the next town over, inaccessible by bike.

'Would you give me a lift?' I asked. 'We could take Mum's car.'

He made a show of thinking about it, but I knew he had nothing better to do. He's spent the whole year sleeping late, synchronising his routine with daytime TV.

'Fine, I'll drive you to Flockhart,' he said. 'But only if you tell me what's going on.'

7

NOW

Chris Chen lived in a big house at the end of a cul-de-sac, set back across an expansive front yard tastefully lined with native trees and veggie planters. There was space in the driveway, but I parked in the street instead. It was steep. I'd forgotten how steep some of the roads were in West Haven. I double-checked that the handbrake was on before stepping out.

I took in the view. The end of the cul-de-sac looked out over Lake Stanton. In the moonless night, the water was black. We used to swim there sometimes in the summer, but it wasn't as refreshing as it might have sounded. The water was murky and brown, and long furry lake reeds brushed against your bare stomach when you swam over them. It was like being caressed by cold fingers.

It had been years since I'd thought about that. Since arriving this morning, more and more things were coming back to me: flashes, glimpses, fragments of memories. Not the big dark stuff – that was always there – but smaller details and feelings. I was starting to remember what it felt like to be young, being present in your world in a way that faded as you grew up, that gleeful unknowingness of what was to come.

Aside from the shape of the lake, everything else had changed. Once overgrown and shaggy, the lawns on the town side had been landscaped and manicured with long rectangular garden beds lined with pine bark and native bushes. The old playground – which, according to Leeson, was haunted by the ghost of Suzie Marlon, a teenager who'd dived into the shallow end of the lake back in the eighties and broken her neck – was gone. In its place was a sprawling adventure park for kids: a complicated mess of climbing equipment, slides, swings and flying foxes. Running beneath this epic playground was the kind of spongey, multicoloured padding that stopped kids from breaking bones when they fell.

As a dad, I'd call that progress. As a former kid, I remember the thrill of nothing being there to catch your fall. There was something special about working without a safety net: your parents not knowing where you were twenty-four seven. Then again, if our parents had paid closer attention to us, maybe I wouldn't be back here under these circumstances.

I shook off my nostalgia, turned back to Chen's house and then flinched. A woman was filming me with her smartphone. She was in her late seventies or early eighties, dressed in a tattered navy-blue robe and Blundstones, standing in her driveway. Her eyes were set deep in wrinkly pockets, glaring at me cautiously.

'Can I help you?' I asked.

'I was about to ask you the same thing,' she said. Then, pointing to a big picture window over her garage, she added, 'I've been watching you prowl around like you're casing the joint.'

Looking closer, I said, 'Mrs Latimer.'

She lowered the phone. 'Yes.'

'I was in your psychology class at West Haven Secondary,' I said. 'You were my teacher. I don't suppose you remember me.'

'No,' she snapped. 'What, am I supposed to be able to remember all my students?' Then, raising her phone again, 'You still haven't told me what you're doing here.'

The years had not been kind to Mrs Latimer. She had been old when she taught me at West Haven SC, but now she was *ancient*. Her eyes had the wild, wandering look of a substance abuser. To be clear, there was nothing to indicate Latimer was a junkie. But her mind, once sharp as a scalpel, seemed to have blunted.

'I'm just here visiting a friend,' I said.

'What friend?'

'Chen.'

'There's nobody with that name in this street.'

'Chris,' I told my interrogator. 'Christopher Chen.'

'Oh.' She slipped her phone into the pocket of her robe and crossed her arms. 'Then what's with all the creeping around?'

First *prowling*, now *creeping*.

'I was just reminiscing,' I admitted. 'Sorry to bother you.'

'With everything happening here, can you see why that might be a bad idea?'

Ah, there it was. The body in the woods had stirred something up in her. The quiet had been broken.

'I can now,' I said.

I started up Chen's driveway with Mrs Latimer's eyes on my back. When I reached the house, I turned. She held my gaze a second longer, then drifted back into her home to a seat by the window, probably.

When I rang Chen's doorbell, a compact guy in a linen shirt answered. He was already smiling, already extending his hand for me to shake.

'You must be Pete,' I said.

'Guilty,' Pete said. 'Yes, I am the one man on this planet crazy enough to marry your old high-school buddy. It's so good to meet you finally. I've read all your books, by the way. Sorry, you must get that all the time.'

'I really don't,' I admitted.

'To be honest, I'm not usually a thriller guy, but when Chen told me he used to be friends with a famous author, I went down to Hidden Books and bought all three. Where are my manners? Come inside, please.'

Used to be friends, I thought. Interesting choice of words.

Pete led me through the house, which was like stepping into an issue of *Interior Design Monthly*. The living room was filled with simple Nordic-style furniture. Ornate wooden lamps cast everything in a warm, cosy glow. There was no television. Instead, everything had been centred around a wood heater, a fire crackling within. Even the logs stacked beside the unit looked curated, hand-picked by a hipster lumberjack. Classical music drifted out of a sleek, modern record player. Did Chris Chen live here?

In the nineties, we'd spent long afternoons in Chen's bedroom, spread out on the carpet playing *Ocarina of Time*. There were nests of dirty laundry on the floor, half-empty bottles of Pepsi Max on the dresser, and a McDonald's cheeseburger he'd left sitting on the windowsill as an experiment. He was sure the sugar content in the bun would stop it from growing mould. That thing sat – unchanged – for months before his dad made him throw it out. It was probably in landfill somewhere now, still fresh. Chen was a kid then, but still, this place was a long way from burgers on the windowsill.

I followed his husband through an arched doorway into an impeccably decorated dining room. There was tasteful abstract artwork on the wall, intimate lighting, and a long table set up family style.

'Take a seat,' Pete said. 'I'll let Chen know you're here. After that, I'll be a ghost. I'm under strict instructions to give you guys some space so Chen is free to relive the many exploits of his youth in private.'

As Pete left, I wondered how much Chen had told him about what happened. Probably as much as I'd told Hannah, which was nothing.

I sat down at the table. There was room enough to host a party of ten – maybe twelve – but it was only set for three tonight. It had been a long time since Chen and I were in a room together, longer still since Leeson was there as well. The thought filled me with a sort of high-school-reunion nausea.

Chen came in thirty seconds later, holding a bottle of white wine in one hand and two glasses in the other. He still looked thirty, the bastard. There wasn't a wrinkle in sight, and his hair was as thick and black as it had been when we were kids.

After setting down the drinks, he gave me an awkward man-hug, then sat at the head of the table. 'It's weird seeing you here,' he said. 'This is my world *now*, and you're my world *then*, and here you both are, colliding. When was the last time we saw each other IRL?'

'IRL?'

'In real life.'

'I know what it means,' I said. 'It just sounds funny coming out of an old man's mouth.'

Chen snorted as he poured each of us a glass of wine. 'If I recall correctly, I am and always will be sixteen days younger than you.'

We drank, and I wished badly I was here for different reasons.

'It was at Mum's funeral,' I said. 'The last time we saw each other.'

'Oh, shit, you're right,' Chen said. 'Sorry, mate.'

I drank. 'I should be the one who's sorry.'

'Why?'

'You live across the street from Mrs Latimer.'

Chen buried his face in his hands. 'Oh God, don't get me started on her. I don't know if she's racist or homophobic or both, but that woman does not like me.'

'Maybe it's because you tried to diagnose her with objectophilia in psychology class.'

He smiled and shook his head. 'I forgot all about that.'

A silence hung over us.

'Has there been news,' I began, 'about the—'

He held up a hand to silence me. 'Let's wait for Leeson to get here.' He frowned and checked his watch.

Something in his tone set me on edge. I took a big gulp of wine. I was drinking too fast but seemed unable to stop myself. 'What's he like nowadays?' I asked.

'Leeson,' Chen said, 'is different. I mean, we're all different. That's life. But Leeson has changed the most.'

'How do you mean?'

'There's a lot of his dad in him.'

'You mean he drinks?'

'Big time,' Chen said. 'That's what I heard, anyway. It's all second-hand. It's not like we catch up for dinner once a week.'

'But he still lives in West Haven?'

Chen nodded thoughtfully, looking down into his glass. 'It's funny how a person can occupy such a huge part of your world for a while and then disappear.'

'Did you and Leeson lose touch because of his drinking?'

He shook his head. 'It happened a long time before all that, around when you moved away. Everything we went through together – something like that either bonds you forever, or the other person ends up reminding you of the stuff you want to forget.'

Now we were both drinking too fast.

'Is he married?' I asked.

'You don't know?'

'Know what?'

With a little smirk, Chen said, 'Remember Shelley Hutchinson?'

'From high school?'

'The one and only. She was – for a time – Shelley Leeson.'

I remembered Shelley Hutchinson as a pretty, energetic redhead, popular with everyone and never cruel. In the social hierarchy, my gang had been somewhere in the middle. We weren't the freaks or the losers; we were those unmemorable in-betweeners. The idea that one of us might marry Shelley was laughable back then.

'How the hell did that happen?' I asked.

'They ran into each other at our ten-year reunion,' Chen explained. 'I don't think they said three words to each other in school, but I guess they found something to connect over as grown-ups. They have three kids together.'

'Wow.'

'You didn't hear it from me, but kid number three was supposed to save the marriage. It didn't work.' He rolled up his shirtsleeves as if preparing for a street fight. 'It's weird you didn't know that.'

'Not that weird,' I said. 'I haven't been back here in years, and Leeson and I don't keep in touch like we do.'

'But there's social media now. You can stalk all your old friends from the safety and privacy of your own home.'

I thought about it, then shrugged. 'I have been curious about him over the years. But …'

'But he reminds you of the stuff you want to forget,' Chen said. 'I do too, I guess.'

We exchanged a long, uneasy look across the table.

The doorbell rang.

We both rose. Chen went to answer the door while I stood there dumbly. Seconds later, he led a massive man towards me through the arched doorway. Leeson was always the tallest of us four but used to be shaped like a beanpole. Now his chest was wide, his shoulders broad. His square-shaped head had been shaved short and tight. If I hadn't known he was a cop already, I could have told just by looking at him.

'Hi, mate,' he said, his tone not cold but not overly familiar. 'Long time.'

We shook hands. Single pump, very formal. His palm was clammy. I noticed he still wore his wedding ring on his other hand.

'Take a seat,' Chen said. 'We're drinking wine, but there's beer or water or—'

'No,' Leeson said suddenly. He must have realised his tone was too firm because he clarified. 'We should talk first.' He glanced back through the doorway into the next room. Pete was in there, kneeling by the record player, selecting his next spin. Leeson turned back to us and said, 'Is there somewhere more private we can go?'

'Let's move to the garage,' Chen said, keeping his voice low.

'Leave your phones,' Leeson said. He took his out and placed it screen-down on the table.

Chen and I exchanged a glance, both of us confused.

'Why?' Chen asked.

'Because, no offence,' Leeson said, 'but I want to make sure our conversation isn't being recorded.'

8

FRIDAY 5 FEBRUARY 1999

The road connecting West Haven to Flockhart is full of big winding hills. Mum's hatchback felt and seemed to exaggerate every pothole. Branches reached out overhead. Scott's face flickered from light to dark as we drove beneath them. He drove too fast, as always, one hand slung casually on the wheel, the other on the gearstick, seat pushed back about as far as it could go. He pulled in too tight behind a logging truck.

I told Scott everything on the way. Well, almost everything. Every few seconds, I checked the screen of Aaron's Nokia, waiting for reception.

Flockhart is nearly twice the size of West Haven (big enough for its own Sizzler and a McDonald's), so as you come down the big hill that leads into town, you can see hundreds of houses spread out on a blanket of yellowy green. Beyond that, in the distance, the mountains. The sky behind them was so flat and blue that the hills looked like cardboard cut-outs, something from a movie set.

We parked outside the Good News Newsagents, which stands halfway up Horn Street, and just as Scott had predicted, the Nokia filled with bars.

'Holy shit,' I said. 'There's a signal.'

'I told you,' Scott said. 'What are you waiting for?'

I brought up the number of Aaron's mystery texter, took a deep breath, and pushed the call button. It started to ring. At first, my heart thudded in time with it; then it beat twice as fast.

'Anything?' Scott asked.

'Shh,' I said.

It kept ringing and ringing. I gave it ten seconds, then twenty more. Eventually, the phone rang out. I wasn't too surprised. Benita had told me she'd tried calling three times with no luck.

'They're not picking up,' I said.

'Leave a message.'

'There's no answering machine.'

I hung up.

'What now?' Scott asked.

'I'll send them an SMS message.'

'Do you know how to do that?'

'Of course.'

I didn't. I'd never sent a text message before today, so it took me ages to figure out how to write using the number keypad and ages again to get the hang of touching those tiny buttons. Scott watched me closely, wincing each time I made a typo and had to go back and fix it. My fingers were too big for the buttons. I don't think this will catch on.

Finally, I managed:

need to talk

Scott leaned in close to watch the screen, waiting for a response. Nothing happened, and nothing would happen for another forty-five minutes. We spent that time talking about nothing, rolling down the windows when the windscreen fogged up and rolling them back up when it got too cold.

At one point, we left the Nokia on the dashboard and ducked into the newsagent. I flicked through an *X-Men* comic book while Scott bought us a couple of Cokes, paid for with some loose change he swiped from the centre console. We drank them beneath the shady awnings outside the shop, trying to hide from the sun.

'How did you know you could get reception in Flockhart?' I asked.

'I don't know.'

'You don't know?'

He looked off and said, 'I've been hanging out with someone here. Her dad is sick, and she's on call to help him, so she carries her mobile phone around and checks it about fifty times a day.'

'*She*,' I said. 'So it's a girl.'

'It's a *woman*.'

'What's the difference?'

'You'll figure it out one day.' He turned to me, raising a smug little smile. 'Actually, who am I kidding? You'll be a virgin forever.'

Suddenly — at least it felt sudden — the Nokia chirped. I grabbed the phone with both hands and read the message:

i knew you wouldnt do it

'What a prick!' Scott said. 'What are you going to write back?'

I considered trying to call the number again, but I was sure whoever was on the other end wouldn't pick up and, if they did, I wasn't entirely sure what I'd say. It was too easy for them to hide behind the screen of their phone. I needed to draw them out of the dark. They thought they were talking to Aaron, so I worked with that.

I texted:

can we meet

I couldn't figure out how to add a question mark, but I doubted that whoever was on the other end would mind. Scott and I waited. Thirty seconds later, the Nokia chirped again.

when?

I wrote:

now

Then I added:

it's urgent

A minute dragged by with no response, then five. I was pretty sure I'd spooked them. Then I got this:

86

bi-lo at 4

The Bi-Lo was back in Fernbrook. Two or three years ago, a Safeway went in on Merrin Street. The Bi-Lo, which had been the town's only supermarket for as long as I could remember, was driven out of business, leaving the building boarded up and empty. The car park is shielded from view, so it's become a local hangout for teenagers having parties. Not that I ever get invited.

Scott and I pulled in at ten to four. There are two entrances, one on either side of the building. Scott backed the car into the space beside the trolley return so we could see anyone coming and going.

The sun had dipped, casting long, yawning shadows over the dilapidated supermarket. The few windows that weren't boarded up were broken. Practically every blank space had been covered with graffiti. A blood-red old couch was in the car park, surrounded by countless empty beer bottles and a dozen long-abandoned shopping trolleys. The bitumen was chipped and potholed, with grass growing through the cracks.

The mystery texter couldn't have picked a creepier place to meet.

'How are you feeling?' Scott asked.

'Fine,' I said.

'No, seriously, how are you? This morning you thought your best bud was dead. That's some dark shit, Justin. How are you dealing with it?'

'I'm fine,' I said again, fighting the urge to cry. 'I just want to know who sent him that message.'

'Why, so you can kick his arse?'

'Maybe.'

Scott smirked.

'What's so funny about that?' I asked.

'Can I ask you a dumb question?'

'What?'

'Why are you so mad?'

'That *is* a dumb question,' I told him.

'Then it should be easy to answer.'

'I'm mad,' I said, 'because this guy told my best friend to kill himself.'

'And?'

'That's not enough?'

Scott leaned back and waited. He was only three years older than me, but sometimes it felt like he was my dad.

'I'm mad at Aaron for not telling me what he's been going through,' I admitted. 'And I'm mad at myself for not knowing. Friends are supposed to protect each other. I didn't even see that he needed protecting.'

Scott asked, 'Do you remember Richard Coyne?'

I said I didn't.

'He was in my year at school. Every other week, he'd come in with bandages on his wrists or ligature marks around his neck from the different ways he'd tried to *kill himself.*' He put air quotes around the words *kill himself*. 'Once, he announced to the class that he was going to dive headfirst off the gym roof after school. Half the school came out to see if he went through with it, but he didn't show. And guess what?'

'What?'

'Richard Coyne didn't kill himself. Carla Delevan did.'

I never met Carla Delevan, but her suicide sent shockwaves through the town. They planted a tree at school with her name on a little plaque at the bottom.

'Carla was quiet as a nun's fart,' Scott said. 'She kept to herself, always handed her homework in on time, and smiled when you walked past her in the corridor. Then, one night, she went home and took too much of whatever she found in her mum's medicine cabinet. No note, no cry for help, just the big dirt sandwich.'

'What's your point?' I asked.

'My point is, some people cry for help, others don't. Usually, it's the people who don't that end up dead. You had no idea Aaron was planning on offing himself because people who plan on doing it — who really plan on doing it — keep that shit to themselves.'

'So, what, I can't do anything to help him?'

'That's not what I said. Be there for him. Be his buddy. If you can catch him when he falls, great, but if you can't, that's not on you.'

I didn't get a chance to process what Scott was saying at that moment — I'm only just starting to process it now, as I write it — because someone was coming.

A figure approached the car — not from the entrances we were staking out, but from behind us. The Bi-Lo car park backed onto a narrow strip of overgrown grass. Beyond that were the back fences of the houses on Koopman Street. They were commission places: small brown brick cubes. The girl must have slipped over from one of them.

She was close to my age, or a little younger — fifteen, maybe. She was dressed churchy in a drab grey ankle-length dress. The sun had dipped but it was still hot, and I'm pretty sure that dress was made of wool. She must have been boiling.

Her hair was straight and dark, her skin milky white.

I was thrown. I had expected a man, maybe even Chen's prime suspect, Tony Darnell, fresh rabbit blood dripping from his lips. Could a girl have sent those messages?

'Stay here,' I told my brother.

I got out of the car. The girl looked at me. I looked at the girl.

'Where's Aaron?' she asked.

'He's not here,' I said. 'I was the one who sent you those SMS messages.'

She spun on her heels and walked briskly in the direction she'd come from.

'Hey,' I called after her. 'Wait.'

She didn't turn around. Head down, hands in pockets, she made a line for the fences. I now saw a narrow path between two houses on Koopman Street.

'Please,' I said. 'I just want to talk.'

She slowed down and turned back. 'Did he do it?' she asked.

'Do what?' I asked.

But of course I knew. A part of me – a vicious, vindictive, angry part – wanted to tell her yes, to see how she'd react.

'Did he kill himself?' the girl asked. 'Is he dead, Justin?'

That caught me by surprise.

'How do you know my name?'

'Aaron talks about you all the time,' she said. 'He showed me a Polaroid he took at school camp. You, Leeson and Chen.'

She glanced at the path between fences — her escape route — as if it were growing smaller. Then she looked over my shoulder to the hatchback. Scott had rolled down the window and was watching us.

'Is that your bodyguard?' she asked.

'My brother,' I said. Then, 'He didn't do it. Aaron's alive.'

She exhaled, ready to burst into tears. But wasn't she the one who'd told Aaron to commit suicide? Why did she look so relieved? They were just two of a million questions I had. But I started simple.

'Who are you?' I asked.

'I'm Faye,' she said. 'Faye Miller.'

She waited, like that name should have meant something to me. Then, when she saw it didn't, she tilted her head and said, 'Didn't Aaron tell you about me?'

'Why would he?' I asked.

'Because I'm his girlfriend,' Faye said.

9

NOW

Chen's garage was cavernous and practically empty, so the sound echoed when he shut the door that connected it to the house.

I'd wondered if this was where Chen kept the relics from his childhood – if Pete was the neat freak and forced him to keep all his old stuff out here – but that wasn't the case. Two items were stacked against the far wall: a small neat toolbox and a smaller, neater plastic crate marked *TO DONATE*. There were rows of steel shelving along the closest wall, all spotless and empty. The concrete underfoot was free of stains and freshly swept. Had Chen got rid of all his old things? Had he purged himself of those years?

A chill seeped into my bones. It was cold in here, away from the wood heater inside the house. I'd left my parka in the dining room (along with my mobile phone), so I held my elbows in my hands and shivered through it. There was nowhere to sit, so Chen and I stood there facing each other while Leeson walked the perimeter, scanning for something.

'What are you looking for, Leese?' Chen asked.

Leeson said nothing. He just kept on looking.

'If you're searching for ant traps, don't bother. Pete thinks they're inhumane. I've seen him devour a T-bone in under three minutes but threaten an ant? Forget it.' He paused just long enough to take a breath. 'That T-bone thing wasn't a gay euphemism, by the way, in case anyone was wondering.'

Chen. He never did figure out when to make jokes and when to keep his mouth shut.

'He's checking for recording devices,' I said. Then to Leeson, 'Do you think we would want any of this on record?'

'I have no idea,' Leeson said. He finally stopped prowling around and turned to face me. 'No offence, but I don't know either of you.'

'What are you talking about?' Chen said.

'I *knew* you both,' Leeson said. 'But you're different now. I'm different too. Once upon a time, our primary objective was to look out for each other, but now we have partners, kids, families. I don't know you. And if I don't know you, I can't trust you.'

'No, Leeson, please, tell us what you really think.' Chen gestured to the garage. 'Are you satisfied this isn't all part of an elaborate sting operation now?'

He shrugged. Then he nodded and said, 'Let's talk.'

'What's the latest about the body?' I asked. 'The news hasn't said anything about identification yet, but the police must be close, right?'

Leeson looked like he hadn't slept for a week. He looked emptied, wrung out like a wet sponge. 'When identifying human remains, there are three key areas that forensics will look out for.' Leeson counted each on his fingers. 'Fingerprints, teeth and DNA.

The remains have been sent to Melbourne for analysis, and there's a very good chance they'll find DNA, at least. In the meantime, a forensic anthropologist will work to figure out age, sex, race and even height. With all this, there's a good chance – a very good chance – they'll identify him.'

'When?'

'Soon,' Leeson said.

'Are we sure it's him?' Chen asked. 'I mean, I know the chances of there being another body out there are slim, but are we one hundred per cent positive?'

'We can't be positive until the police are,' Leeson explained. 'But there are some things that haven't gone public yet. Clothing was found with the remains. A badly decomposed pair of cargo trousers and a mostly decayed sneaker.'

'That's pretty generic,' Chen said.

'The body was found in the valley below the ledge.'

That shut Chen up and sent a jolt directly to my heart.

The ledge.

It had been a long time since I'd thought about that place. For a moment, I was a kid again, standing outside the mouth of the cave, looking up at the rocky outcrop high above, a black silhouette against a slate-grey sky.

'Is there anything else we need to know?' I asked.

'Officially, the cause of death is still unknown,' he said. 'But anything like this is treated as suspicious.'

'What does that mean?'

'Foul play is assumed.'

'What does *that* mean?' Chen asked.

'A homicide detective is on his way up from Melbourne. Bob Eckman. I haven't met him. If and when the remains are identified, he'll have questions for all of us.'

'What do we do until then?' I asked.

'Wait,' Leeson said.

I'd never been good at waiting.

'In the meantime, you should head home, mate,' Leeson said. 'You turned up in West Haven days after the body did. That's not a good look. People will talk. If they haven't started talking already.'

Chen murmured something I didn't catch. He looked boyish for a moment, a glimpse of the Chen from *then*, not *now*. He massaged his left hand with his right, fingering a needle-thin scar that ran horizontally across his palm, faded and pale. I had a matching scar on the palm of my hand, Leeson too.

Turning back to Leeson, I said, 'I'll go home tomorrow morning.'

'Good,' Leeson said.

It was a relief to be told to go home. Being helpless together, it turned out, wasn't all it was cracked up to be. Why not feel helpless alone in the comfort of your own home?

I hesitated. 'Chen said you saw it, Leese.'

Leeson looked at me.

'The body,' I clarified.

He sighed.

'Everything was laid out on a tarp in an onsite lab we put up at the scene,' he said. 'When I went in to look, I had this dumb idea that I might recognise him. But there's hardly any of him left.'

A fresh chill crept up my spine.

'Nature reduced him to parts,' he said. 'Decomposed, weather-beaten, pulled apart and spread by animals. After another few years out there, there would have been nothing left. At the end of the day, we're all just sacks of meat.' His big chest rose and fell. 'Maybe I'll take that drink now, mate.' He looked at Chen. 'Mate?'

Chen was crying. He briefly let his hands dangle at his sides, then brought them up fast to cover his face. I did nothing. All the social cues I'd learned since being a teenager fell away, and I was a kid again, gangly and awkward, unsure of what to say or do.

Leeson said, 'You need to pull it together, Chen. If we go back in there and your husband sees that you've been crying, he'll have questions.'

'I know,' Chen said, sniffling.

'Unless he already knows,' Leeson said. His tone was colder now, probing. He watched Chen closely, gauging his response. 'Have you told Pete anything about it?'

Chen straightened up. 'Of course I haven't.'

Leeson turned to me next. 'Does your wife know?'

'She's my ex-wife now,' I said. 'And no. I've never told a soul about what happened. Everyone who knows is in this room.'

'What about you?' Chen asked Leeson.

'What *about* me?'

'Have you told anyone?' Chen's eyes were dry again now. 'Does Shelley know?'

Leeson held his gaze. 'I'd never make her carry something like that.'

'I wish we didn't have to carry it either,' Chen said. 'You know my first thought when I heard the news?'

Leeson and I waited.

'I was watching TV,' Chen went on. 'Pete had gone to bed, and I was half asleep myself. There was an ad for the eleven o'clock news. *Human remains found in West Haven.* Then they went right on talking about who'd won the football and what the weather would be on the weekend. I thought I'd dreamt it. Then, when I realised it was real, I thought, *Good.*'

Leeson fixed Chen with a baffled look. He stood towering by the garage door, arms folded across his chest, hands tucked neatly beneath his armpits. 'Good?' he said.

'Yep,' Chen said. 'I thought, *Good.* I thought, *Thank God.* These past two decades have been hell for me. They've been hell for all of us. What we did — *what we had to do* — it fucked me up. It broke me. When I heard the news, I thought, maybe, after all these years, we could start to fix ourselves. It was a relief. Like, my whole life was about to fall apart, and everything would be exposed, but at least I could stop living in the dark like a fucking mushroom.'

Leeson's eyes sparked with panic, then anger.

'What are you saying, Chen?' he asked.

Chen looked down at the scar, closed his hand into a fist and lifted his eyes to meet mine. 'I'm not saying anything, Leeson. I think I'm just drunk.'

Leeson glanced over to me, then took one quick step forward. My instincts flared. I braced myself for a burst of sudden violence. I could just about see Leeson grabbing Chen by the shirt collar, hoisting him into the air and then slamming him down against the hard concrete floor like a limp doll, listing all the horrific things he'd do to him if he ratted us out. But Leeson didn't reach for Chen. He sat down on the cold concrete floor. Chen and I followed suit, and soon all three of us, grown men, were sitting cross-legged in a circle.

Leeson said, 'Nobody calls me Leeson anymore. Everyone calls me Geoffrey now. Everyone except for you two.'

'Want us to switch to calling you Geoffrey?' I asked.

'No.' Leeson shrugged. 'I'm getting used to it. First, it felt like you were talking to someone who wasn't in the room anymore. Now it just feels, I don't know, familiar.'

I looked from him to Chen and back again, seeing first the aged, worn versions of my old friends, then the children they used to be. Something in me shifted open. 'You know what *I* thought when I heard the news?'

'What?' Chen said.

'I thought, *Wow, it actually happened.*'

'How do you mean?'

'Over the years, I'd almost convinced myself it had never happened,' I explained. 'If there's one thing I'm good at, it's detaching.'

'You spent twenty-five years in denial,' Leeson said.

'I guess so. I had to. It was a survival mechanism. It got a little easier when I left West Haven. It got easier still when I got married, had a kid and my career started taking off. I allowed myself to get so distracted that it all started to feel like a bad dream.'

It felt good to talk about all this out loud. This was what support groups must feel like.

'Your turn, Leese,' Chen said. 'What did you think when you heard the news?'

'When the call came in, I was at the station, running the front desk because Rach was on her lunchbreak,' Leeson said. 'I was reading about how to keep rabbits away from your veggie garden. Until last week, rabbits were my biggest problem. Imagine that. Then it came over the radio that a surveying team had found what looked like human bones, and my world just … stopped. I didn't feel relieved and hadn't convinced myself it had never happened. I felt everything, all the time.' Moisture built in his eyes. 'I thought, *This was inevitable.* Because something like that doesn't stay buried, no matter how deep you dig the hole.'

He looked down at the palm of his hand and sniffed. 'But we'll get through it,' he said. 'We'll weather this storm like we weathered the last one. By sticking together.'

We all go free or no one does, I thought.

We were quiet for a moment.

Then I said, 'Hey, Leeson?'

'Yeah?'

'I can't believe you married Shelley Hutchinson.'

He smiled. 'Bet you weren't expecting that.'

'It surprised me more than when I found out Chen had turned gay.'

'I didn't *turn* gay,' Chen said. 'I was always gay.'

'But when we were teenagers, everything was about tits and pussy with you,' I said.

'Classic overcompensation,' Chen said. 'That should have been your first clue.'

We went back inside and ate and drank and kept on talking for a while. The icy years we'd spent apart began to thaw. We were like old friends at a reunion.

Like kids.

We said goodbye at the end of the night, and I started the short drive back into town. My mind felt foggy at the edges, dreamlike. It took me a minute to remember I was drunk. I'd had too much to drink in the short time I'd spent at Chen's place, and now it felt less like I was driving somewhere and more like the Prius was stationary and the world was rolling towards me on a giant treadmill.

I shouldn't have been driving, especially not in West Haven. The forest roads curved and dipped. The high beams were on, but they barely penetrated the dark. It was a different sort of dark out here on the forest roads. I'd forgotten that.

I rolled down the window to let a gust of cold air into the car. Headlights flickered through the trees on the road behind me, getting closer. A few seconds later, a police car pulled in tight behind me. Damn. There was nothing like the threat of being pulled over by cops to sober you up. I eased off the pedal, even though I was driving under the limit. But now it felt as if I were moving too slowly. That was suspicious. But then I put my foot down too hard on the pedal, and the car lurched forward.

Red and blue lights would flash any second now, I thought. I saw visions of the breathalyser, the white tube being stuck into my mouth, of being taken to the station for a blood test and having to call Hannah to come to West Haven to pick me up because her ex-husband was driving while shit-faced.

As the road dipped into town, I entered a fifty zone and eased off the pedal again. I checked the rear-view. In the dull glow of the town lights, I saw that it wasn't a cop car at all. It was a station wagon with roof racks. An older guy with a disinterested expression was driving.

I exhaled, but the prickly heat of paranoia remained. As strongly as I'd felt the pull towards West Haven this morning, I now felt the urge to leave. I was eager to throw my things in my bag and hit the road in the morning. I might have driven back to Melbourne tonight if I wasn't drunk. Maybe I'd go to Hannah's place, make love to her, wake up in the morning and make pancakes for Steffi.

In an alternate reality, I thought.

In this reality, I pulled in to the Golden Fern Motor Inn, fished the big wooden key ring from the centre console, and stepped out into the cold. Before I reached my door, I paused to look across the street. The dark blue Subaru Forester was back, parked outside the Uniting Church. Someone was behind the wheel. It was too dark to see more than a silhouette, but it felt like I was being watched.

I considered going over there, but I was too drunk – and too much of a coward – so I slipped into my motel room instead and locked the door behind me.

The room was hot. I'd accidentally left the heater on before leaving and was thankful for it. I shook off my jacket, opened my laptop and fell onto the bed. My Facebook profile was still open from earlier. There were two new notifications.

You and faye miller are now friends

And

faye miller has sent you a message.

I opened the message.

I've decided to tell the police what I know.
But we should talk first.
When can we meet?

10

FRIDAY 5 FEBRUARY 1999

It took some convincing, but Scott gave Faye Miller and me the back seat of the hatchback and agreed to take a walk. We stared at each other, neither knowing where to start, both of us listening to the *tik-tik-tik* of the warm engine and baking in the sunlight coming in through the windows.

'I'm not that surprised he didn't tell you about me,' she said after a while, with a strange, sad little smile. 'I asked Aaron not to tell anyone about us. But I also know you're his best friend, and there aren't many secrets between you guys.'

I used to think that was true as well.

'Why did you want to keep it a secret in the first place?' I asked.

'If my dad found out I had a boyfriend, he'd lock me in my room until my eighteenth birthday. He told me that.' Her smile went away. 'If he knew the rest, he'd probably disown me.'

'The rest?'

'Aaron and I do ... stuff.'

'What sort of stuff?'

She blushed. 'You know,' she said. 'Sex stuff.'

Now it was my turn to blush.

But it was also starting to sound pretty fishy. I could buy Aaron vanishing without a trace. I could even believe he was harbouring secret suicidal thoughts. But not telling me he did *sex stuff* with a girl was just impossible. Besides, what sort of girl sends her boyfriend to a ledge to jump off?

'What school do you go to?' I asked.

'I'm homeschooled,' she said.

'What's that?'

'Just what it sounds like,' Faye said. 'I still go to school, but it's at home. Mum and Dad are my teachers. It's super weird, I know. It's Dad's twisted little way of protecting me. My family is pretty religious.'

That explained her wardrobe, at least. But churchy outfit or not, Faye was cute. I hadn't noticed that before. She had a long, prominent nose that reminded me of Ingrid Jensen, a Norwegian exchange student who'd been in some of Scott's year ten classes. She came over to the house sometimes. She was tall and blonde and reminded me of a Viking warrior. Faye was short with dark hair but could have been Ingrid's younger sister.

'How much do you know about Jehovah's Witnesses?' she asked.

'Nothing,' I admitted. 'Other than that my mum hates it when they turn up at the house uninvited.'

Faye laughed. It was a light, pretty sound.

'Turning up at houses uninvited is part of the gig, but not everyone slams a door in your face,' she said. 'Sometimes you even get invited inside.'

'It works that way with vampires, too,' I said.

She frowned. I felt bad for saying it, even though I shouldn't have.

'That's how Aaron and I met,' she said.

'You knocked on his door?'

Nodding, she said, 'He was home alone. He made it clear he wasn't looking for a big religious conversation or anything. But he was happy to talk, so we did that for three hours straight. Then, when I left, I wrote my number on the back of a *Watchtower* magazine and gave it to him. I didn't know if he would call or not.'

'But he did.'

'We started talking pretty much every night,' she said. There was a fire in her eyes. I think she was telling me the truth. 'He'd have to call me so it wouldn't show up on our bill, and he had to wait until after my parents were asleep. I'd turn the volume of our little cordless phone down and make sure I picked up on the first ring. Sometimes, it wouldn't even ring at all. I'd answer, and he'd be on the other end of the line. Like we were psychically connected or something.'

'What did you talk about?'

'Everything. Nothing.' She looked me in the eyes. 'We talked about you, sometimes, and the other guys.'

'Were you trying to convert him or something?' I asked.

'In the beginning, that's what I told myself, and we did talk about God sometimes,' she said. 'But it wasn't really about all that.'

'What was it about?'

'Love, Justin,' she said. 'Aaron and I are in love.'

'Then why did you tell him to kill himself?'

A wrinkled, defensive crease appeared between her eyes. For a second, it felt good to watch her smile vanish.

'I wish we weren't meeting like this,' she said. 'You're such an important person in Aaron's life. I feel like I know you. I feel like I *like* you.' She took my hand in hers. I cringed. I wanted to shake it off, but I froze. 'But you think I'm a monster.'

'How would your family feel if they knew what you did?' I asked. 'Isn't suicide a sin?'

She let go of my hand.

'Do you know what faith is, Justin?' she asked.

'Are you going to teach me about the Bible now?'

'Faith is evidence of things unseen. When I sent Aaron that message, I had faith that he wouldn't go through with it. I didn't know. Knowing is different. But faith is what allowed me to tell him about that place.'

'So you were, what, calling his bluff?'

'I was showing him the light,' she said. 'Aaron and I talked a lot about the afterlife. Not just about what Witnesses believe but what different people believe around the world. Paradise, heaven, reincarnation, ghosts. Even the idea that this life is all we get. I once asked him why he was so interested, and you know what he said?'

I thought about what he'd told me at the pool that day and took a punt.

'*Don't you ever feel like just getting it over with?* I said.

Faye blinked. Then nodded. 'So you know he was having suicidal thoughts?' she said.

I didn't reply. I didn't know that. But maybe I was supposed to.

Faye said, 'When Aaron told me that, I said I could relate.'

'You've had suicidal thoughts as well?' I asked.

She nodded, then tugged down the sleeves of her jacket to cover more of her hands. 'Have you been to the ledge?' she asked.

I told her that Chen, Leeson, Benita and I had followed the directions earlier that day.

'I go up there sometimes with kids from my youth group,' she said.

'Seriously?'

'Yeah. Why?'

'That place was covered in beer bottles and graffiti and at least one used condom,' I said.

She started smiling again. This girl was always smiling.

'Nothing is what it looks like from the outside, Justin,' she said. 'We go up there sometimes to blow off steam. Sometimes, I'd go by myself and throw things off. Like that Björk song, do you know it?'

I shook my head. 'What kind of things?' I asked.

'Just little things,' she said. 'Carl Collins, a guy from church, gave me a mood ring for my birthday last year, and I thought it was really special. Then I found out he'd given one just like it to Catherine Love, so I took it to the ledge and threw it off.'

'Did it help?' I asked.

'I was over him before that ring hit the ground,' she said. 'There's a power to that place. You go out there, and all your problems feel smaller. Know what I mean?'

'Not really,' I admitted. Then I remembered what Leeson and I had found dangling from a tree branch in the valley. 'Wait a second, did you throw a doll's head over the cliff? We found one this morning, hanging from a branch.'

Her face darkened a little.

She said, 'It sounds like you found Darcy. Dad gave her to me when I was a kid.' She didn't elaborate, and I didn't press her on it. There were more important things to worry about. 'The point is that there's a reason I told Aaron about that place. I knew — scratch that, I had *faith* — that when he got up there, standing right at the edge and looking down, he'd realise he couldn't go through with it.'

'Why?' I asked. 'Because of, like, the majesty of God or whatever?'

'No,' she said. 'Because up there, it's all just so obvious. You look down and think, *I wouldn't even make a dent in those trees.* The world is indifferent.'

'That doesn't sound very churchy,' I told her.

'Probably not,' she said. 'But that's how it felt when I thought about jumping.'

I remembered what Scott had told me about the difference between Richard Coyne and Carla Delevan. Some people cry for help; others don't. There was something about how open and honest Faye was that made her story less believable. I don't know. It was pretty intense. Maybe I'm looking for excuses not to believe her.

'What if Aaron *had* jumped?' I asked.

'He didn't,' Faye said.

'But what if he did?'

She frowned and said, 'Then his demons would have won.'

'What demons?' I asked. I surprised myself by thumping a fist into the back of the seat in front of me to emphasise my point. My voice echoed against the roof of the hatchback, startling Faye. 'What does Aaron have to be so fucking sad about?'

She flinched, her eyes wide and frightened, one hand reaching for the door handle, the other pulled up over her face, cowering like a dog in thunder.

I wondered if she'd been hit before.

'I'm sorry,' I said. 'I'm just trying to be a good friend. Please, if you know something, tell me.'

She turned to look out through the front windscreen. Scott was over by the Bi-Lo, cupping his hands against a dark old window to look inside, well out of earshot. When she turned back, her posture was stiff, her gaze ice-cold. 'He really didn't tell you, did he?'

'Tell me what?' I asked.

'How well do you know Aaron's stepdad?'

11

NOW

I've decided to tell the police what I know.
But we should talk first.
When can we meet?

I stared at the message on my laptop and waited for Leeson to pick up his phone. Faye didn't know the whole story – at least, I hoped she didn't – but she knew a lot of it. Meeting her had set everything in motion. Then we were West Haven's Most Unlikely Couple for a while. We were close. Sometimes we talked about what happened. How much had I let slip?

'Yeah?' Leeson said when he came on the line. He was outside somewhere. I could hear the chirps of insects and the howl of the wind. I heard something else, too: ice rattling around inside a glass.

'Sorry to call so late,' I said.

'Is everything okay?'

'Yeah,' I told him. 'No. I don't know. I got a message from Faye.'

'Okay.'

'She wants to meet.'

'How does she know you're in West Haven?'

'I'm not sure she does,' I said. 'But listen to this.'

I read him Faye's message.

'How much does she know?'

'I'm not sure.'

'What did you tell her?' he asked.

'I didn't tell her anything,' I said, hoping he didn't pick up on the uncertainty in my voice.

'You were with her for years, mate.'

'You were with Shelley for years, too,' I said. 'Did you tell her?'

That silenced him. He took a sip of whatever it was he was drinking. I heard the ice clink again. 'Do you have any idea what she's talking about?'

'Maybe she saved the text messages she sent, but I doubt it. And even if she did, I'm not sure they could hurt us, could they?'

'I don't know,' Leeson said. 'I don't think so. Do you swear to me that you never—'

'I didn't tell her anything,' I said. 'I swear.'

Leeson took another drink. 'Does she have any reason to hurt you?'

'Hurt me?'

'Was it a bad breakup?'

'It was twenty years ago.'

'Still.'

'I'll meet with her,' I said. 'I'll find out what she knows.' I glanced around my motel room. I guessed I'd be staying in West Haven a little longer. 'Leeson?' I asked. 'Are you still there?'

'No more over the phone,' he said. Then he hung up.

Turning my attention back to the laptop, I replied to Faye's message:

When and where?

I stared at the screen.

While I waited for Faye to write back, I performed a mental post-mortem on our relationship. Even after all these years, it hurt to look back on it. The way arthritis flares sometimes when it rains. Faye and I had been so certain of our love, the way only teenagers can be. But our demise was inevitable.

By the time we were seventeen, we were living in each other's pockets but fighting more than we weren't. I could be possessive sometimes. She liked to push my buttons. We couldn't live with each other. We couldn't live *without* each other. We planned to move to Melbourne together. I wanted to be a writer; she wanted to be a visual artist. We were going to be starving artists together. Then, the night before we were supposed to leave, we had an apocalyptic argument. I can't even remember what it was about. But the next day, I went to Melbourne on my own. I left her behind.

So yeah, she did have a reason to hurt me.

Running on nerves and pure impulse, I grabbed my phone and brought up Hannah's number. Then, without giving myself time to wonder if it was a bad idea – it was – I called her. There were three long rings before she picked up.

'Hi,' she said in a sleepy voice.

That voice was a cool drink on a warm day.

'Were you asleep?'

'No. Yes. But it's fine. Is everything okay?'

'Yeah, I'm fine. Everything's fine.'

'You don't sound fine.'

I gripped the phone hard. 'I was just hoping to hear Steffi's voice. I didn't realise how late it was.'

'Steffi's been fast asleep since eight, and there is no chance in hell I'm waking her. So my voice will have to do.'

Despite everything, a smile rose on my face. Her voice *would* do.

'How was bedtime?' I asked.

'Well, apparently, I don't sing lullabies as well as you, which is total bullshit because you know I can hit those high notes.'

'Oh, I know. I remember you belting out Mariah Carey at Jackie's karaoke night.'

'Steffi's worried about you, you know.'

I hesitated. 'What makes you say that?'

'She's not herself.'

'I haven't told her anything.'

'She's intuitive,' Hannah said. 'Sometimes to the point of being creepy. The other night, I swear she read my mind. I was thinking about how I'd oversalted the sprouts, and Steffi pushed her plate aside and said, *It's okay, Mummy. I wasn't going to eat them anyway.*' She paused. 'She's not the only one who's worried about you.'

'You don't need to worry,' I said.

'It was on the news,' she said. 'The body's being tested with some new DNA technology.'

'It's not a body, Han.' *Nature reduced him to parts.* I heard the TV in the background. The football was on. Hannah hated sports. 'Is Tim there?'

She was quiet. Then, 'You're not allowed to be jealous.'

'I'm not.' I was. 'That's not why I asked.'

'Why did you ask?'

I shook my head. This conversation was going south. 'I don't know,' I admitted. 'Maybe I *am* jealous. But I'm also glad you've found someone. You deserve to be happy.'

'Oh.' She paused. 'Well. Thanks.'

My lips were dry. My throat itched.

I wanted another drink.

'I'm sorry I couldn't make you happy, Hannah,' I said.

Her tone darkened. 'Can we not do this?'

'It's my fault,' I told her. 'I'm not sure I ever admitted that to you out loud. But the marriage. How it ended. It was me. I fucked it up. I fucked *us* up.'

She paused. 'Are you drunk?'

'A little,' I said. 'But that's not what this is.' The words were tumbling out of me now. 'Right towards the end, when we were always fighting, you told me something I didn't understand until tonight.' There was silence on the other end of the line. Hannah must have stepped into a different room, away from the TV and away from Tim. 'You said I didn't see you. Even when we were in the same room, even when you were standing right in front of me. Do you remember that?'

'I remember,' she said. 'That was one of our more colourful arguments.'

I leaned forward on the edge of the bed, once again assuming the crash position. 'I get it now,' I said. 'I didn't see you because I wasn't *there*. Not really.' I wiped tears from my eyes. I hadn't even realised I was crying. 'It's like there was an amazing movie playing out in front of me, and all I had to do was look at the fucking screen. But I didn't. I couldn't.'

'It's okay,' Hannah said.

'It's not.'

'We're all a work in progress, right?'

'Don't do that. Don't let me off the hook. You were the best thing that ever happened to me, and I blew it up.'

She didn't speak, but I knew she was still there because I could hear her breathing. I heard a shudder. She was crying too.

Finally, she asked, 'Why?'

'Why what?'

'Why weren't you there?' She sniffed. 'What was it you were so distracted by?'

I almost told her. I almost told her everything. But something stopped me – a big monstrous hand clamped over my mouth, and a sinister voice whispered, *We all go free or no one does*. When that hand unclasped, my head was straight again.

'Sorry,' I said. 'I didn't mean to get so deep. I'm just a little drunk and nostalgic, that's all.'

'You're not answering my question,' she said. 'When you weren't there with me, where were you?'

On the ledge, I thought.

'I'm going to let you go, Hannah,' I said.

'Seriously?'

'Yeah. It's late. I'm tired.'

'To be clear, you called me late at night to give me the apology I've been waiting years for, and you rip open a deep emotional wound, and then, just as we're finally getting somewhere, *you're tired*?'

I didn't know what to say, so I said nothing.

Hannah sighed. 'I don't know why I expected anything else.'

'I'm sorry, Han—'

'That's the third time you've apologised to me during this call.'

'I didn't mean to rip open a wound.'

'Yet here I am, bleeding,' Hannah said.

There was a chasm between us, filled with everything I hadn't told her. All those secret things I'd clung to, the way a man clings to the mast of a sinking ship.

'I might not be home for a while, Hannah.'

'What are you talking about?'

'I might be in a little trouble.'

She hesitated. 'What kind of trouble?'

Bap-bap-bap. A sudden knock at the door. Three firm raps.

'I have to go, Hannah,' I said.

'Of course you do,' she said.

'There's someone at the door—'

But she was already gone. The line was dead.

Bap-bap-bap.

Aside from Chen and Leeson, nobody knew I was here. I got up from the bed and tugged back the curtain to look outside. A big wooden meter box obstructed my view of the door. I scanned the car park, half expecting to see a police car. But my lonely little Prius was the only car there. The dark blue Forester was still parked outside the church across the street, empty.

Bap-bap-bap.

I opened the door.

It was him. The man in the cargo pants and black hoodie. He was holding a tyre iron in his left hand. His right was closed into a fist. His hood was pulled up, but now that I could see his face, there was no mistaking who it was. That nose, those eyes – it was like looking at an old photo.

Or like seeing a ghost.

'I told you never to come back here,' he said.

Then he slammed his fist into my face.

12

FRIDAY 5 FEBRUARY 1999

If Mum knew I rode to Aaron's place in the fading dusk light, she'd shit a brick. But ride there I did, pumping the pedals hard up the steep inclines, hugging the shoulder of the road, especially on the corners, hoping that any cars that came charging up behind me would see the little red tail-light and give me some space. I got honked at twice, and one guy shouted out his window to *get the fuck off the road*. But I made it to Aaron's in one piece.

When I dismounted and pushed my bike up the driveway, full dark had fallen. There are no streetlamps that high on the mountain. There was a little moonlight flicking in through the trees and the orange glow of the Wynn residence. It was creepy, but mainly because Aaron's stepdad was home. His red four-door ute was parked beneath the carport. Halfway to the house, it occurred to me that Devin might even greet me at the front door and say, *Hey-ho, kiddo, what's new?* the way he sometimes did.

How was I supposed to act around him, knowing what I did now? A strange fear gripped me, not so much a fear of *now* but a fear of *then*. If Devin had done what Faye said, I had been visiting his lair for years. It was like coming back to a treehouse you'd spent your childhood playing in, only to learn a snake had been living beneath the floor the entire time.

On my way up the front steps, I noticed Benita sitting on the porch swing again. She wasn't smoking a cigarette this time, but she was fiddling with the Bic lighter, rolling and sparking it compulsively. She seemed neither happy nor sad to see me. I wasn't a blip on her radar.

'Hi, Benita,' I said.

'Hey, Justin.'

'Is Aaron here?'

Benita scoffed. 'Mum won't let him out of her sight. I think she'll put a leash on him soon and one of those ankle trackers they stick on people under house arrest.'

'What about Devin?' I asked.

'What *about* Devin?'

'Nothing.'

She noticed the phone in my hand. 'Is that Aaron's?'

'Yeah,' I said. 'I accidentally took it home. I thought I'd better give it back.'

'Give it to me,' she said. 'I'll hold on to it for him in case he gets any more freaky messages.'

I considered telling her about Faye, then decided that it was Aaron's secret to spill. 'Is he okay?' I asked.

Benita looked at me, her face hidden in the shadow of the porch. 'He's lucky to have you, Justin. But look out for him, okay?'

'Of course. It's what best friends do.'

'No, I don't mean look *after* him, I mean look *out* for him.' It sounded like a warning.

'What do you mean?' I asked.

But Benita just shook her head and looked away over the dark neighbourhood. She slipped a pair of headphones on and hit play on her Sony Discman. It was a Nirvana album, playing loud. I took that as my cue to leave.

I moved towards the front door, but it swung open before I could knock. Aaron's mother, Lucy, came at me fast, arms outstretched, eyes wide and wet. On instinct, I took a quick step backwards. Lucy Wynn was a kind woman, but in all the years I'd known her, she'd never hugged me until tonight. She'd barely even touched me, but now her meaty arms were wrapped around me and squeezing tight. With her mouth so close that her breath tickled my ears, she said, 'We got him back, Justin. We got our boy back.'

'Yeah,' I said. Then, because I wanted to fill the silence, 'Thank God, right?'

Lucy ended the hug but kept hold of my shoulders. 'Thank God,' she echoed, nodding.

Considering how good-looking her daughter is, Lucy's a plain woman. Plain and big. The word *homely* comes to mind. God, I hope Aaron never reads this. Her hair is dyed black, but there are always grey roots showing. Her skin always looks sore and splotchy, and her nose is always red. Mum thinks she drinks a lot.

'Can I see Aaron?' I asked.

'He's in his room,' she said, then frowned. 'He's playing with his old toys, Justin, but don't tease him about it, okay? He's emotional. I think maybe he's regressing. Do you know what that means?'

'I think so,' I said. 'Like, he's acting like a kid and stuff.'

'That's right. He's acting like he used to, probably because life was easier when he was little. Then again, it was easier for all of us back then. Has Aaron talked to you, Justin?'

'Talked to me?'

'Has he told you why he ran away?'

'No. Sorry.'

Her pupils were big black circles. I wondered if she might have taken something.

'I don't think he's ready to talk,' she said. 'Not to me, anyway. You might have better luck. Come on in out of the cold.'

She pulled me inside, shut the door and stood at the top of the hallway, watching me walk down to Aaron's room. On my way past the arched doorway that looked in on the kitchen, I saw Devin sitting at the table. He was staring off into space, a half-drunk beer on a coaster in front of him. Filtered through what I now knew about him, he looked different. His big round face, usually warm and goofy, suddenly seemed sinister.

He turned in the direction of the doorway and spotted me. Blinking out of whatever trance he had been in, he gave me a soft, tired smile and said, 'Justin, hi. God, what a day, right?'

It was warm inside, but prickles of cold, shivery sweat broke out on my back. 'Right,' I said. I started down the hallway.

'Justin.'

I stopped.

'Come here for a sec,' Devin said.

I drifted into the kitchen, keeping my distance, feeling cautious.

'We need to work together on this, Justin,' he said.

'What do you mean?'

'We can't let something like this happen again.'

'What am I supposed to do?' I asked. The words came out with hard edges, but I couldn't help it. I didn't like the idea of Devin making it my fault when it was so clearly his.

'Lucy and I can do our best to talk to him and try to figure out what's going on in his head, but you probably know him better than either of us now,' Devin said. 'Your teenage years are like that.' He slid the beer across the table and asked, 'Want a sip?'

I stared at it, wondering if this was some kind of test. Devin laughed.

'I was ten when I had my first beer,' he said. 'My dad came home late from the pub. He'd had a few. He called me into his den — he had one of those — and two icy cold ones were waiting there. One for him, one for me. It tasted like shit, but that didn't matter. I wanted to be just like him.'

When he saw I wasn't going to touch the beer, he picked it up and put it to his lips. 'Your dad isn't around much, is he, mate?' Devin said.

'Not for a while,' I admitted.

'That can leave a big hole,' Devin said. 'When things with Lucy and me started to get serious, I was terrified of meeting her kids. I remember the first night I came over for dinner. Benita was as cold as an ice queen, not that I judged her. She was eleven and probably thought I was trying to replace her dad. But Aaron was just so warm right from the start. He asked me to play Nintendo with him, then laughed his arse off when he saw how bad I was at Super Mario.'

He drank again, smiling at some distant, rose-coloured memory, then looked away. I saw my moment to escape and took it.

I don't know the whole story about Aaron's dad, why he left, or even when. Aaron never talked me through the timeline, but what I'd pieced together from fragments of conversations over the years was this: Aaron's dad, Joseph Wynn — the family still used his surname, even Lucy, I wasn't sure why — had an affair, which broke up the marriage.

Depending on Aaron's mood, this happened either because Joseph was a lowlife prick who couldn't keep his little dick in his pants or he was forced into the arms of another woman because Lucy was hell to live with. The truth is probably somewhere in the middle. At times, Lucy can be uptight and pretty needy. Is that enough to justify her husband fucking someone else? No. But I know from my own parents that when one person has an affair, it usually means something isn't right in the relationship.

When I was little, I believed everyone was either good or bad, created in God's image or the Devil's. Now I know everyone has a little bit of both.

Joseph and his mistress stuck around West Haven for a while, and Aaron and Benita stayed with him every second weekend. But soon, for reasons that are still a mystery — to me, at least — he moved away. He now lives in Sydney with the woman he had an affair with. Somewhere along the way, they got married. Technically, she's Aaron's stepmother now, but he never talks about her. I think her name is Claire.

God, I should know that about my best friend, right?

I've seen precisely one photo of Joseph Wynn. Lucy probably took the rest down and burnt them years ago. But Aaron kept one, a Polaroid, stuck to the door of his wardrobe among a sea of other photos and magazine cut-outs. It's almost lost beneath a picture of Spider-Man Aaron painted with watercolours and a hideous photo of Benita mid-sneeze that he keeps there to mess with her. The photo shows Joseph in a hospital room, holding a freshly born Aaron, gazing down at him like this baby is the most amazing gift he's ever received. Aaron has his eyes.

I knocked at the bedroom door.

'Yeah,' Aaron called from the other side.

I pushed open the door and stepped inside.

Aaron was sitting cross-legged on the floor, intensely focused on a pile of toys. He'd dragged out all the old classics, Ninja Turtles, G.I. Joe, He-Man, and even a couple of ancient *Star Wars* figurines. The action figures were arranged into a sprawling landscape, two clear sides locked in battle.

'Hi,' I said.

He looked up and then immediately turned his attention back to the toys. He said, 'Hey, man.'

'Mind if I hang out for a while?'

'Whatever,' Aaron said.

He went on moving action figures around his makeshift battleground, not playing with them, exactly, but finding the right spot for each one, like a film director setting up for the perfect shot.

I reached over and plucked out a Donatello toy.

'These used to be so hard to get,' I said. 'Toyworld had about a million Splinter figures, but the actual turtles were like gold.'

Aaron took the figurine back and placed it where it had been.

'Chen was the first one to get them, remember?' I said. 'He had to go all the way to Daimaru.'

Comic books were spread out on the bed behind him. *X-Men, Spider-Man, Batman*. All the greatest heroes. I cleared a space to sit down.

'Why did you bring all this stuff out?' I asked. 'Your mum thinks you're regressing.'

He frowned. 'It's not that.' He moved Han Solo and raised the little plastic hand so that the little plastic blaster was aimed at Rocksteady's face. Then, gesturing to the toys, Aaron said, 'I miss doing shit like this with you.'

'Playing with toys?'

He nodded. 'It's like, I got too old for toys, but I still haven't *outgrown* them. Know what I mean?'

I didn't, but I said I did.

'Lately I've been thinking about how we're in this weird in-between place,' he said. 'We're too old to play with toys but too young to drive. Too old to believe the world is safe and free of monsters, too young to do anything about it.'

He looked up at me.

'I know you want to know why I ran away,' he said. 'But can we just, like, not talk about it? It doesn't have to be a big deal.'

I was tempted. The idea of just leaving it all alone and going back to how things were sounded wonderful. But it was too late for that. I already knew too much. I'd already changed.

'I know why you ran away, Aaron,' I said.

'What are you talking about?'

'I met your girlfriend,' I said. 'Faye Miller.'

'Faye's not my girlfriend.' He shook his head. 'Shit, maybe she is. I don't know.'

'Why didn't you tell me about her?' I asked.

'There's a lot of stuff you don't know, Justin.'

'Stuff you told her.'

'She wanted to listen.'

'And I didn't.' I wasn't being defensive. I was stating a fact. I surprised myself when I reached for Aaron's hand and held it. Aaron surprised me when he squeezed my hand and kept it there. Tears prickled in both our eyes.

'If you still want to talk,' I said, 'I want to listen.'

'How much did Faye tell you?'

'She said your stepdad is a bad guy.'

'Devin's not a bad guy,' Aaron said. 'He's a monster.'

13

NOW

For a while, everything was black.

I woke but didn't wake, caught briefly between two worlds, Wake and Sleep, Now and Then. With one foot still firmly in each, I felt cold hands around my throat. I didn't open my eyes. I didn't need to. I knew what those hands belonged to, could recognise the touch of bony fingers and the feel of dead flesh hanging off in strips. It was the corpse. That dead but undead thing I'd first glimpsed in the storage cage, then again beneath Steffi's bed.

It was a dream. I knew that. But in another sense, it was more real than anything in my waking life. It held more power over me than anyone. More than Hannah. More than Steffi, even.

Its hands closed around my neck. I couldn't breathe. It began to throttle me, squeezing my throat and shaking back and forth in sudden jerking movements. The sound of rattling bones was deafening. The stench of death seemed to settle over me and everything else like a veil.

The corpse shook me so hard that parts began to come loose. Bits of bone and old tissue and organs broke off and fell to the floor around me.

When at last I opened my eyes, expecting to see the hollow face of the corpse screaming back at me, it had been reduced to parts, scattered across the floor of my motel room. All that was left intact was a pair of skeletal hands, and those were still groping at my neck. From somewhere in that world, Beyond Awake, the corpse whispered: *We all go free, or no one does.*

As I exited that cool, frightening place, a light globe came into view. It hovered overhead like one of Leeson's UFOs. I tried to sit up, but a blast of white-hot pain behind my eyes kept me down.

But I was awake. I was safe for now.

We all go free, or no one—

'Hey, mate, are you okay?'

I couldn't see who it was, nor did I recognise the voice.

'Can you hear me?' the voice said.

I noticed the door to my room was wide open. My legs were poking through the frame, lying across the welcome mat, getting wet from a misty sideways rain.

'Mate,' the voice said, closer now. 'Do you need me to call an ambulance?'

I managed to lift my head. It was the skinny kid from reception. He was kneeling beside me, his face lit up with sheer panic. I tried to talk, but there was a delay between my brain and mouth.

'Is he gone?' I asked eventually. I pointed across the street to the church. Craning my head to look over the kid's shoulder, I saw that the Subaru was gone. Despite the pain in my head, I was thankful he'd only punched me, instead of using the tyre iron.

'There's no one else here,' the skinny kid said. 'I was on my way to the storage shed to get more TP when I found you like this. What the hell happened to you, man?'

'I …'

'Who did this?'

'I can't …'

'I'll be right back,' he said. 'I'm going to call the cops.'

'No.' I grabbed the kid's hand. 'No cops.'

'At least let me get you to the hospital,' he said.

'I'm fine,' I lied. 'Just help me up, would you?'

He took hold of my shoulders and hoisted me up. The pain in my head grew so intense that all I could do was grit my teeth and moan. I caught a whiff of metal in the air, then realised it was the blood inside my nostrils. Waves of pain were radiating out from a spot above my left eye. I gave it an exploratory poke, then winced. My fingers came back wet with blood.

'You should get that looked at,' the kid said. 'There's a first-aid kit under the desk at reception. I've never opened it, and it's been there from before I started working here, but bandages don't expire, right?'

'The first-aid kit,' I said. 'That's a … that's a good idea.'

The skinny kid stepped over my legs and out into the rain. I wished I could remember his name. He ran back towards reception in a hurried, bobbing motion. His mop of blue hair flapped up and down. It reminded me of a Muppet. I might have smiled if my head wasn't pounding like a jackhammer.

In the few minutes he was gone, I found my feet and crossed to the bathroom with slow, wobbly steps. I slapped the switch with the heel of my hand, but the bathroom lights were too bright. I switched them off again and studied my reflection in the dull light from outside. There was a raw, open wound on my face, hot with sticky blood. I dabbed at it with a fresh face cloth, turning the fabric from blue to purple, wincing through the pain.

My phone rang in the next room. It took me an age to get back to bed, but my mobile was still ringing when I reached it. Hannah was calling. She'd be worried about me. My call to her was practically a cry for help. Come to think of it, it *was* a cry for help, something I now regretted. She wasn't my person anymore. I had trouble remembering that sometimes. I wasn't her person either; it wasn't her problem to fix.

I sent the call to voicemail.

The skinny kid returned with a dusty first-aid kit, talking fast. 'Okay, so there's some Band-Aids and stuff in here, and I found a couple of tabs of Disprin in Cal's pigeonhole. Cal is like super old – older than you, even – so her locker is full of medicine.'

'Thanks,' I said. 'You can just leave that stuff here.'

'Uh, the thing is, this stuff is motel property.'

'Charge it to my room,' I said.

My phone rang again. Hannah was calling and again I sent it to voicemail.

The kid ran a hand through his wet blue hair. 'Well, if you're sure you're okay, I should probably get back to work.' He paused. 'Hey, listen, don't die on my shift, okay?'

I swallowed something hot and wet. Then I managed to raise a smile. 'How long's your shift?'

'I'm on until midnight.'

'It's a deal,' I told him. 'But I meant what I said before. No cops, okay?'

'Are you in some kind of trouble?' he asked.

'No trouble,' I said.

He hovered briefly, gave an odd little bow, spun on his feet and disappeared into the rain. I shut the door behind him and hobbled back to the bathroom. I dissolved two Disprin in a mug of water. The mug had the motel logo on it – THE GOLDEN FERN MOTEL: *Have a golden time!* I necked the contents and squinted through the taste.

Who still used Disprin?

I tried to unzip the first-aid kit, but my motor functions weren't fully working, so I gave up. Instead, I peeled off my clothes and collapsed into bed.

The pain behind my eye fell into a throbbing rhythm. Yet, somehow, I managed to fall asleep. As I drifted off, I hoped the corpse wouldn't be waiting for me.

The next morning, the pain in my head had retreated. The cheap motel pillow was wet under my head. I'd gummed it up with blood. My mind felt clear; there was only one thing on it. Leave. Go. Run.

I told you never to come back here, the ghost had said. I should have listened. To hell with sticking around to see Faye and feeling helpless together. I had run away from West Haven once. I could do it again. I had run from the trauma of my childhood, from Faye, from Hannah too. Hell, I was practically an expert. Yes. That was my new plan. Run. Run until I was out of track. Then keep running.

After getting dressed and throwing everything I'd brought back into my overnight bag, I plucked up the courage to check my phone. Hannah had tried calling four times last night. I should have called or texted to apologise and tell her not to worry. Instead, I put the phone back in my pocket.

I slung my bag over my shoulder and gave my room one last cursory look. Then I swung open the door, moved to step out, and just about bowled over the woman standing on my doormat. Her hand was raised into a fist. I'd caught her seconds before she knocked.

'Good morning,' she said.

She was heavy-set, dressed in jeans and a too-big puffer jacket. She had broad, solid shoulders and stark white-grey hair. There was a big, confident smile on her face. I had no idea who this woman was.

'Can I help you?' I asked.

She noticed my Band-Aid and wrinkled her nose. 'You didn't have that ouchie in your headshot.'

'Excuse me?'

'Sorry,' she said. 'I recognise your face from the photo in the bookshop window. You're a local celebrity around here. Full disclosure: I haven't read your books, but don't take it personally. I'm one of those horrible people who wait for the movie.' Then, gesturing to my Band-Aid with her chin, 'What happened?'

'I walked into a tree.'

It was a bad lie, but I was still catching up.

'Here,' she said. 'One of these is for you.' She was cradling a cardboard tray with two takeaway coffees. She put one in my hand and said, 'I hope almond milk is okay. My wife's gone vegan and keeps sending me videos of sad mama cows and their babies, so I guess I'm a vegan now too.'

I took the coffee because that's what you do when someone hands you one. But I repeat: I had *no* idea who this woman was. 'Thanks?' I said.

'No worries, but I'm less generous than you think. I just wanted one for myself, and felt guilty turning up with nothing for you.' She shook her head and laughed. 'Oh gosh, I didn't even introduce myself yet, did I? See what I'm like before I drink my morning coffee?'

She fished around for something in the pocket of her puffer jacket, then showed me a badge. 'I'm Detective Bobbi Eckman with Victoria Police,' she said as she pocketed the badge. 'Do you have a few minutes to talk?'

14

FRIDAY 5 FEBRUARY 1999

Devin's not a *bad guy*. He's a *monster*. That's how Aaron put it, and after hearing all the gory details, yes, I can confirm that's the case.

A monster.

Yesterday, a monster was something out of a Stephen King book or a John Carpenter movie. It was a creature pulled from the pages of *High Strangeness Monthly*. Something glimpsed in a grainy photo.

But yesterday was a long, long time ago. That's how it feels as I write all this down, and that's how it felt at Aaron's place as he laid it all out for me, as I sat as still as I could on his bedroom floor, hands on my knees, eager to absorb everything my best friend said but terrified at the same time.

'I was twelve when it started,' Aaron said. 'Well, maybe it started before that, but that's when I noticed something was happening.'

If *yesterday* felt like a long time ago, *twelve* felt like another lifetime.

'That would have made Benita thirteen,' he said. 'It was late. The first time, it was after midnight, I think. I can't remember why I got out of bed, but it was probably to take a piss. You know what my bladder's like.'

I did. When Aaron slept over, he always parked himself by the bedroom door because he took, like, thirty pisses a night. Aaron kept talking.

'I was on my way past my sister's room,' he said. Long pause. 'Her door opened.' Longer pause. 'Devin came out.'

I held my breath.

'It was dark,' Aaron said. 'But we had a night-light in those days — remember, the He-Man one?'

'I remember,' I said.

'Yeah, well, the He-Man night-light was on, so Devin's face was lit up. He had this look on his face ... If not for that look, I probably wouldn't have thought anything of it. It was like he'd been sprung. Like he'd been caught someplace he wasn't supposed to be.'

'What did he say?'

'Nothing,' Aaron said. Then he thought about it. 'Actually, he told me to go back to bed. So I did. He waited until I'd shut my bedroom door before he went back to my mum.'

'Then what happened?'

'For a while, nothing. He was really nice to me after that. Like, the next day, he took me to school early so we could get Maccas for breakfast in Flockhart. I kind of just forgot what I'd seen, and I hadn't really even *seen* anything anyway. He could have been in Benita's room for plenty of innocent reasons. Maybe she'd had a nightmare and cried out, and he'd gone in to check on her. I probably would have forgotten all about it if it had been just that one time.'

'But it wasn't the only time,' I offered. We were still sitting in the sea of old toys. Without thinking, I picked up a G.I. Joe and turned it over in my hands. I got the appeal. It was weirdly comforting. Maybe I was regressing too.

'No,' Aaron said. 'That wasn't the only time. About a year or so later, Devin lost his job with a building company in Harper Lake, and before he found a new one in West Haven, it started to happen more often. It'd be late. I'd hear his footsteps in the hall. Then I'd hear Benita's bedroom door creak open.'

'Did you hear anything else?' I asked, not wanting an answer. But Benita had told me the walls were so thin that she could hear Aaron crying at night.

Aaron shook his head.

I said, 'Are you sure he was … you know.' I couldn't finish the sentence.

'What else would he be doing?' Aaron said. There was shame on his face. 'You probably think I'm a pussy. I should have done something. I *know* I should have done something. But he's a grown man — and I was just a kid. And now look at me, playing with these fucking toys. I'm still a kid.'

I put down the G.I. Joe. 'Did you talk to Benita about it?'

'Not until later,' he said. 'Because right around my twelfth birthday — I remember coz that's when I got my BMX — Devin and Mum were fighting a lot. I used to pray they'd get a divorce. But it didn't matter as much anymore because while they were fighting, he stopped going into my sister's room.'

'Do you think your mum knew?'

Aaron shrugged. 'If she didn't, she should have. Parents are supposed to protect their kids. It's, like, their whole job. And if she did know and didn't kick his arse out – well, I can't even go there in my head.'

'What happened next?'

'Next, Devin became the guy he advertises to be. He was nice and fun and generous and goofy and embarrassing. He acted like a dad. We were happy. We were a family. This'll sound weird or fucked up or both, but I decided that I'd made the whole thing up. Like I'd dreamt it or something. How could the guy I knew *now* have done that *then*? It made more sense that it was some freaky and twisted thing I imagined.'

His face darkened. 'Then there was this big Christmas party at the end of last year. Devin went to the pub with all his contractor mates and came home shit-faced. The air changed when he stepped through the door. He looked the way he had that first night when I caught him coming out of Benita's room. Right there, at that moment, I knew I hadn't dreamt anything. Worse than that, I knew he would go into Benita's room again.' He sniffed. Tears were flowing down his cheeks. He didn't bother to wipe them. 'Unless I did something about it.'

'Did you?'

He shook his head. 'I came up here to my room and put the stereo on,' he admitted. 'I let it happen.' There were more tears now.

'Did you try talking to Benita about it then?' I asked.

'I wanted to.' He shook his head. His face had turned red and splotchy. As he finally wiped the tears away, he said, 'Do you ever just do or say something fucked up and then wonder where it came from? Like, does it ever feel like there's a demon inside that takes over sometimes?'

I wasn't sure what he meant, but I nodded anyway.

'The next day, that demon took over,' he said. 'I waited until Benita was alone – I didn't want Devin or Mum to hear – and it was thirty degrees that day, and Benita was sunbathing on the lawn. She was wearing a bikini. And I don't know. It just pissed me off. I wasn't mad at her, but the demon went after her anyway. I told her to put some clothes on. I called her ...' More tears. 'I called her a slut, Justin.'

'You didn't mean it,' I said.

'It doesn't matter. I took it out on her. And I remember wanting her to bite back, you know. I wanted her to get mad at me or hit me or something. But she just looked hurt and embarrassed. Then she went inside, put jeans and a jumper on, and sweated through the rest of the day.' He sniffed hard and wiped his eyes with his fingers.

'Why didn't you tell me about all this?' I asked.

'I just couldn't.'

'But you could tell Faye.'

He looked hurt by that. 'I know what you must think of her,' he said. 'But she wasn't trying to convert me or anything. She doesn't even believe in God anymore. We just talked. She has a way of getting people to open up. She's special, Justin.'

'Do you love her?' I asked.

'I don't know,' he said. 'How can you tell if you love someone?'

'I have no idea.'

He seemed to think about it for a second. Then he shrugged and said, 'Yeah, I guess I do.'

'Why didn't you tell me about her?'

'She asked me to keep it a secret. Her dad is, like, super religious.'

'I wouldn't have told anyone,' I said.

Aaron didn't reply. There was more to it than that. Maybe he was worried that the guys and I would laugh at him for going out with a Jo-Ho. To be fair, we probably would have.

'Why did she tell you to kill yourself?' I asked.

'It wasn't her idea,' Aaron said. 'It was mine.'

I noticed how fast my heart was beating.

'Do you really want to die?' I asked.

'Part of me does.'

'The demon part?'

He thought about that. Then, he shook his head. 'The *me* part,' he said. He looked down at his toys for a second. When he looked up again, he seemed older. 'When Dad moved out, I became the man of the house. I know it sounds stupid, but the man of the house is supposed to protect his family.'

It didn't sound stupid to me. I guess I'm lucky to have Scott.

Then Aaron said something chilling: 'If you're not brave enough to stop the monsters, then you're probably a monster as well.'

'So you planned to commit suicide because you're not brave enough?' I asked. 'Sorry, Aaron, but that's just, like, so dumb. Don't you think killing yourself would hurt Benita even more?'

'You don't get it, Justin.'

'You're right. I don't.'

'Have you ever felt completely powerless?' he asked. 'Have you ever felt like you don't want to be here? I'm not talking about West Haven. I'm talking about the planet. You asked me why I didn't tell you about all this. This — right here — is why. You don't get it. You don't know.' His jaw tightened. 'You can't help. And honestly, that's not even on you. Nobody can help. Not even Faye.'

I didn't think about this then, but now that I'm replaying our conversation in my head, I can see the twisted logic behind Faye's plan. She knows she can't help Aaron. He needs to help himself. Sending him to the ledge was insane and bogus and risky, but I get it now. She had faith he wouldn't go through with it. She bet on Aaron for the win.

'So,' I said. 'Are you, like, over it now?' I asked.

'Over what?'

'Over wanting to kill yourself?'

'All I know is that I'm back here now, at home, in my bedroom. Nothing's changed. *Nothing has changed.*'

Devin is still a man. Aaron's still a boy.

He sagged back against the bed, emptied of something.

'You have to tell your mum, man,' I said.

He shook his head firmly. 'Mum's lonely, Justin. After what my dad did to her, she's so scared of being by herself that she'd go into hardcore denial mode.'

'What about Benita?'

'I can't.'

'What about the police?'

'There's no proof. Benita would have to admit it, and then everyone would know about it. You know what this town is like. This shit would brand her for life.' He glared an accusation at me then. 'You can't tell either, Justin. Not the cops, not your mum. Not anyone.'

'I won't.'

'Promise.'

I took a deep breath. Then said, 'I promise, Aaron.' Then, I suppose because I was feeling grown up, I added, 'This isn't your fault.'

'Uh-huh,' he said. 'Yeah. Thanks.' But he didn't mean it. It was total lip service.

'What are you going to do now?' I asked.

'Well, I can't kill myself,' Aaron said. 'So I suppose I'll have to kill Devin.'

My blood turned cold.

'Will you help me, Justin?'

It took me a second to answer. 'Are you serious?'

He held firm for a moment, then blinked and shook his head. 'Nah, mate,' he said. 'Bad joke, that's all.'

15

NOW

There was only one chair in my motel room, which Detective Eckman had dragged out from the desk and sat on. I was perched on the sagging mattress. Eckman pointed to the pillow I'd slept on last night, covered with blood, and said, 'Do you think they'll charge you extra for that?'

'Maybe,' I said.

She glanced around the room. 'From the look of this place, they might not even notice. Are your books not selling well?'

'Excuse me?'

She spread her hands. 'Why else would you be staying in a place like this?'

'I'm a simple man with simple needs,' I said. I was trying to be charming.

'They've got me staying at a cute little Airbnb halfway up the mountain,' Eckman said. 'The first thing I do when I get to an accommodation is inspect the place with my black light. It drives my wife crazy, but I sleep better knowing there's no blood, semen or urine on the walls. I'm not sure I could say the same for this place.'

'What can I do for you, Detective?'

Eckman sipped her coffee, set it down on the little round table by the window, and then checked each pocket of her parka twice. Finally, she took a pen and notepad from her pocket and asked, 'Did you hear about the human remains found in the forest near here?'

Her tone was breezy and casual, as if she had just asked about a new restaurant opening in town that I just had to try. Eckman was at least a whole foot shorter than me but had the presence of a much larger person. The word *formidable* came to mind. If I leapt off the bed right now, I was confident I could reach the door, probably even the Prius, but this woman wouldn't let me out of the car park.

'Yes,' I said. 'I heard.'

'I'm working with a team that's trying to identify the remains and figure out how they ended up dead.' She cocked an eyebrow and smiled. It was a smug, dangerous little thing. 'Pretty weird timing, huh? You turn up in West Haven three days after a body is found?'

'Not really,' I said.

'What would you call it?'

'A very unfortunate coincidence.' I tried to smile, but all I could manage was a grimace. How did this woman know where I was staying? Could Leeson have told her, or had the guy at the reception desk called the cops about what happened last night? There was a bigger question. What was the detective doing here? Had Faye talked to the police already and, if so, what had she told them?

Eckman clicked her fingers in my face and asked, 'Are you still with us?'

I blinked out of my panic. 'What?'

'You zoned out on me,' Eckman said. 'Maybe you've got a concussion.'

'I'm fine,' I said.

'What are you doing in West Haven?'

Inhale. Exhale. Be still, my trembling hands. I tucked them under my butt and tried to swallow my nerves. I couldn't tell her why I was there. Leeson had been right when he pointed out how suspicious it looked: me turning up in town after a years-long absence, a few days after a body was discovered. So I reached for the most believable lie I could think of.

'I'm here working,' I said.

'Writing?'

'Promoting,' I told her. 'I'm doing an author talk in town.'

'What's that?' she asked.

'I talk a bit about my writing and sign some books.'

Eckman got her pen ready. 'When is it?'

'Tonight,' I said.

The lie began to grow before my eyes.

'Where?' she asked.

'A local bookseller.'

'Like, a bookshop?'

'Yeah.'

'Does it have a name?'

'Hidden Books,' I said.

That detail went into Eckman's notepad. Damn. If Eckman checked up on my story – and after meeting her for all of five minutes, I knew she would – my lie would come undone. Why hadn't I said I was visiting friends, hiking or taking a ghost tour? Any excuse would have been better than the one I'd pitched.

'Do you come back to West Haven often?' she asked.

'Not really,' I told her.

'How long has it been?'

'A few years.'

'I bet it's changed a lot since you grew up here.'

'Everything changes and nothing changes,' I said.

She leaned back, sipped her coffee, and studied me. 'Everything changes and nothing changes,' she echoed. 'That's small towns for you. I live in one myself. On an island, actually. When I come home, it feels like coming *home*. Does it feel that way for you?'

'No,' I admitted.

'Why not?'

This time, I went with the truth to keep things simple. 'When I left this town, I left some bad memories behind.'

'Like what?'

'Nothing I feel like revisiting now,' I said. My head hurt, and all I wanted was to close my eyes for a second. 'I don't know anything about the body in the woods, Detective. If I did, I'd tell you. If I could help, I would.' Then, because I couldn't help fishing, 'I heard you don't even know who it is yet?'

'Who told you that?' Eckman asked.

'I read it in the newspaper,' I said.

'Don't believe everything you read in the papers.' She smiled again. Then, looking at the wound on my forehead, she asked, 'How did you *really* get that cut on your face?'

'I told you. I—'

'Walked into a tree, right.' She paused. 'That's your story and you're sticking to it.'

'It's not a story—'

'Can I tell you about the night I had last night?'

I didn't know what to say, so I said nothing.

'It was around midnight,' she said. 'I was still at my desk for reasons that remain a mystery. The station in this town is smaller than the one in Belport, so you hear everything. I heard a commotion at the front desk, so I, ever the procrastinator, wandered out to look at what was going on. Melissa, the constable on duty, was taking a statement from a very twitchy man in a black hoodie.'

I held my breath.

'He wanted to report an assault, which isn't unusual,' Eckman said. 'The unusual part was, he was the one who carried out the assault, not the other way around. He was scared about getting in trouble and wanted to get ahead of it. He was there to confess.'

I knew where this was going, but I let her get there anyway.

'He told Melissa that he'd come from the Golden Fern Motor Inn, having just punched someone in the face.'

Inhale.

'When Melissa asked him what provoked the assault, he said that if the cops wanted to know about the body in the forest, we should come to you.'

Exhale.

There it was.

'So,' I said. 'You spoke to Scott.'

★

The last time I saw Scott (if you didn't count the time he stalked and attacked me) was three years earlier, on a warm March day at West Haven Cemetery. All things considered, it wasn't a bad place to spend eternity. The graveyard was built on a slope. The grass swept down to the edge of West Haven State Forest.

It had been a hot summer — the summers were always hot up there — so the grass was yellow. A light, warm breeze moved through the trees. Birds chirped. Insects buzzed. It was peaceful there. I didn't believe in God or an afterlife, but there was something nice about the thought of all those corpses feeding the trees. The circle of life, I guess.

I had just buried my mother.

Mum died of breast cancer. By the time they found the tumour, it was too late for surgery. They put her on chemotherapy and radiation, and she fought like a motherfucker. But in the end, it killed her.

She never remarried. She dated a few guys here and there, but none of them stuck. It was hard not to blame myself for that. I changed in the summer of '99. My outlook, my personality, my soul: they all darkened. So Mum poured her entire focus into me. I became the centre of her universe. When you give a kid that much energy, there isn't much left over for anyone else.

Then I just left.

Mum was part of West Haven, which meant she was part of what I'd been running away from. I'd abandoned her the way I abandoned Faye. It didn't feel like I had a choice at the time, and maybe I didn't. But sometimes I wondered if the tumour started to grow when I left. When she got sick, and later, after she was gone, I started reading studies about the link between stress and cancer. Stress hormones could inhibit a process called anoikis, which killed diseased cells and prevented them from spreading. It also drove people to smoke, drink, overeat and become less active, all of which increased the risk of cancer. All of which, towards the end, my mother did.

I wondered if I'd killed her.

Scott didn't come down to her grave. He hung back instead, hovering with cousins, distant relatives and friends. Even on the sunlit day, he looked shadowy. Once, he had been a calm, steady force in my childhood. He was confident and cool. He wasn't much older than me but had always seemed wise and worldly. That version of him had been stripped away over the years. Now, I didn't know him at all.

He was waiting when Hannah and I got back to the car.

'Where are you going?' he asked.

'Home,' I said.

He'd glanced at Hannah then, who looked lovely in a bright summer dress. She read the not-so-subtle social cues on Scott's face, then let go of my arm and took the car keys.

'I'll put the air con on,' she said. 'Take your time.'

Scott waited until she'd slipped behind the wheel and started the engine before he spoke again. He was dressed in a cheap, too-big suit. The sleeves on his blazer were an inch too long, and he'd hemmed the trouser legs himself with safety pins. He'd lost a lot of weight in recent years. It made him look like a kid dressed in grown-up clothes.

'How are you?' he said.

It was a tricky question to answer at a funeral, so I shrugged and said, 'I don't know. Okay, I guess. How are you?'

He answered my question with a question. 'Are you happy?'

I stared at him.

He cast his eyes into the graveyard and then the dense forest wall beyond. 'You have a daughter, a wife, you're a famous writer now—'

'I wouldn't say *famous*.'

'Are you happy?'

I thought about it. 'Broad strokes, yeah, I guess I'm happy.'

'Good,' Scott said. 'Then don't come back.'

'Excuse me?'

He pointed down to Mum's grave, still just a deep uncovered hole in the ground. 'She's gone, so you have no reason to come back to West Haven. So now, when you leave, stay gone.' He looked me in the eyes as he spoke. Small wrinkles at the edges of his mouth twitched. 'Don't come back to West Haven, do you understand?'

I just shook my head, feeling a little bewildered. 'Or what, Scott?'

Or I'll turn up unannounced at your motel room and knock you out, he might have said. Instead, he stuck his hands in his pockets and walked away.

'Yeah,' Detective Eckman said. 'I spoke to Scott.'

Slumped back in the motel chair with her fingers threaded neatly over her belly, Eckman was the image of a sated diner. She rocked back slightly, the front chair legs lifting an inch off the carpet, the back ones groaning under the weight.

'Things between me and Scott are …' I started. But I wasn't sure how to finish the sentence. Even as someone who made their living with words, some things were beyond explanation. There were colours and feelings and dark places beyond language. Instead, I went with an old favourite. 'Complicated.'

'That much is obvious,' she said, looking at my wound. 'Was the attack provoked?'

It hurt to think about the gulf between me and Scott. There had been a time when he looked out for me. My mind flashed to my second year of high school. Dave Billers had me cornered in the bathroom and tried to make me drink water from one of the toilet bowls. He presented me with two options. I could scoop some out and take a small sip, or he would shove my head into the bowl and flush. Sad as it may seem today, I was genuinely — *genuinely* — considering the first option when Scott came in and rescued me. After chasing Dave off, he reminded me that if I was ever in trouble, all I had to do was find him. The following year, he left high school, and we were forced to deal with Dave on our own. But damn, it had felt good to have Scott in my corner. In my life.

Now I was pretty sure he hated me.

'Do you usually take this long to answer a question, or is it the head injury?' Eckman asked.

'Will Scott get into trouble?' I asked.

'I don't see much reason to pursue charges unless you want to make a complaint against him.'

'No,' I said firmly.

'Good,' she said. 'That means less paperwork for me. And honestly, your little fight is the least interesting part about what happened. The thing that has the old juices flowing is what Scott said about the body in the woods.' Then, holding my gaze, 'Why would he think you know something about that?'

'Do you know what happened in this town in the summer of 1999?' I asked, knowing she must.

'We have a file about that this thick,' Eckman said, making a big C with her fingers.

'There were rumours when it happened,' I said.

'There usually are.'

'Some of those rumours were about us.'

'*Us?*'

'Me and my group of friends.' I put my hands flat on the bed beside me. 'They were *false* rumours, Detective. Make sure you make a note of that in your pad. But some people still believe them.'

'Like Scott?' she asked.

'Like Scott,' I said.

Eckman tilted her head and considered me as if I were a piece of abstract art hanging in a gallery, and she was trying to figure out if I meant something more than a few splashes of paint on the canvas.

'Is there something else, Detective?' I asked.

'That depends.'

'On what?'

'Do you have anything else to tell me?'

'No.'

'Want to take a minute before you answer?'

'I don't need to,' I told her.

She flipped her notepad shut and tucked it into her pocket. Then she changed the subject so fast it gave me whiplash. 'Have you ever cooked lobster?'

'... Huh?'

'I spent a year of high school as an exchange student,' she said. 'My host family lived in Portland, Maine. They go crazy for lobsters over there, and when you try one, you know why.' She made a chef's kiss.

'But they never quite tasted the same after I found out how they're cooked.'

I waited.

'When a lobster dies, bacteria build up quickly and wreck the meat,' she said. 'So you need to start cooking them while they're alive. When they put them in the pot, the water's cold, then they turn up the heat so slow that the lobster doesn't know he's being cooked until he's being cooked.'

'Okay,' I said, slowly. Because how the hell do you respond to something like that?

'Don't wait until the water's boiling, mate,' she said. She stood up and started off.

I felt a surge of relief, knowing I would, in seconds, be on my own. She reached the door, opened it, and then turned back.

'I'll see you tonight,' she said.

I blinked back at her. 'Tonight?'

'At your book signing,' Eckman said. 'That sounds like fun.'

'What made you change your mind?' Lisa Wu asked.

She was dressed in a tight black T-shirt tucked into tighter, blacker jeans. An old Cure track was playing in the background. She'd been unboxing new releases when I came in, and she added little *2-4-1* stickers while she talked.

'I'm not sure when I'll be back in West Haven,' I said. 'Besides, an in-store event at my old local would be a bit of a full-circle moment. I used to wander these shelves, imagining what it would be like to see my own book here one day. And here I am.'

I'd rehearsed this part on the short drive over.

Dull morning light fell in through the shop window, spelling out *HIDDEN BOOKS* backwards on Lisa's face. Her expression was somehow even stonier than usual. She had offered to host a book signing when we last spoke. Why was she making me beg for it now?

'The extra book sales wouldn't hurt either,' I added.

'They wouldn't hurt at all,' she admitted. She perked up a bit. 'I'm thinking we do an in-conversation here in the shop, a reading if you're happy with that, followed by a Q&A and book signing.'

'Great,' I said. 'How about tonight?'

She looked startled. '*Tonight?*'

'I'm only in town for a few days,' I said. 'Look, I know I'm not Harlan Coben. I'm not expecting a full house.'

She looked at my beat-up face.

'Walked into a tree,' I told her.

'Can I be honest with you?' Lisa asked. As if she'd ever been anything but. 'I think we could get a good turnout, even on short notice, but maybe not for the reasons you'd hope.' She took a well-chewed pen from behind her ear and chewed on it more. 'You have readers in this town, for sure. But in West Haven, you're famous for a different reason.'

I waited.

Lisa asked, 'Would you be comfortable going there during our conversation?'

'Going where exactly?' I asked, even though I already understood.

'Can we talk about what happened here when you were a kid?'

What choice did I have? I'd promised Detective Eckman an event, and now I had to give her one. So I dug deep, dragged up a smile, and said, 'Anything that'll get butts in seats.'

It wasn't a question of being okay with it.

With a triumphant nod, Lisa said, 'I'll get it onto our socials before lunch.'

My phone chirped. It was a Facebook notification – a private message from Faye Miller.

Where are you?

Damn. I'd forgotten about Faye.

16

SATURDAY 6 FEBRUARY 1999

I woke early to watch Saturday morning cartoons. I didn't actually *watch* them. I just *looked* at them. I needed to switch off, to fill my head with a swirl of meaningless colours. If my brain was full, there'd be no room to think, and if there was no room to think, it meant I didn't have to think about Devin creeping into Benita's bedroom and Aaron walking to the end of the ledge and letting gravity take care of the rest.

A long day stretched out ahead of me. Usually, the first thing I'd do on a weekend is call Aaron. Then we'd meet up with the guys and go to the pool, hike up to the gorge or play N64 at Chen's house. But I didn't feel like seeing anyone. Home, hot and uncomfortable as it was, felt safe. Aaron didn't feel safe. I had the strange sense that his drama was contagious, like an illness or virus.

I promised not to tell anyone what he'd told me, and I meant to keep that promise, but at the same time, this problem was way too big for just the two of us. Also — and God, this is so awful to admit, and I'd never say it out loud – Aaron didn't actually *see* Devin do anything to Benita, so even he couldn't be sure. I could ask her about it but, again, I promised not to tell anyone, which brought me back to the same place.

I couldn't talk to Benita. I couldn't speak to anyone.

I wouldn't let Aaron down again.

The pipes in the walls started to scream. Mum was in the shower because she worked on Saturdays. She drifted in ten minutes later, smelling like conditioner, drying her hair with a towel and drinking black Nescafé.

'You hungry?' she asked.

'No.'

'What are you watching?'

'I don't know.' I wasn't being a smartarse. I really didn't know. My eyes were staring at the screen, but my mind had drifted far away. I refocused. A big blue cartoon superhero bounded across the screen. '*The Tick.*'

'Oh. Fun,' Mum said. She sat down. 'Have you spoken to Aaron?'

'Not today.'

'Will you visit him again, do you think?'

'I don't know, Mum.'

She sighed. Then she stroked my hair. I pulled away. She made a strained little sound like she was offended, and I got that she was trying to be nice, but it was hot and sticky, and I didn't feel like being touched.

'Have any interesting dreams last night?' she asked.

'I don't remember,' I told her.

She looked at her watch again, then looked back at me with a pitying face.

'I'm okay,' I told her. 'Go to work.'

'Are you sure?'

I nodded. She got up as Scott came into the room, draped in the tattered old dressing-gown he'd had for years. It was purple once, but time had faded it to pale grey-blue. Mum made a big show of looking shocked, then went to the window and looked into the sky.

'What are you doing, Mum?' Scott asked.

'Checking if there are any pigs flying around,' she said. 'I haven't seen you up before nine for years.'

'It's too early for jokes,' he said.

'It's never too early for jokes.' Mum finished her coffee on the way to the front door. 'Have a good day, you two. If you go out, don't forget to slip-slop-slap. It's going to be another scorcher.'

She left. Scott drifted into the kitchen, dropped two slices of Wonder White into the toaster and came back to the sofa. He scratched himself and yawned.

'Why *are* you up so early?' I asked.

'I've got plans,' he said. 'I'm going over to Flockhart.'

'To see that girl?'

'None of your beeswax.' He looked at me. 'Are you okay, mate?'

Everyone was worried about me today.

'I'm fine.'

Scott picked the remote up from the coffee table and turned off the TV.

'What are you doing?' I snapped.

'I'm going to say some things now, Justin. I want you to listen to them carefully because they're not easy things to say, and I don't plan on repeating them.'

I didn't turn to face him, but I could see him behind me in the reflection of the dark TV.

'You're going through something heavy,' he said. 'When I was your age, I went through some heavy stuff too, believe it or not, so I know a little bit about it.'

I doubted that.

'There are things I couldn't tell Mum,' Scott said. 'Things I really couldn't even tell my friends. In those times, I wished I had a big brother.'

I turned to look at him to see if he was fucking with me.

His face was heavy and severe. He said, 'When Dad moved, he took me aside to give me this big, pre-prepared speech.'

'Seriously?'

In a deep voice, Scott said, '*Now that I'm not going to be around as much, you're the man of the house.*'

The man of the house. That was what Aaron had tried — and failed — to be. What had driven him to the ledge.

'That's dumb,' I said.

'I agree with your assessment,' he told me.

'Did he really say that?'

'He did. Like he was ever the man of the house.' Scott looked away and picked something from his nails. 'When he told me to look out for you, I thought, *Fuck you, Dad*. He didn't need to tell me that. I know I give you a lot of shit, Justin, because that's what brothers do ... but I've always looked out for you.'

'Gee, thanks, Dad,' I said. Scott flinched as if he'd just been punched. 'Sorry.'

'Look, it was easy to keep an eye on you and your shit when you were a little kid. All I had to do was watch for bullies and make sure you didn't break your neck getting off the trampoline. Life is different now. I can't help you if I don't know what's happening.' His toast popped in the kitchen. He got up, then paused to turn back. 'You have a big brother, Justin. Don't ever forget that.'

I wanted to say thank you. I wanted to tell him he didn't need to worry about me, but I sensed that I might break down in tears if I tried to form those words. So I just sat there instead, staring at my reflection in the telly, saying nothing. A while after that, the phone rang. Scott went to pick it up. Then he called out that it was for me. I went into the kitchen and asked who it was.

'Aaron,' Scott said. Then, lowering his voice, 'He sounds weird.'

'Weird how?' I whispered.

Scott shrugged and handed me the phone.

I took a deep breath. Then, into the phone, I went, 'Hey, man.'

'Get a pen and a piece of paper,' Aaron said. Scott was right. He did sound weird. He sounded older. The line was terrible too.

'Where are you calling from?' I asked.

'A payphone,' he said. 'Do you have the pen?'

'Why are you calling from a payphone?' I asked.

'Justin.'

'Where are you?'

'*Justin.*'

'Sorry.' We keep a lined notepad beside the phone for taking messages. I told him I was ready. Then I copied down what he told me. It was an address on Bowman Street. I'd never heard of it. 'Where's that?' I asked.

'Old West Haven,' Aaron said. 'How soon can you get here?'

'I don't know, I'll have to check the Melways. What's going on, Aaron?'

He made a big wheezing sound but didn't answer my question. 'I need you, Justin,' he said.

It was hot in the kitchen, but I felt a chill in the air.

'I'm on my way,' I said.

'Thanks, mate,' he said. 'And Justin?'

'Yeah?'

'Just you, okay? Don't bring the guys.' Then he hung up.

I set the phone back down and stared at it. Then I made two quick phone calls: one to Chen and one to Leeson. I'm not sure why. I was mainly acting on instinct. Something about Aaron's voice had scared me. I guess I thought there was safety in numbers. Or maybe — to quote *The Wonder Years* soundtrack — I needed a little help from my friends.

After making the calls, I looked up the address in the Melway. Old West Haven is a long stretch of burnt-out old properties that back onto the forest. We had a pretty bad bushfire up here when I was little. It ripped through those places like they were dry leaves.

After mapping out a route, I pulled on my sneakers, put on some sunscreen and stepped out into the baking sun. That was someone else. That was *him*. Me *before*. A stranger. Another kid that looked just like me. A doppelgänger, Leeson would call it. That other me wheeled the Mongoose out of the carport and pedalled off down Westlake

Drive. Later, when it was all done, he — *I* — came back to the house as someone else.

Chen and Leeson were waiting for me at the corner of Elm Street and Castle Creek Hill Road, sitting on the nature strip in the shade of a big tree, whispering to each other. They both stopped talking and looked up as I rolled in. I set the Mongoose against the small brick wall on the corner and took my helmet off. My hair was already soaked with sweat.

The guys circled up.

'What's going on?' Leeson asked.

'Is he fucking gone again?' Chen said. 'Because if he is, I'm sorry, I'm not going back down into the valley. My One Stars were so filthy my mum put them through the washing machine, and now they look too new.' He gestured to his feet. His shoes were spotless. You might think that's a good thing, but if you turn up at West Haven Secondary wearing new shoes, it's like an invitation to stomp on them. Dave Billers and those other guys say, 'I'll wear them in for you,' and then step on the toe. High school is like the Wild West, I swear.

'He hasn't run away,' I said. 'At least, I don't think so. He called me from a payphone and said he needs us.' I paused. 'Actually, he said he needed me. Full disclosure: he asked me not to invite you guys.'

Leeson and Chen exchanged an uneasy look.

'What's going on, Justin?' Leeson asked again.

'I don't know,' I told him.

A brown station wagon rolled past. The driver, a middle-aged woman with curly hair, gave us a curious look before moving on.

There was no way the woman could hear us — why would she even be listening? — but I waited until the car had turned off Elm and onto Merrick Court before talking again.

'Look,' I said. 'Aaron is going through some stuff. Big, heavy, fucked-up stuff. Now he needs me, and I don't know why, but I know I can't do it alone.' I looked at Chen, then Leeson, then back to Chen. 'Aaron needs me, and I need you.'

'What kind of stuff?' Leeson asked.

I took a deep breath. Then I broke my promise to Aaron. I told them about Devin, about Benita, about Aaron's plan to kill himself and Faye's plan to help him. They listened with wide, pitying faces. I should have felt bad for breaking Aaron's confidence, but I didn't. I felt relieved.

Or, as Chen put it: 'You look like you just ripped the world's biggest fart.'

Leeson and I didn't laugh, but we didn't blame Chen either. He always made jokes when he was nervous.

'I do feel like I was holding something in,' I admitted.

'I'm glad you told us, Justin,' Leeson said. He put a hand on my shoulder. 'We've got this. We're brothers, all of us.'

Chen stood up, dusted grass from his knees, and strapped on his stackhat. 'Where are we meeting Aaron?'

'Old West Haven,' I told him.

'So what are you pussies waiting for?' he said. 'Let's mount up.'

It was a long ride over to Old West Haven. The houses grew shabbier the further we got from the town centre, and we had to get onto Balarang

Highway, a stretch of nothing with fields and paddocks on either side of the road. The grass was burning yellow. The bitumen was hot. We had to ride single file because a semitrailer would thunder past every few minutes and just about blow us off our bikes.

There was no shade, and the sun was getting higher and hotter. When I applied sunscreen in the morning, I'd slathered it onto my face but forgot to get my arms, and now I could feel them burning. It was like we were crossing the Sahara on camels. I pulled in behind Leeson and Chen, both of them hot and bothered, but neither of them complaining, and I thought about how far we'd followed Aaron this week. First, we followed him into the mountains; now, we were following him into the desert.

Blissfully, Bowman Street was lined with big overgrown gums. When we pulled off the highway, it felt like the temperature dropped five degrees and, away from the roar of the trucks, we could hear each other speak again. Not that there was much to say.

'This neighbourhood is dead,' Chen said.

'A ghost town,' Leeson said.

We spread out on the street, handlebar to handlebar.

'Do you guys know the legend of Screaming Sharon?' Leeson asked.

We didn't.

'Sharon was a beautiful teenage girl who went to West Haven Secondary,' he explained. 'When the fire came through here, she was taking a bath, listening to her Walkman. The volume was up so loud that she missed the call to evacuate. She was boiled alive in the tub.'

'Damn,' I said.

'Bullshit,' Chen said.

Ignoring him, Leeson said, 'Her ghostly screams can still be heard on full moons. That's why they call her Screaming Sharon.'

Bullshit or not, this part of town did feel haunted. There were no cars, no people, no noise. There were just collapsed old houses, empty paddocks fenced in with barbed wire, and lots of crows. But as we put some distance between us and the highway, we started seeing signs of life. There were still no people, but there was at least some evidence that people had been there.

The houses on this end of the street were in various stages of demolition and reconstruction. We cruised past a big yellow Bobcat, parked and quiet for the weekend, and a huge wooden skeleton of a two-storey house. There were cement mixers and stacks of lumber behind temporary fencing. People were finally starting to build in Old West Haven again.

'What's Aaron doing all the way out here?' Leeson asked.

'I have no idea,' I said. 'Look, I guess that's where he called from.' I pointed to a payphone outside a small concrete milk bar that looked like it had been closed since the seventies. 'We must be getting close.'

Soon we arrived at two empty blocks of land, flattened and stripped back to dirt. The next block along was the address Aaron had given me. We pulled up outside and looked in, none of us in a hurry to get off our bikes and go inside.

It was a big family home. Well, once upon a time, that's what it had been. Now, it was somewhere between being gutted and renovated. Some of it was brick, other parts were exposed wooden frames with plastic sheeting stapled over them. The plastic was foggy — is *opaque* the word? — so you couldn't see inside. One strip had come loose and was flapping in the warm breeze like a Halloween ghost.

There was a massive pile of debris outside on the nature strip. A toilet had been dumped on its side, dripping black liquid into the gutter. Nearby, a kitchen cabinet lay in pieces alongside a stack of door handles and a broken mirror. The driveway was dry mud. A ute was parked there. I felt sick when I saw it.

'That's Devin's work car,' I said.

'Shit, do you think he's here?' Leeson said.

'Is this a trap?' Chen asked. 'Have we been lured here by Devin so he can flick our beans?'

'Not funny, Chen,' Leeson said. 'By the way, we don't have beans. That's girls.'

'Whatever,' he said.

I wanted to go home. 'Where's Aaron?' I looked up the street, but there was nobody around. There was no sign of Aaron. I checked my watch. It was like déjà vu.

'He must be inside,' Leeson said. 'Look.'

He pointed. Aaron's ten-speed was lying on the other side of a bank of temporary fencing, half-covered with a dusty old tarp as if he'd hidden it on purpose. The breeze died down. The plastic Halloween ghost stopped flapping. Everything fell still. Even the crows stopped squawking.

'The Oz Factor,' Leeson said.

'Again with the aliens?' Chen said. He was the first off his bike but made no sign of going inside. 'Well?'

Leeson and I dismounted, and we all walked our bikes over to the temporary fencing. There was a gap wide enough to fit through if we moved in single file. One by one, we stashed our bikes near Aaron's, then regrouped at the front door. Although it wasn't so much a *door* as a sheet of plywood designed to keep the weather out. Someone — Aaron? — had slipped it to one side to pass into the house.

We all went inside.

It was dark and cool away from the sun. The air smelled like freshly cut plaster and dust. A short hallway opened into a larger room — probably a living space. Spotlights were set up in each corner, but they were switched off. It took a second for my eyes to adjust. When they did, a sawhorse came into view by the window, which was covered with more of the same foggy plastic sheeting. A yellow extension cord was coiled beneath it like a snake.

'Hello?' Chen called.

His voice echoed around the chambers of the building frame and came back distorted. There was no answer.

'Aaron?' I called.

Nothing.

Then a small voice called from the next room. 'In here,' he said.

It was Aaron.

Chen and Leeson both planted their feet. As if they'd both taken part in a silent vote, they looked at me. Apparently, I was to head in first. I stepped into the room, which was smaller. There was a toolbox to one side of the doorway. A half-empty Big M carton sat on top, alongside a tape measure and level. If I had to guess, this room would be a kitchen one day, but it was hard to tell.

Being inside a house like this was strange, with the old version being dismantled and thrown away and the new version only half-built. Is *transitional* a word? If so, that's what it felt like. But when you stop to think about it, everything is transitional.

'Aaron,' I called. 'Where are you?'

A silhouette stepped away from the wall. 'Don't come any closer,' Aaron said.

'Why not?'

Nothing.

'Why not, Aaron?' I asked again.

Half concealed in the shadow of freshly nailed plasterboard, Aaron took a deep, shaky breath. Then he took a small step towards me. In the dull sunlight falling in through the plastic sheeting, I saw blood on his hands.

'Jesus,' I said. 'What happened? Are you okay?'

'I'm okay,' he said. 'It's not my blood.' His breathing was ragged and uneven, like he'd just run a marathon and only now remembered he had asthma.

The hot summer breeze kicked up again, howling through the cracks in the house and thumping against the chipboard walls. It sounded as though the house were alive, some yawning creature that had swallowed us without thinking, like a basking shark sucking up krill.

'If it's not your blood,' I said. 'Then whose blood is it?'

He shook his head and said nothing. He didn't want to answer the question. And it was like, newsflash: *I don't want you to answer the question either!* But he had called me here for a reason. Had he left blood on the payphone?

There was movement behind me. Chen and Leeson shuffled into the room. They kept their distance, keeping me between them and Aaron, like I might protect them from whatever was happening. Correction: *whatever had already happened.*

'Jesus, man,' Chen said. 'Is that blood?'

Aaron glared at me and said, 'I told you not to bring them.'

That just made me angry. I didn't feel bad for telling them about Devin and Benita. I was glad they were here, and I wasn't going through all this alone. 'What the hell happened, Aaron?' I said.

'It's too fucking dark in here,' Leeson said.

He stepped out of the dark, grabbed the corner of a plastic sheet that had come loose from a big glassless window frame, and yanked it down. Light poured into the room. I blinked against it. Outside, an ancient tin shed stood across an overgrown yard, wild with tangled blackberry bushes slowly eating a rusted-out old fire pit. A deflated basketball sat inside the fire pit, half burnt.

When I looked back at Aaron in the light, I saw more blood. It wasn't just on his hands but in his hair as well. There was also a smear around his eyes where he kept wiping the tears away. His expression was distant. He kept looking down at his hands as if they weren't his.

'Why is your stepdad's car here, Aaron?' Leeson said.

Still looking at his bloody hands, Aaron said, 'I tried to bring it in off the street before anyone saw it.' He looked up. His eyes were full of sorrow. 'But the keys are in his pocket. I can't go back in there.' He started to cry. 'I can't do it, Justin. I just can't.'

'Can't go back where?' I said. Then, trying to keep the piss-in-your-pants fear from my voice, 'Is Devin here?'

Aaron took a short step forward and collapsed into my arms. He clung tightly to my back and sobbed into my T-shirt until it was wet. I held him. What else could I do? I tried not to think about his bloody hands on my clothes and skin. Chen watched us, mouth slung open, trying to catch up. Leeson watched us too, crying now, almost more than Aaron.

'It was an accident,' Aaron whispered.

I stepped out of the hug. Aaron kept hold of my shoulders. He'd stained my white T-shirt pink.

'What do you mean, Aaron?' I asked. 'What was an accident?'

He opened his mouth, then closed it. Then he let go of me. He'd been squeezing so hard that my skin felt raw.

'Where is he, Aaron?' I asked. 'Where's Devin?'

He pointed to a shadowy doorway that led to a corridor. The sunlight spilling in through the window didn't penetrate it. I turned to Chen and Leeson. Leeson was crying into his hands. Chen was whispering to himself, shaking his head back and forth. Neither one of them was particularly eager to move.

Aaron was staring at me, pleading for something I couldn't give.

'Wait here,' I said. As if any of them were planning on coming with me.

I had never felt like the leader of the group before. If anything, our little gang was usually a democracy. We all agreed to something or none of us did. But leaving them there and walking towards that shadowy door felt symbolic, like I was stepping over an imaginary line. No, not stepping *over* – stepping *up*. I wondered if this was how it felt to be a dad. A real dad, I mean. Not one like mine or Devin. But the kind of dad who did bad things so his kid didn't have to.

I stepped into the corridor with the same sick, nervous pang I'd felt when crawling onto the ledge. Aaron grabbed hold of my arm. More blood on my skin.

'Are you sure?' he whispered. 'It's not ... it's not too late for you.'

Of all the horrors I was about to live, this moment would haunt me the most. In his confused way, Aaron was offering me an escape. A life raft. An *out*. Why didn't I take it? Why didn't I leave? Why does anyone fight against their gut? Why do dogs return to their owners after being beaten? Why do we do stupid, ugly things for the people we love? There are a lot of reasons, and there are none.

I was learning a lot about myself this week.

'It's okay, Aaron,' I said. 'Everything's going to be okay. We're here now. You're not alone.'

Fresh tears spilled from his eyes, cutting a clean line through the blood. I turned away and walked into the corridor. The darkness ate me up. The air was ripe with the smell of paint or glue or silicone. Another gust of wind tore through the house, screaming and moaning. The wind was hot. I was hot too. My skin felt prickly. I wiped my forehead with the back of my hand. It was slick with sweat. I touched my chest; I could feel my heart thumping. When I reached the end of the hall, I turned back. Aaron was watching me with a desperate, pleading expression.

There was a room at the end of the corridor. It was a large space with another doorway off the far wall, leading into what would one day be an ensuite or a walk-in wardrobe. There was a nail gun and a circular saw set against one wall, both plugged into a yellow power board caked in old mud. Above them was a large picture window without glass. More white plastic had been stapled to the frame. It moved in and out with the wind, like lungs.

Sunlight fell through the plastic, spotlighting a bloody heap on the floor.

I went closer.

I'd never seen a dead body in real life before today.

17

NOW

Faye lived in a Californian bungalow on South Forest Road, a densely populated area in walking distance of West Haven's main drag. Close to a dozen wind chimes were hanging from the porch, clinking together madly in the breeze. Metres and metres of fairy lights were wrapped around the posts on either side of the front steps. It was the middle of the day, but they were switched on, glowing and blinking weakly against the wet, grey day.

I was struck with a rush of nerves as I rang the bell. It had been a decade since I last saw Faye and two since we'd last slept together. There was almost too much to catch up on, too much time between us.

A tall woman answered the door. Had Faye always been that tall or had she just stopped walking with hunched shoulders?

'Hi, Faye,' I said.

'Oh my goddess, let me look at you.' She folded her hands beneath her chin and studied me warmly. 'This is weird, right?'

'Really weird.'

'But nice.'

'Definitely,' I said. 'I'm sorry I'm so late. Something urgent came up this morning and—'

'Forget all that,' she said. 'It's been ten years. What's an extra hour?'

I looked at her. The lines around her eyes had deepened over the years, and she had slightly misrepresented herself with her profile picture (but then again, didn't we all?), but she was still beautiful.

She took me by the arm and led me into a small, cosy living room, where a wood heater was crackling with fire. The smell of burning wood reminded me of home. The space was busy with throw rugs, cushions, taxidermy and big canvas paintings. The art had all been made by the same person and, aside from a handful of forest landscapes, all the subject matter was the same – a dark-haired woman with a striking nose and an elongated neck.

'They're self-portraits,' Faye said. 'It's like, totally vain, right?'

'No,' I said. 'I like them. Especially this one.'

It was an abstract nude hanging above the television in prime position, etched with charcoal. The breasts were like sinister eyes, the pubic hair and upturned triangle spilling dark red blood. Faye laughed, stood back and admired the painting as if seeing it now for the first time.

'I made that after I found out I had endometriosis,' she said. 'It's about infertility. It reminds me of my twenties. God, I wish I still had a body like that. What do you think about my new nose?'

'I liked the old one, but this one's nice too,' I said. 'You look great, Faye.'

Mild flirting.

'You too,' she said. Her gaze lifted to the Band-Aid on my forehead.

Off her look, I said, 'I walked into a tree.'

We sat side by side on a sofa draped in shades of blue and purple.

'Congratulations on your books,' she said. 'I read the first one.'

'Oh. Did you like it?'

'You know, I've written a novel. Well, I haven't actually *written* it yet, but it's all in my head. I had so much free time during the scamdemic that I thought, *why not write a book?*'

'Scamdemic?'

'COVID,' she said. 'That whole thing was a test to see how blindly people will follow the government.' I hoped she was joking, but her face was straight. 'Anyway, when the sheeple were out sticking mandated poison into their bodies—' Uh oh '—I was writing. It's like, I'm a visual artist first, but sometimes a canvas isn't enough. I'd love to pick your brain about it when it's done.'

'Sure,' I said, hoping that simple promise would never come back to haunt me.

I couldn't say I was surprised by all that scamdemic stuff. Evolving politics and the pandemic had revealed many people's inner kookiness, but Faye had always been eccentric. In the time we were together, she went from a 'recovering Jehovah's Witness' to a 'practising Wiccan' to a 'non-practising Wiccan' to an 'atheist' before settling on an 'omnist' (someone who believes in a fusion of faiths – to this day I'm unsure if she made that last one up).

'Faye, can we talk about the message you sent me?'

I've decided to tell the police what I know.

She frowned. 'It's about the human remains they found in the forest,' she said. 'I have information that will blow the case wide open. I'm going to tell the police. I've meditated on it, and it's the right thing to do. I don't need your blessing to tell the authorities what I know, but I'd sleep much easier knowing I had it. Do you understand?'

My heart climbed into my throat and waited there. 'What information, Faye?'

She stood up and offered me her hand. I took it. She led me across a short hallway and into her bedroom as if she intended to seduce me.

The dresser was piled with multicoloured jewellery, and another wind chime, made of blue and red crystals, hung from the ceiling. The bed had two big wrought-iron posts. A dreamcatcher hung from one post, a Native American headdress on the other. I was pretty sure Faye had never heard of cultural appropriation. The window gave an unglamorous view of the backyard – pyjamas, bras and underwear hanging from a Hills Hoist, like ducks in a butcher shop window.

She drew the curtain.

Maybe she did intend to seduce me.

She lit a candle on the dresser, then drifted to the bed and slipped her hand under the pillow. She brought out a small red leather book and clutched it between her hands, handling it delicately like an uncooked egg. There was something ceremonious about the way she moved. Every action seemed deliberate and performative, as if there were a studio audience just beyond the fourth wall that only she could see.

'The body in the woods,' she said. 'It's him.'

'They haven't formally identified the remains yet,' I said.

'It's him.' Her tone was firm but apologetic. And she was right.

'How can you be sure?' I asked.

With her eyes on the little red book, she asked, 'Have you ever heard of automatic writing?'

'I have,' I told her. 'Automatic writing is when someone claiming to have psychic abilities allows a spirit to manipulate their hand.'

Faye offered a surprised smile.

'Leeson told me all about it when we were kids,' I said.

'I forgot you used to be into stuff like this,' she said. 'Maybe you won't think I'm crazy after all.'

Too late for that, I thought.

'Why would I think you're crazy, Faye?'

'Because every night since his body was found, his ghost has visited me.' She put the red book into my hands. 'He speaks through me. I transcribe whatever he tells me onto the page.'

I just stared at her. Had she called me here for this?

'His ghost …' I started.

'… sends me messages,' Faye said. 'See for yourself.'

The expression on her face was desperate and pleading. So, with weary eyes, I opened her book and looked inside. There, in chilling, scrawled biro, as if written with the left hand of a right-handed author, were the same two words, over and over.

moon river moon river moon river moon river moon river moon river moon river moon river moon river moon river moon river moon river moon river moon river moon river

Over and over, on and on.

'Any ideas?' Faye said.

'About what?'

'The message,' she said. 'It has to mean something, right?'

I closed the book and asked, 'Are you a Jerry Butler fan?'

'Who's that?'

'He sang "Moon River".'

Faye sighed. 'You think I'm crazy.'

Yes.

'No,' I said. 'Faye, is this what you plan to show the police?'

She took the book back, traced it with her hand, and sat on the bed. 'I know they'll probably think I'm a tripper, but I couldn't live with myself if I held something back that could solve the case.'

A wave of relief crashed over me. Unless the police took testimony from beyond the grave, Faye had nothing.

'Faye.'

'Yes?'

'You have my blessing.'

She looked like she might cry. Instead, she threw her arms around my neck and pressed her body into mine. She whispered in my ear, 'Thank you.'

I couldn't help but feel sorry for her. Whatever had become of this woman, I had known the girl once.

She took a short step backwards. 'Are you sure Leeson won't mind?' she asked.

I froze. 'Leeson?'

'He turned up on my doorstep last night around midnight, stinking of whisky,' Faye said. 'No call, no message. Nothing. I don't even know how he knew where I lived.' She must have seen the concern on my face because she said, 'I don't mind that you told him we were meeting. There were never any secrets between you boys.'

If she only knew the half of it …

'What did Leeson want?' I asked.

'He wanted to know what I knew.'

'What did you say?'

'That I'd have to talk to you first.' She clutched the book to her chest. 'He made it pretty clear that if I didn't keep my mouth shut, there'd be trouble.' She shook her head. 'Makes you wonder what he's hiding.'

I wasn't the only one in town making myself look suspicious.

'I'll talk to him,' I said.

'Be careful,' Faye told me. 'I've known a lot of men like him over the years.'

'Men like him?'

'Leeson is a desperado,' she said. 'Only the goddess knows what people like that are capable of.'

18

SATURDAY 6 FEBRUARY 1999

My grandfather died when I was nine, and his funeral was an open casket, but I couldn't bring myself to look. Scott did. Later, huddled together at the kids' table with my cousins at the wake, he described what he saw.

'It was him, but it wasn't,' Scott had said. 'It was like they made a replica of him out of clay and make-up. He didn't look dead, but he didn't look alive either. He looked unreal. Not unreal as in cool. But unreal as in ... well, *un-real!*'

But Devin didn't look unreal. Devin just looked dead. He lay on his side, one leg tangled over the other as if he'd tripped. One arm was resting beneath his head. The other was twisted beneath his body at an unnatural angle. It made me think of waking up with pins and needles in my arm. The left side of his head — the side facing up — was covered with blood and flecks of something white or yellow or both. Like spilt cereal, I thought then. Now, thinking back, I think they were chunks of bone.

He was facing away from the doorway.

I drifted across the room, sticking to the wall, keeping my eyes on the body like a zookeeper circling a darted lion, making sure he'd loaded it with enough tranquilliser to keep it down.

I peered through the crack between the plastic and the wooden frame when I reached the window. The street was quiet and empty. Turning back, I looked at Devin's face without thinking. His eyes were open and staring. His expression was frozen, his mouth slightly open, his brows knotted in the middle. He didn't look scared or shocked. He looked confused. As if he just didn't understand. He didn't look like the monster Aaron said he was. He looked like my best friend's stepdad: a god in my childhood, a familiar, mildly comforting presence in my life.

I threw up.

It suddenly came on, gushing like a cracked water main. I hadn't eaten breakfast, so it was mostly clear liquid and bile. It splashed against Devin's Blundstones. I'd seen those boots a million times, set neatly beside the doormat outside Aaron's house, covered with clay and dirt from worksites. I used to think those were the boots of an honest, hard-working man. A *dad*.

There was a small shape across the room, a metre away from the body, outside the spotlight of the window. I went over to it. It was a blood-splattered hammer. My heart kept thumping. I could just about hear it. It made me picture a ticking clock, counting down to zero.

'Shit,' I had time to whisper before I barfed again.

The floor creaked.

For a brief, frightening moment, I pictured Devin rising from the floor, limbs twisted, blood spraying, pale hands reaching out, groping the air, clawing at me. But it was just Aaron. He stood between the corridor and the room, inching up the line but not stepping over it. I think they call that the *threshold*. Husbands are supposed to carry their new wives across it — something about never being able to turn back.

'What's that smell?' he asked.

'I threw up,' I admitted. 'Sorry.'

'That's okay,' Aaron said. 'That's normal, probably.' He stared at Devin.

I inserted myself between Aaron and the body, wanting to protect him from it somehow. 'What happened, Aaron?'

He was backlit by the plastic lighting so that I couldn't see his face. 'It was self-defence, Justin,' he said.

'He hurt you?'

'He tried to,' Aaron told me. 'I knew Devin was working today. Usually he makes a point of not working weekends, but he underquoted the owners to get the job of renovating this place, and the quicker he gets this house finished, the quicker he gets paid. After you came to my house last night, I got an idea.' He paused. 'It was a dumb one, I guess.'

'What idea?'

'I had to get Devin out of my life. Out of my family's life. But I also knew I wasn't strong enough to fight him. So I came here to give him an ultimatum. I told him to leave West Haven. Leave my mum, move out of the house. I told him never to come back. Or else ...'

'What?' I asked.

'Or else I'd tell the cops about Benita.' Aaron took a breath. 'It was the first time I'd said anything to him about it out loud. He must have known I knew, but we never talked about it. He didn't even bother pretending.'

'What did he say?'

'He didn't say anything,' Aaron said. 'He just turned vicious, like a wild animal or something. He ran across the room at me. Put his hands here, around my throat.'

The hot, sweet-and-sour taste of vomit clung to my mouth. 'What happened next, Aaron?'

'I reached out, and there it was.' Aaron pointed to the bloody hammer on the floor. 'As if it had been waiting for me.' He looked at me, his eyes hollow shapes in the dark. 'I thought he was going to kill me, Justin. He didn't give me any choice.'

He wiped at his eyes.

The sound of a car engine rumbled up the street. I held my breath and went to the window. Looking out through the crack, I watched an olive-green Jaguar roll past. The driver was smoking a cigarette and singing along to a pop song. Then the car was gone. A bird squawked somewhere outside. It seemed strange that birds would go on squawking. Didn't they know what had happened in here? Didn't they know what we were going through?

'Are you going to tell on me?' Aaron asked.

Tell on me. That seemed like such a childish way to put it. You *tell on* people who do something naughty. You don't *tell on* people for something like this.

I said, 'Maybe if we tell the police about Devin ...' I couldn't even get the rest out.

'I'll go to prison, Justin,' he said.

'You're only sixteen ...'

'My life will be over. My mum, Benita — their lives would be over too.'

As I stared at my barf, I realised that running away was still an option. Right now, this was still Aaron's nightmare. It didn't have to be mine. But the window to leave was small and closing fast. The longer I stood in this room, the more incriminated I was. Strangely, I missed my dad. Then I thought of my brother and what he'd told me.

You have a big brother, Justin. Don't forget that.

'Do you know what you're asking, Aaron?' I said.

He stepped out of the darkness. 'Yes,' he said. 'And I know this isn't fair on you and Chen and Leeson, but you're my best friends. I need your help. If you tell anyone about this, I'm dead, Justin.'

Dead didn't feel like a figure of speech here. It wasn't like I'd be dead if Mr Green found out I hadn't read the assigned chapter of *Lord of the Flies*, or I'd be dead if Mum caught me sneaking some of her riesling out of the box she keeps on the bottom shelf of the fridge. Here, dead meant *dead*. Italics, underlined, dead. I could picture Aaron going back out to the ledge, walking out and looking down into the valley below. He hadn't been able to bring himself to jump before, but now ...

Saying yes — keeping his secret — was saving his life. Right?

'What do you need us to do?' I asked.

'Help me clean this place up,' he said. 'Help me get rid of the body.' He took a deep breath. 'And never tell another soul.'

Aaron Wynn is my best friend, and I love him.

What else could I say?

Five minutes later, the four of us sat cross-legged in the front room of the house, talking in hushed, entirely surreal whispers.

'It's too risky to move him while it's still light outside,' I said. 'We have to wait until it gets dark.'

'My parents will get worried if I'm not home for dinner,' Chen said.

'We'll all go home first,' I explained, formulating the plan in real-time as it came to me. 'Then we'll all sneak out and meet back at midnight at our spot.'

'I can't go home,' Aaron said.

'You have to,' I told him. 'Benita said your mum already has you on a short leash. If she thinks you've run away again, she might call the cops. Devin's not going home, so you have to.'

Aaron nodded reluctantly.

Somehow, I was already detaching myself from the situation. My body wasn't going anywhere. But that didn't mean my mind had to stick around. I figured that when the job was done, I'd deal with whatever emotional fallout there would be – I was already pretty sure I'd never get a good night's sleep again – but there was only one way through this: switch to autopilot.

Softly, Chen asked, 'Where will we put the ...' He couldn't bring himself to say *body*. 'Where are we going to put him?'

'I haven't figured that part out yet,' I said. 'But in the meantime, we need to scrub this place down. Police can detect, like, tiny traces of blood, so we need to be thorough. We can't leave any fingerprints behind either. I noticed some old gardening gloves outside. We should put those on. We'll also need something to clean with, sponges and bleach. Does anyone have any money?'

We all turned to Chen. He always had money.

'I've only got a fiver on me,' he said. 'I guess I can pop home and get some more.' He turned to Leeson. 'Will you come with me to help me carry whatever we buy?'

'No,' Leeson said. Leeson hadn't said a single word since discovering Aaron covered in blood. He hadn't stepped foot in the back room where the body was either. He crossed his arms, cupping his elbows as if hugging himself.

'Fine,' Chen said. 'You can wait here.'

'No,' he said again. It wasn't clear if he was talking to us or himself.

'You all right, mate?' Chen asked.

'No, I'm not.' He stood up and dusted off his knees. 'I'm going home.'

I noticed Aaron look over at a flat-head screwdriver that had rolled into the corner of the room to gather dust. His expression was stiff and cold.

'We can't let you go,' he said.

Leeson opened his mouth, but Chen spoke for him. 'Can't *let* him?'

Leeson sighed. He didn't look frightened. He just looked tired. 'I won't tell anyone,' he said. 'But I won't help you cover it all up, either. I'm sorry. I just ... I can't give you that.'

Aaron said, 'How do I know you won't run straight home and tell your mum everything that happened?'

I felt a sudden, hot wave of anger at that. 'He just told you he wouldn't tell, Aaron.'

'I want him to promise.' Aaron looked from Leeson to Chen to me. 'I want you to all promise. This secret stays with us. It stays in the group.'

Chen shrugged. 'I promise.'

'Leeson?'

Leeson sighed again. 'Yeah. Whatever. I promise.'

Aaron turned to me and asked, 'What about you, Justin?'

'I promise,' I said.

As Leeson drifted towards the front door, Aaron called after him. 'Make sure nobody sees you leave,' he said.

Leeson nodded but didn't turn around. He stepped outside into the blinding sunlight and was gone. I was the next on my feet. It was time to get to work.

Chen found a roll of plastic sheeting in the front room, the same that had been used to cover the walls and windows. I helped him drag the roll to the master bedroom, then helped spread it out on the floor to wrap up Devin's body.

'What now?' Chen asked.

'We lift him on to it,' I said. 'Here, I'll grab the feet, and you two get his hands.'

'I don't want to touch him,' Aaron said.

He was standing on the threshold between the room and the hallway again, unwilling or unable to step over it.

'Me neither,' Chen said. 'What if we just roll him?'

It wasn't a terrible plan under the circumstances. Chen and I positioned ourselves behind Devin. Chen sat down on his butt, braced himself with his hands, and pressed against Devin's back with his feet. I put my hand on his shoulder. I expected it to feel stiff and cold, but it felt like any other body.

On the count of three, we pushed. Devin tumbled onto his back. His hand flung out from beneath him and made a horrifying crack against the floor, the frightening snap of bone. Only it wasn't a bone. It was just his watch. Its face was broken. Its arms had stopped moving.

We finished the rest of the job in silence. I don't want to go into detail about it. It's not that it was so traumatic or anything, although it was. It's that I don't remember it all that clearly. It's a bit of a fog. Maybe my brain was too busy in the moment that it didn't bother saving much for later, or maybe I was already starting to repress stuff.

I remember this: when we had Devin's body on the plastic, I tucked in each of his arms. Chen still refused to touch him, and Aaron was yet to step back into the room. Then I took one last look at his face: the open eyes, the surprised mouth, the curious little knot on his forehead. Then Chen and I wrapped him up, using the whole roll of plastic wrap. After that, we tied the plastic to his feet and head with an extension cord as if fastening a loaf of bread.

Chen and I fell back, breathing heavily.

'Oh man,' Chen said. 'This is ...'

'Don't,' I told him. 'I can't talk about it. If I talk about it, I'll think about it and if I think about it ...'

'I get it,' Chen said. He pointed. The blood-splattered hammer lay halfway across the room. 'Shit, we should have wrapped that up with him. What are we going to do with that?'

I looked over to Aaron, waiting for him to answer, but he didn't say anything. He wasn't crying anymore. His eyes had glazed over, like frosted glass, as if he'd slung a *CLOSED* sign over a shop window. Chen looked at me instead, his reluctant, unelected leader.

'I'll take care of it,' I said.

I turned my T-shirt inside out before I left the house because there was blood on it. The air outside was sweltering, the sun hot and bright overhead. Still, it was good to get out of that house. Taking care to make sure the way was clear, I pulled out onto Bowman Street and started pedalling as hard as I could.

I'd wrapped the hammer twice in a long strip of plastic pulled from one of the temp windows at the worksite. I held it tight in one hand and kept the other firmly on the handlebar.

Being away from the house made it easier to think. I wasn't sure if that was a good thing. Thinking allowed the total weight of what had happened and what was *happening* to settle on my shoulders. Strangely — or maybe it wasn't strange at all — it wasn't Devin's body I thought about on the ride. It was how Aaron had glanced down at the flat-head screwdriver when Leeson told us he was going home.

We can't let you go.

I looked up at the sky, swimming-pool blue, and wished it was raining. Rain would cool the road down, and there'd be something comforting about it too — something to do with washing sins away.

As I rolled onto Castle Creek Hill Road, past the war memorial and into the town proper, I passed more and more people. The streets were busy with Saturday traffic. The footpath was buzzing with joggers and dog walkers.

A couple were in the park, setting up for a first birthday, tying a big bunch of blue and white balloons to the post of the pavilion. A twenty-something-year-old woman carried a handful of paper cups and plates over to a patch of grass, where another woman laid out a picnic blanket. A gang of teenagers — most of whom I recognised from West Haven Secondary — hovered beneath the awnings outside the video shop, looking bored. Nobody looked at me, but it felt like everyone knew where I had come from, where I was going and what I was carrying with me.

As I cut across the intersection of Castle Creek Hill Road and Shelley Street, I noticed a police car parked at the bus stop. The lights were off, but the engine was running, probably to keep the air con working. There were two cops inside. Neither of them was holding a speed gun, so they weren't there to catch people going over the limit. From what I could tell, they weren't eating or drinking either, so they weren't on a lunch break. It was as if they were waiting for something.

As if they were waiting for me.

There was no way for them to know I was cradling a murder weapon or that my friends — and fingerprints — were waiting for me in a half-finished house on Bowman Street with a dead body inside it. Still, my cheeks went red, and I began to sweat even more than I already was. It felt like I was carrying a sign above my head that said *ARREST ME*, with an arrow pointing down in my direction.

I thought about turning around or at least crossing the street to avoid the cops, but both of those things would have made me look more suspicious. So I rolled right past them. The passenger-side window was down. The police officer on that side — a skinny guy with a flat-top haircut — held my gaze as I pedalled along. For reasons unknown, I tried to smile at him: a big, cheesy, nothing-to-see-here kind of grin. But I was nervous as hell and couldn't quite manage it. Instead, I offered him a twisted sneer. He turned in his seat to watch me pass, then said something to his partner.

Seconds later, the cop car pulled into the street, three-point-turned and started after me. I didn't turn around but kept an eye on them in the little side mirrors I'd stuck on the handlebars. I popped up the gutter and onto the footpath, waiting for the cop car to pass. It didn't. Instead, they slowed right down. Then the lights came on: a big show of blues and reds. People on the footpath ahead of me turned to see what was going on.

'Hey,' the skinny cop called from the open window. 'Pull over, mate.'

I stood on the pedals and craned my neck to look behind me. All at once, I understood. *Leeson*. He had left the worksite and gone right to the police station. He'd told them everything. He had spilled his guts. One friend had killed someone, and the other two were cleaning the mess. The cops had probably put out an APB and were now cruising the streets of West Haven looking for us. There was no time to warn Aaron and Chen. No time to do anything but – *run?* – pull over.

I stopped outside the chemist. People inside were peering at the flashing lights. The cop car rolled up to the footpath, but the skinny guy in the passenger seat didn't get out. He waved me over. I did as I was told. He was younger than I had first expected, hardly older than Scott. His trousers were huge, cinched tight with a big belt, like something out of a weight-loss commercial.

'What's your name, mate?' he asked.

The other cop, a slightly overweight woman with a disinterested look on her face, rested her hand on her side-arm.

'Well?' the skinny cop asked.

'Huh?' I said.

'It shouldn't be a hard question, mate,' he said. *'What's your name?'*

'Oh,' I said. 'It's Justin.'

'Justin what?' he asked.

'Huh?'

'Justin what?'

'Smith. Justin Smith.'

He jotted my name down in a little notepad, then flipped it shut. 'Well, Justin Smith, do you have something you want to tell me?'

I shifted my grip on the hammer. I didn't know what to say, so I said nothing.

Tapping the crown of his head, the cop said, 'Forgetting something?'

'Huh?'

'Thousands of words in the English language, you reach for *huh* a lot.'

'Huh.'

'Christ,' he said. 'Your helmet, mate. Where's your helmet?'

My helmet.

My helmet.

A surge of relief swept over me. With the numb panic I'd felt leaving the worksite, I'd forgotten to strap on my stackhat. This would have been cause enough to freak out on any other day. Today, it was wonderful.

'I'm so sorry, officer,' I said. 'I forgot to put it on.'

The cop cocked his head and sized me up for a beat. He must have known there was something up because I kept fidgeting with the damn hammer.

'What's in the bag?' he asked.

He pointed to the hammer.

'Videos,' I said. 'I'm returning them.'

Jabbing a thumb back the way they'd come, he said, 'The video shop's that way.'

'Oh,' I said. 'Right.'

The skinny guy's partner yawned behind the wheel.

'Promise me you'll walk your bike home, and I'll let you off with a warning,' the skinny cop said.

'I promise,' I said. It was the second promise I'd made that day. 'And again, I'm sorry. This never happens. I won't let it happen—'

'Uh-huh,' he said. Then he waved me off.

I walked my bike back towards the video shop until the cops were around the corner and out of sight. Then I turned and rode as fast as I could. I didn't stop until I got to the train station.

Repeating the journey I'd taken with Chen, Leeson and Benita just one day earlier, I locked the Mongoose to the chain-link fence across from the station, then snuck past the covered ticket counter. Then I jammed myself between two vending machines to hide and waited a long nineteen minutes until the 12.13 train hissed into the station.

Three or four passengers got off. Around twice as many got on. When the train rolled out of the station, I waited for the platform to clear then leapt onto the tracks and legged it into the forest. I ran until I ran out of steam and had to walk briskly, my head spinning around like the girl from *The Exorcist*, looking out for trains.

It was cooler inside the tunnel of green that cut around the side of the mountain, but it was darker, too, and there was less room to move if a Melbourne-bound train came barrelling up behind me. When I caught my breath, I started running again, holding the hammer tightly in both hands. The further I went, the heavier it felt. When I reached the stone spray-painted with an *X* and ducked onto the narrow trail that would take me over the mountain, it was almost too heavy to carry.

I tucked the hammer into the waistband of my jeans when I made it to the steep embankment. I needed both hands — and feet — free to climb. Hand over hand, foot over foot, I climbed up the rocky wall. Like last time, I read the graffiti as I passed: *PRACTISE PEACE, SORRY — PLANET CLOSED, IF GRAFFITI IS A CRIME MAY GOD FORGIVE US.* Then I lingered on a line that said, *CHANGE IS COMING — ARE YOU READY?*

I climbed on.

At the top of the embankment, I stepped through the stand of trees and out onto the clearing. The forest stretched out before me. I didn't slow down.

When I reached the ledge, I spread my hands flat and crawled towards the edge. I slid on my belly for the last metre and a half. When I reached the lip of the ledge, I rose to my knees and looked over.

Way below, the canopy of trees shifted and danced in the wind, moving in unison like one great organism. There was a magic to this place. Staring down into the green void, I thought: *This place doesn't care about what I've done — what I'm a part of. This place is indifferent. This place is ready — and eager — to swallow up our secret.*

I took out the hammer, wiped my fingerprints from the plastic as best I could, and tossed it over the edge. It seemed to hover briefly in midair, then sailed quickly down, down, down, where it disappeared into the trees.

I stayed there for a while, clinging to the rock. Looking down into the valley, everything suddenly felt very obvious. We needed to bring Devin here, I decided. The forest swallowed the hammer. It could swallow the body, too. It could swallow him forever, and it'd be like none of this ever happened.

19

NOW

I wasn't exactly sure what I was going to say to Scott. He needed to stop telling the cops I knew anything about the body, for one thing. But there were reams of unfinished business between us. We could spend the rest of the day unpacking our past. Or he could punch me again.

Scott had inherited the house on Westlake Drive. I pulled up across the street and sat in the warm car for a beat. The place was exactly how I remembered it: the same yellow bricks and brown window frames, the same small tidy lawn, even the same garden gnome, standing guard on the front step, his paint faded and chipped. I wondered if the same family photos would be hanging in the hallway or if Scott had taken them all down.

The dark blue Subaru Forester was parked in the carport. I half expected to see the Mongoose leaning against the wall of the house. Whatever happened to that bike? As I stepped out of the car and started towards the house, a wave of nostalgia hit me so hard I nearly lost my balance: a collage of memories, most of them good. Overcooked chops and open pizza boxes, laughter, action figures and sleepovers, camp-outs in the backyard, long nights talking about which girls we liked and long days in front of the telly, watching videos. Childhood.

I noticed a curtain twitch in the lounge room window. I couldn't see Scott, but since coming back to West Haven, I'd become pretty good at knowing when he was watching me. I ignored my fear and nerves and kept my eyes on the front door. I was halfway across the lawn when my phone chirped with a text message. I glanced at the screen, expecting to see Hannah's name there, but it was a number I didn't recognise. The message said:

Call when you get a chance. Tim.

I paused. Tim. As in, Hannah's Tim.

I couldn't imagine why he'd be contacting me. Maybe something had happened to Hannah or Steffi. For a moment, I forgot all about the twitchy curtain. I turned back to the car and dialled Tim's number.

Until now, I could count the number of words Tim and I had exchanged on two hands. We said hello sometimes if he was at Hannah's place when I dropped Steffi off, but he usually stayed inside, and Hannah rarely invited me in when he was there. I didn't know if that was his hang-up or Hannah's, but I was in no rush to get to know this guy, so I hadn't made much of an effort. To *know* Tim would be to humanise him, and to do that was to accept him as part of Hannah's life. Part of Steffi's life. A stepfather. The thought of that made me nauseous.

He picked up and said, 'Thanks for calling.'

'Is everything okay?' I asked.

'Have you talked to Hannah?'

'Not since last night. Why?'

'She's gone.'

'What are you talking about?'

'She left before we got up,' Tim said. 'There's a note saying she'd be back later tonight but she didn't say where she was going. I tried calling and texting, but she isn't responding.'

'What about Steffi?' I asked.

'She's here,' Tim said. 'She's fine.'

'Can you put her on?'

'Yeah, in a sec, mate.' His tone was cold. 'What did you and Hannah talk about last night?'

'Nothing,' I said.

'Nothing?'

'I don't know. Life stuff.'

'Well, whatever it was, it stressed her out. She was up half the night chewing her nails down to the skin.' He sighed. 'Look, mate, Han is special to me. I care about her. You can't just call her whenever you feel like it.'

'Are you asking me not to talk to your girlfriend, Tim?' I reached the Prius and turned back to the house. The curtains didn't move. 'I'm still her husband, you know. On paper, at least.'

'I'm telling you to think about Hannah,' he said. 'You'll always be part of her life because of Steffi, but she's fragile. When you call, you rip her open. I've watched it happen, and it needs to stop.'

'No offence, Tim, but this really isn't any of your business.'

'Hannah's my business. You should know I'm not going anywhere, mate.' He sighed again. 'I'm not asking you to pull your head in. I'm asking you to be a man.'

Be a man.

What does that even mean?

There was a rustling sound as Tim's phone changed hands. Then the lovely sound of Steffi's voice filled me up.

'Hi, Daddy!'

'Hey, Little Bean,' I said. 'Are you doing okay?'

'I'm great,' she said. Then, 'Well, I think I'm great. I don't know how to tell sometimes. Tim's phone is different from yours and Mum's.'

'Oh, yeah?'

'Hey, Daddy, did you know Alia has *two* dads?'

'Who's Alia?'

'Alia from school,' she said. 'She wears red glasses and then sometimes black ones, and the black ones glow in the dark.'

'Who needs glasses that glow in the dark?'

'Dad, you're interrupting my trail of thought!'

'It's a *train of thought*.'

'Train? That doesn't even make any sense. Trains go on tracks. Tracks can't be interrupted.'

My heart swelled. 'Good point,' I said. 'You were talking about Alia's two dads …' I got back in the car and, for a moment, forgot about Scott. I forgot about everything.

Steffi said, 'So, Alia has two dads, and they all sleep in the same house. They sleep in the same bed and everything.'

'Uh-huh.'

'So I was thinking … maybe I could have two dads—'

'Steffi …'

'Because if I had two dads, then you could move in here with Mum and Tim.' Kid logic. 'You don't have to sleep in the same bed or anything, but wouldn't it be nice all living in the same house?'

I could have cried. 'That would be nice, honey,' I said. 'But with Alia's dads, it's different. They're a couple. Me and Mummy …'

'Yeah, yeah, Mum already explained it to me,' she said. 'Do you know where she is?'

Sensing movement, I glanced at the rear-view mirror. A shiny red RAV4 had just pulled onto Westlake Drive and was slowing down. 'I do know where she is, actually.'

'Where?'

The RAV4 parked behind me. A familiar – and furious – face looked out from behind the wheel.

'She's here,' I said. 'I have to go, Little Bean.'

Hannah and I got out of our cars and met in the chilly street. She looked as though she'd dressed quickly: baggy pair of blue jeans with the cuffs rolled up, oversized jumper, unwashed hair, no make-up. It was the kind of raw, unfiltered, indoor look you usually reserved for your partner. She still looked beautiful to me.

'How did you find me?' I asked.

She held up the screen of her phone for me to see. A tracking app was open, marking my location with a little blue dot. 'You're still logged in on the Family Tracker app. Because technically, you're still family, which means when you call someone in the middle of the night to say you're in trouble, then stop answering your phone, I have to dump our daughter with a boyfriend who's already threatened by you to come to your rescue.'

She glared at me, anger shifting into concern when she noticed the Band-Aid on my head. 'Do I even want to know how you got that?'

'Your boyfriend is threatened by me?'

'Really? That's what you took from all that?' She lunged forward, then pulled up short. She drew her hands into fists, a boxer in a title fight. She looked ready to punch me. I hoped her swing wasn't as good as Scott's. Suddenly – almost violently – she hugged me. She smelled nostalgic and safe, like a cosy wood fire on a rainy Saturday afternoon. She stepped out of the hug but held on to me.

'I thought you were …' she started but couldn't finish.

'You thought I was what?'

'When you called last night … it sounded a lot like a goodbye.'

The muscles in my chest contracted. My bowels thrashed like fresh-caught fish in a bucket. I knew these symptoms well. I'd lived with them – or tried to – for twenty-four years. Guilt. Like a crushing wave. Like all the people in your life would be better off not knowing you. That the world would be better off without you in it.

'I shouldn't have called you,' I said. 'I'm sorry, Han.'

She dried her eyes and shivered against a breeze so sharp it seemed to have teeth. 'Christ, I forgot how cold it gets up here in the winter.'

'You get used to it,' I told her.

Hannah asked, 'Can we talk in the car?'

We slipped into the warmth of her RAV4, Hannah behind the wheel and me on the passenger side. She turned on the engine to get the heater going. A Morrissey song started playing. She'd been listening to him on the way up. Morrissey was my favourite singer; I'd introduced Hannah to his music. She switched it off.

'How was the drive?' I asked.

'Long,' Hannah said. She looked off through the windscreen, lost for a moment. Then, quietly and completely without venom, 'We were never going to work, were we? You and me. The marriage.

The way it all just fell apart. It was inevitable. We were always going to run into an iceberg. There would never be enough lifeboats.'

'Han—'

'I'm not here to fight,' she said. 'I have no interest in unpacking our shit. We're beyond that. *I'm* beyond that. I know how it happened. I want to know *why*.'

'It's more complicated than that,' I said.

'It really isn't,' she said. 'Last night, you said you didn't see me. There's a reason for that. Your mind was always someplace else. For a while, I thought it was because of your work, but the truth is you were here. You were always *here*. In West Haven. In your childhood. You were stuck here and you still are. And I don't know why because you never told me. You never let me in. You never trusted me.'

'I trusted you, Hannah—'

'Not fully. Not enough.'

It started to rain. Little droplets banged against the glass, concealing the outside world from view, drawing a curtain over the old house on Westlake Drive. Hannah wiped her eyes. She was crying again.

'We're done,' she said. 'You can't call me in the middle of the night anymore to tell me you're in trouble. You can't apologise for fucking up our marriage and then disappear. You can't lean on me anymore.'

'Okay.'

'I'm not finished. You can't lean on me anymore … unless you let me in. Tell me why you've been stuck in this place ever since you left it.'

I wanted to tell her, but a powerful, profound fear gripped me. And guilt. Always guilt.

'Please,' she said.

She put her hand against my cheek. Her fingers were still cold from the icy air outside. It made me picture the corpse, skeletal hands groping for my throat. I leaned away, shook my head, and said, 'I can't.'

Hannah gave a small, deflated nod. 'If you won't let me in,' she said, 'then you have to let me go.'

I closed my eyes, and in the darkness there I saw all the things I had kept hidden from her. I slung open the passenger door. Cold air swept into the car. I glanced back at Hannah, could feel her drifting … drifting … out of reach. I was still in love with her. I think she was still in love with me too. I shut the door, still in the car.

Then I asked, 'How comfortable are those shoes?'

Hannah lifted a sneaker and gave it a quizzical look.

'Start the car,' I told her.

She started the car.

'Where are we going?' she asked.

'You'll see.'

The West Haven railway station had received a revamp over the past several years. The foundations were the same – two sets of tracks, two brick platforms and a covered counter at the top of the concrete slope, but now there was a bank of unmanned ticket machines at the entrance and half a dozen small LCD screens mounted at intervals, displaying digital timetables. The colour scheme had changed too. Once, it had been covered in various shades of grey. Now it was white and blue.

'I didn't bring my Myki card,' Hannah said as we approached the electronic barricades (also new). In her haste to get out of the house, she'd forgotten to bring a jacket, so I had given her my parka to wear. She was swimming inside it. 'Where are we going?'

'You won't need your Myki,' I said.

One of the barricades was open in case anyone needed to get through in a wheelchair. Hannah and I slipped through it and out onto the platform. There were no staff and nobody else on this side of the platform. There were a handful of passengers on the opposite side, waiting for a train. An elderly couple sat together beneath the awnings, huddled together out of the wind. A woman and her dog stood nearby, both dressed in winter jackets. Further up, four teenage boys crowded together around a smartphone, laughing. For a moment, I saw my own face among them and the faces of my friends. The old gang.

'The next train is in six minutes,' I said, checking one of the LCD screens above our heads. 'After that, there's a window of thirty-one minutes. That should give us enough time.'

'Enough time for what?' Hannah asked.

'Hey, are you hungry?'

While we waited for the next train to come – and go – I bought us each a KitKat from the vending machine and pocketed them. Hannah stopped asking where we were going. For now, at least, she seemed content to follow on this cryptic little journey. The train rolled into the station one minute early, hissing and idling on the opposite platform as passengers hustled in. When it pulled away, Hannah and I were all alone at the station.

I held out my hand and asked, 'Do you trust me?'

She stared at it a moment, maybe seeing it for what it was – a red pill/blue pill moment. She didn't give me an answer, but she did take my hand and allow herself to be led to the end of the platform. When we reached the wire perimeter fence, I looked both ways to check that the coast was clear, then jumped down onto the tracks.

Hannah gasped. 'What the hell are you doing?' she said.

'Come on,' I told her. 'We should move fast before the next train.'

She just stood there, gaping down at me. 'You're crazy,' she said.

'I know.'

'This is dangerous.'

'I know that too, but you asked me to let you in or let you go,' I said. 'I'm not ready to let you go, Hannah.'

A small fearful smile rose on her face. Then she nodded, rolled up the sleeves of her parka – *my* parka – and leapt down onto the train tracks.

Just as I had during the summer of '99, we followed the tracks deep into the bush. There was near silence for a while, just the sound of our footsteps over wooden railings and crushed rock. Then, as if we were tuning into a radio station, the sounds of the West Haven forest rose around us: the wind moving across creaky branches, the gurgle of frogs and the far-off sound of rushing water. We heard the eerie laugh of a kookaburra.

'It's beautiful,' Hannah said. 'I love that sound.'

That beautiful sound was a warning. When kookaburras laugh, it's a territorial call. A caution to stay away. I didn't point that out, but I couldn't help wondering if the birds knew something I didn't.

The trees rose impossibly high above us. To one side of the tracks, the earth plunged into a dark wet valley foaming with ferns and moss. To the other side, the wall of the valley rose steeply. I looked at the trees, rolling on and on into a collage of green. I used to love this forest when I was a kid. It had been like the set of a fairytale or the world's best Zelda game. It had felt magical. Haunted, but in a good way, by fairies and goblins and elves instead of ghosts and demons. Now it just felt haunted.

I pointed. 'There it is.'

The stone stood where it always had but was half consumed by vegetation. I had to strip some vines back to be sure. There it was. A big *X* in faded, time-worn spray paint. The trail behind it was mostly gone, but I could just make out a thin line of dirt between the grass and moss. The air smelled like damp earth – the scent of my childhood.

'It's not much further,' I said. 'Follow me.'

As she stepped off the train tracks and onto the trail, Hannah gazed around with childlike awe. Her nose and ears had turned red from the cold. I could see her breath. 'How did you ever find this place all the way out here?'

'A Jehovah's Witness told me about it,' I said. 'Watch your step.'

We followed the trail as it hooked and turned and climbed up the mountain, pressing through giant wet palm leaves and grappling over slippery moss. The journey felt longer than I remembered it. My thighs began to ache and twice I had to pause to catch my breath. I was not a young man anymore.

Hannah reached the end of the trail first. She spread her hands and asked, 'What now?'

'Now we go up.'

I gestured up the stone embankment, slick with rain. The graffiti was still there but long faded and unreadable.

'Seriously?' Hannah said.

'Just follow me and watch where I put my hands and feet.'

'No, I'll go first. That way, if I slip, you'll be there to break my fall.'

Smiling genuinely, I watched her scale the wall quicker than I ever had in my youth, moving with confidence from crack to groove to branch to foothold. She had the toned, limber body of an athlete, and now all those Pilates classes were paying off. When she reached the top, I lumbered up behind her like an old chimp, nearly slipping twice. When I was close enough to the top, Hannah offered me her hand and helped me the rest of the way up. Then, hands on hips, she performed a slow spin, taking in our new surroundings.

'The air is fresher up here,' she said.

'We're nearly on top of the mountain,' I told her. 'Here, look at this …'

I led her through the tree line and out onto the rocky clearing. The wind howled up the valley and over the cliff face. This place was untouched by time. It could just as easily have been the nineties. Or three hundred years before that.

'My God,' Hannah said, holding her hands out to steady her balance against the wind. 'That view. This place. It's stunning.'

'We used to call it the ledge,' I said.

'I can see why.'

The ledge loomed beyond us, cutting a straight horizontal shape into the landscape. We eased towards it, careful not to get too close to the edge. Far below, the valley shifted and moved with the wind. Not much had changed up here, but the view had. West Haven had nearly doubled in size over the past two decades. It used to feel like the forest was lapping at the edges of town. Now it seemed the opposite was true. That filled me with a deep, existential sadness. For some reason, I found myself thinking about Steffi.

We found a dry spot at the edge of the clearing to sit down, in the shadow of an ancient fir tree. I cracked open both KitKats but, despite the hike we'd just been on, neither of us was hungry.

'Why did you bring me here?' Hannah asked.

'Because this is where it started,' I said. 'And this is where it ended.'

'I'm listening,' she said.

I took another deep breath. Then I let her in.

20

SATURDAY 6 FEBRUARY 1999

Before going back to the house on Bowman Street, I stopped by the West Haven Visitor Centre. There was an old lady behind the front counter. She was reading a book but when she saw me, she marked the page, put it aside and asked if I needed help finding anything.

'Do you have any maps?' I asked.

'Are you looking for anything specific?'

'Not really,' I lied.

She smiled at me. But it wasn't a nice smile. It was more like she was suspicious. I'm guessing she didn't get too many sweaty teenage boys through the door. She pointed me to a long wooden rack at the back of the room. I headed to the maps, passing a display of brochures and postcards, a few shelves of stuffed kangaroos and a long glass cabinet with weird stone jewellery for sale. The old lady and I were the only ones there. There were no tourists, which makes sense now that I think about it. West Haven isn't really a place you come to. You either live here or you pass through.

There were three maps to choose from. One was a town map surrounded by ads for local businesses. One included Flockhart and had little illustrations to mark popular hikes, lookouts and attractions. In West Haven, the lake and the war memorial were both marked as 'tourist destinations', which was pretty much the funniest thing I'd ever heard. I took the third map marked *Regional*. This one showed a lot more of the area and a decent chunk of West Haven forest.

I unfolded it on the glass cabinet, found the train station, then followed the tracks with my finger, deep into a field of green. The ledge wasn't marked on the map (I hadn't expected it to be) but I was pretty sure that with a little time I could figure out where it was. We obviously couldn't bring Devin with us the way we usually went, but I was thinking we could find another way in, maybe via a hiking track or a four-wheel-drive trail.

A sudden chill ran through my body. I couldn't see a fan or air-con unit, but it was freezing inside, the way old stone buildings get. I looked over at the old lady. She was still watching me, still smiling. I folded the map in a hurry and asked, 'How much is this?'

'Maps and brochures are free,' she said.

'Really?'

'Really,' she confirmed. Then, looking at the map, she said, 'Is that for a school project or something?'

'Definitely,' I said. Why I chose *definitely* instead of *yes* or *sure* or *uh-huh* is anyone's guess. 'Thanks, bye.'

I was halfway to the door when the old lady said, 'You're Janet's boy, aren't you?'

'You know my mum?' I asked.

'From the butcher shop,' she said. 'Which one are you, Scott or Justin?'

'Justin,' I said.

'She talks about you two a lot,' the lady said.

'Oh. Sorry.'

She laughed. 'Why are you sorry?'

'I don't know. Me and Scott are pretty boring.'

'I ask after you,' the lady said. 'I was worried about your mum. After your dad left. I hope you and your brother help with the chores.'

'Definitely,' I said. There was that word again.

I inched my way towards the exit.

'Tell her Carol says hi when you see her,' the lady said.

I promised I would, then thanked her again and hurried outside. The sun was hot and high when I stepped back onto the footpath. I'd left the Mongoose in the shade of a tree. With the map stuffed in the back pocket of my shorts, I pushed my bike up Castle Creek Hill Road. I didn't want to get sprung riding without a helmet again. I'd wait until I got to the other side of the crest before mounting up.

The strip of shops across the street from the visitor centre had been busy when I pulled in, but now it was deserted. Most people were probably hiding inside to escape the heat or flocking over to the public pool. Most people, but not all.

'Hello, Justin,' a voice said behind me.

I knew who it was before turning around. Dave Billers. He was coming out of the milk bar with his hand inside a packet of CC's. He was wearing footy shorts and nothing else. He'd taken off his

T-shirt and stuffed it in his pocket. It trailed behind him like a tail. His bare chest looked greased up and toned.

I kept walking.

'You owe me a football, mate,' he said, keeping pace. 'You better fucking bring one to school on Monday or — hey, slow down, fag — you better fucking bring one, or I'll make you and your fag friends eat dog shit.'

I'm not sure what came over me then.

After everything that had happened over the last few days, Dave Billers seemed smaller, somehow. Or maybe I got bigger. Like a growth spurt. Because it isn't just Dave. Everything feels smaller now. Mum, Scott, West Haven. Even the Mongoose.

Whatever. It doesn't matter. What matters is that I dropped my bike and turned around. Dave flinched. God, that felt good.

'Stay away from me,' I said. 'And my friends.'

He laughed and said, 'Or what, fag?'

'Or I'll smash your teeth in with a fucking hammer!' I said that. I *actually* said that. It might have all gone differently if Dave's gang was around to back him up, and maybe those words will come back to bite me on Monday when I go back to school. But somehow I don't think so. 'Now fuck off.'

Dave grinned. But his eyes were beady and scared. He took a step backwards, still watching me, and said, 'Whatever, fag.'

Then he walked off. He looked over his shoulder after a few steps to check if I was still looking his way. I was. I watched him to the corner of Shelley Street until he was around the corner and gone.

Then I exhaled.

I picked up the Mongoose and considered riding it, helmet or not. But then I changed my mind. Better not to push my luck.

When I got back to the house on Bowman Street, I felt a surge of relief (because the police weren't there), followed by a wave of gut pain (because Devin was). After checking that the coast was clear, I slipped in through the gap in the temp fencing and stashed the Mongoose alongside Chen's BMX and Aaron's ten-speed.

All was quiet in the house.

Chen was waiting in the hall. When he saw me, he called back down the corridor, 'It's just Justin, Az.' Then, to me, 'Did you get rid of the hammer?'

'It's gone,' I said. 'How's it all going here?'

'I think we're nearly done cleaning,' Chen said. 'All that's left is, well, the big part.'

'I have an idea about that,' I said, pulling out the map. 'How's Aaron?'

Chen lowered his voice. 'He's, like, zoned out or something. Can't say I blame him.'

'How are you, Chen?'

'Ask my future therapist.'

Aaron came down the hall, stripped to his singlet. He looked at me with hot, wet eyes, then gave me a quick man-hug. It lacked the emotion of our last one. This one was more ...

... is *transactional* a word?

'I moved the ute onto the vacant lot next door,' he said. 'You can't see it from the street. What's with the map?'

I told them my plan.

We sat down on the floor and crowded over the map. I found a builder's pencil on the sawhorse and used it to circle the spot on the map where I was pretty sure the ledge was. The train tracks — marked with a little dotted line — were the fastest and most direct way in, but that was off the table.

'What about this road here?' Chen said. He pointed to a narrow brown line that rolled out in big loops and curves, snaking its way around the mountain. 'It's not a main road,' he said.

'Probably a four-wheel-drive track,' I said. 'There wouldn't be much traffic on it, but some of those roads are pretty wild.'

Chen asked Aaron, 'Do you think Devin's ute could handle it?'

Aaron didn't say anything. He was staring at the map but his mind was someplace else.

'Az?'

'Huh?' He blinked out of his trance. Chen asked again. 'I think so,' Aaron said.

'Will you be okay driving?' I asked.

All four of us had our L-plates, but Aaron was the only one who knew how to drive a manual. He nodded.

Back on the map, I followed the dirt road with the tip of the pencil, then drew a little *X*. 'We can park here, then go the rest of the way on foot.' I checked the legend, then measured the distance with my thumb and forefinger. 'It's like, a kay to the train tracks, then another one to the trail.'

Chen looked back at me with a grave face. Neither of us said it, but we were both thinking it. Carrying a body all that way wasn't going to be easy. It might not be possible.

'We should get a copy of the train timetable so we can time it out right,' I said.

'I'll get one on the way home,' Chen said. He looked at his watch. 'Speaking of, we should all get going.' He took a big breath. 'Meet back here at midnight?'

'Midnight,' I said. 'That work for you, Aaron?'

'Huh?' he said. Then, 'Yeah. Midnight.'

'There's a few last bits of evidence to get rid of,' Chen said. He picked up a backpack beside the front door and took out two pairs of shorts and two T-shirts. As he passed them to me and Aaron, he said, 'I dug these out of my wardrobe. Wash them before you give them back. Actually, just keep them.'

I unfurled the T-shirt he'd given me. It was faded pink with the words *FBI: FEMALE BODY INSPECTOR* printed in white block letters. The shorts weren't much better. They were bright green with a rip halfway up the leg.

'Seriously?' I said.

Chen said, 'You want to risk dumping those clothes in the laundry basket for your mum to find instead?'

'Good point.'

Chen had brought a set of clothes for himself as well. The three of us stripped quietly to our underwear in the dark of the house and got changed.

When we were done, we went into the backyard, plucked the deflated basketball out of the fire pit, and put our bloody clothes in instead. We found a half-empty bottle of turps in the shed and soaked everything. Then Chen set it alight. He'd brought matches. West Haven had a total fire ban all summer, but I doubted anyone would notice the smoke all the way out here. The three of us stood around the pit, watching the flames, none of us complaining about the heat, none of us talking until the job was done.

Later that afternoon, after getting home and scrubbing myself raw in the shower, I collapsed in a heap on the bed and spent the next few hours staring at my clock radio. Time dragged. Midnight seemed a long way away. Then I got up, sat down at my desk and started writing.

My head is buzzing.

It's only seven.

Even so, I should get ready. I should stop writing and get ready. Can't forget to pack a torch. Hopefully I won't need to use it. Hopefully there's enough moonlight to see most of the way. We'll be less conspicuous that way and

Sorry. Mum just barged in. I got such a fright I nearly jumped off the bed. I spun the computer monitor towards the window so she wouldn't read what was on-screen. I need to be more careful.

Shit. I'm crying again. Why was I such an arsehole to Mum? When she came in I blurted, 'Jesus, Mum! Don't you knock?'

She isn't used to me snapping at her. Mostly because I never — *ever* — snap at her. But my heart has been pounding at double speed all afternoon and my brain is buzzing like a bug zapper and I can't remember the last time I ate anything and I'm scared that if I do put something in my mouth I'll barf it right back up again, an encore of my performance at the house on Bowman Street.

Mum said, 'Okay, Grumpy. But in my defence, I've been calling you for ten minutes. Dinner's ready.'

'I'm not hungry,' I told her.

'Why are your wedding pants out?' she asked, pointing to the back of my chair, where I'd slung my black hoodie and the only black pants I own. Mum calls them wedding pants but the only place I've worn them is at Pop's funeral and my year ten formal.

I shrugged.

Mum was leaning in my bedroom doorway with a glass of riesling in her hand, and a tea towel slung over one shoulder. She looked tired. An unfair, vicious voice in my head whispered: *You have no right to be tired. Your life is nothing compared to the day I've had.*

She pointed to my computer. 'What are you writing?'

'Just something for school,' I lied.

'Have you seen the Melways?' she asked.

I shook my head, then remembered I used it earlier today to plot the route to Bowman Street. Damn. Had I left it open?

'Yeah,' I said. 'Sorry. I took it out of the car.'

'Why?'

'Something for school,' I said again. Yep. The same lie twice.

'The same project you don't want me to look at on your computer?' she asked. 'You just about threw that thing out the window when I came in.' She fixed me with a long, suspicious look. Then she let me off the hook. 'Just make sure you put it back in the hatchback when you're done. I have no sense of geography.' She hovered. Mothers are mystical creatures. I swear sometimes she can tell something's wrong by smell alone. 'Did you see Aaron today?'

I didn't know how to answer her.

'Yeah,' I said.

'What'd you two get up to?'

'Nothing.'

'How's he doing?'

'I don't know.'

'You didn't ask?'

'I guess not.'

'Men,' she said. She looked at me with those hooded gentle eyes of hers. 'How are *you* going, Justin? You've been through a lot this week, little mate. Your best friend disappeared and reappeared like the world's lousiest magic trick. That's a lot to process.'

And the rest, I thought.

'I'm here if you want to talk,' she said.

'Uh-huh.'

'You sure you don't want something to eat?'

'Yeah, Mum. I'm sure.'

'You look pale. I hope you're not getting sick. I really think you should eat something, Justin. You need some fuel in that tank to—'

'I don't want any fucking food, Mum,' I yelled at her. 'I don't want anything. I'm not a little kid. I don't *need* you!'

Fuck. Why did I say that?

The saddest part wasn't the way my mum's eyes pricked with tears or the way she recoiled, as if I'd just thrown boiling water at her. It was that what I'd told her was true.

I'm not a kid anymore.

I'm not a *man* yet, either.

Where the hell does that leave me?

I wanted to take it back. Or if not that, I wanted to tell her I was sorry. But I knew in that fragile, pathetic moment that if I opened my mouth and started talking, everything would pour out of me. So I didn't say anything. I just looked down at my hands. Mum didn't say anything either. She took a small sip of wine, whipped the tea towel off her shoulder and left.

I followed her to the door, closed it behind her, and started to cry.

I'm still crying, even as I write this.

But Mum is tomorrow's problem.

It's time to get ready.

Pretty soon it'll be time to go.

Signing off for now.

Wish me luck.

21

NOW

'No.'

'Hannah?'

'No,' she said again. 'That's not true.' She started breathing heavily, as if on the verge of an asthma attack. 'None of that happened.'

'I wish you were right about that, Han,' I said. 'Hey, just breathe, okay?'

She stood up. I reached for her hand. Her skin was hot.

'Don't touch me!' She pulled her hand away, red-faced and trembling. She looked at the parka on her shoulders and, as if suddenly remembering it was mine, tugged it off. She dropped it onto the wet stones and took two quick steps backwards. Her ponytail had come loose on the hike up to the ledge and now a strand of hair was dancing wildly around her face in the wind.

'Why did you tell me?' she hissed. She covered her face with both hands and started to sob. I moved towards her and placed a hand against her back. She had sweated through her jumper. Viciously, she shrugged my hand away. 'I said *don't fucking touch me.*'

Through darkened, narrow eyes, she glared at me. No, that's not quite right. She glared *into* me, at the corners of my mind and my heart and my soul. *My truth.* It was as if she was just now seeing me for the first time and was repulsed.

'Why did you tell me?' she snapped again.

'Because you asked me to, Hannah,' I said.

She shook her head in disbelief. 'I didn't ask for *this.*'

'You asked me to let you in,' I told her. 'This is what I've been carrying on my shoulders for twenty-four years—'

'And now you've put that weight on me.' She wiped her tears. Her eyes were wide and white-hot. I'd never seen rage in her like this, had never seen it in anybody. 'You should have let me go.'

'Hannah …'

'If you were a better man – a *good* man – you would have let me go.'

This was a mistake.

What had I expected to happen, that Hannah might hold me in her arms like a mother and tell me everything was going to be okay?

'I was just a kid, Hannah.' My voice was pitiful and desperate.

She turned as if to leave, then spun on her heel and marched back like a malfunctioning toy. 'Don't do that.'

'Do what?'

'Don't use your childhood as a shield,' she said. 'I was a kid too once, you know. The worst thing I ever did was shoplift a *Dolly* magazine from the milk bar my mum worked at. This is different. This is …'

'What?'

She glared at my soul again.

'*What*, Hannah?' I said. 'Were you going to say *evil*?'

'No,' she said. 'I was going to say *unforgivable*.'

We just stared at each other. A silence fell between us. It was hard to tell if time had stopped or was still flowing as normal. Then Hannah screamed: a raw, primal reaction. Her voice carried on the wind and echoed around the valley thirty metres below us.

I tried to touch her again and again she pulled away. Through tears she asked, 'What am I supposed to do with this?'

'I don't know,' I admitted.

She screamed again, then took a step backwards. She moved too close to the cliff face. I grabbed her hand and tugged her to me. She whimpered: a dreadful, desperate little sound, as if I'd meant to push her over the edge. She looked terrified.

Terrified of me.

'Stop,' I said.

'Stop what?'

'Stop looking at me like that.' I let her go, then balled my hands into fists. 'Stop looking at me like you're …'

'Like I'm what?'

'Like you're scared of me.'

She stepped backwards, moving too close to the edge of the cliff again. 'But I *am* scared of you. I don't know you. I don't know who you are … Who are you? *Who are you?*'

'Hannah—'

'*Who the fuck are you?*'

Shame and guilt and fear and desperation swept up from somewhere like wind off the valley.

'Are you going to tell on me?' I asked. It just came out that way. I seemed to be regressing.

'If I say yes, will you let me leave?' Hannah asked.

My heart broke in two.

'How could you even ask me a question like that?' I said.

'I need you to answer it.'

Subconsciously – or perhaps consciously – Hannah shifted into a defensive fight stance. After Steffi was born, Hannah had become obsessed with protecting her in any and all possible scenarios, so she started taking Krav Maga classes once a week. I wondered if she'd ever considered having to use her skills against me.

My heart broke again.

'Hannah,' I said. 'Of course I'll let you go.'

She read my face, then relaxed her stance a little. She backed away slowly, ready to run if she needed.

'For what it's worth, I thought I was doing the right thing,' I told her, weakly. I was sobbing now. 'What I did then, and telling you about it now. I thought it was the right thing to do.'

'It's not worth much,' Hannah said. She kept walking.

'I don't know what I'm supposed to do now,' I called after her. 'Tell me what to do, Hannah. Tell me what to do and I'll do it. Please, just tell me what to do.'

Hannah faltered, turning back. For a moment she looked at me the way she used to.

'Telling the truth *was* the right thing to do,' she said. 'But you confessed to the wrong person.' She turned away again.

'Are you going to tell the police?' I asked.

This time she didn't turn around. 'What do you think?'

But she was gone before I could give her an answer.

I stayed at the ledge for a long while after Hannah left, thinking about what she'd said, wondering about what she was going to do with the information I gave her, hoping she got down the stone embankment okay and knew to watch for trains as she walked on the tracks. I might have stayed there longer – might never have come down at all – if my phone hadn't started to ring.

It was funny when you thought about it. Not too long ago, there was hardly any mobile reception out here. Now you couldn't escape it if you tried.

I answered the call.

'Where are you?' Leeson asked. 'It sounds like you're standing in a wind tunnel.'

'Nowhere,' I said. Telling Leeson I was at the ledge would invite questions I was unwilling to answer. 'What's up, man?'

'Have you left West Haven yet?'

He was calling to check up on me.

'Not yet,' I admitted. 'There's some stuff I have to take care of first.'

'Good,' he said. 'Can you meet me?'

'Why?'

'There's been a development,' he said. He sounded scared. 'A big one.'

I grabbed the phone with both hands. 'What kind of a development?'

'I don't want to go into it over the phone.' He told me where to meet him. Then he hung up.

I picked up the parka Hannah had dropped, zipped it on, and started back down the mountain, casting one long look back over the ledge.

★

The West Haven police station is a baby shit–brown brick building with rusted-out gutters and a flagpole but no flag. It was as if the Victorian Police Force was waiting for it to collapse in on itself because it would be cheaper than hiring a demolition team.

I checked the car park for Hannah's RAV4. There were several police vehicles and a crime scene van, but the rest of the spaces were empty. That didn't mean Hannah wasn't on the phone to Detective Eckman right now. There was a chance – a good chance – that I'd take one step inside the station and get arrested.

By the time I stepped through the automated doors and into the stuffy warm waiting area, which smelled like stale dust and mouse shit, I was soaked from head to toe with rainwater and sweat. It had been a long walk back from the ledge, not just because I'd had to shimmy down a wet stone embankment and hike four kilometres along the train tracks, but because I'd also left the Prius on Westlake Drive, parked outside 'Scott's house' (I still hadn't got used to calling it that) and had to travel the rest of the way on foot.

The reception area was brightly lit with fluorescent tubes. One of them was faulty, blinking on and off like a strobe-lit fever dream. Stacked against the far wall was a tall pile of packing boxes and smaller piles of retired office equipment that had been left to gather dust: a fax machine, a photocopier and an ancient computer monitor. A slate-grey hard drive stood next to it, with a Post-It note that read, *DON'T THROW AWAY – CONTAINS POLICE REPORTS.*

A young desk constable bobbed behind a wall of pandemic-era plastic. She glanced up at the Band-Aid on my head, then stiffened. 'Can I help you?' she asked, a little cautiously.

'I'm here to speak with Leeson.' Then I clarified. '*Sergeant* Leeson.'

'Is he expecting you?'

'Yeah.'

The desk constable sized me up. Then, nodding slowly, she said, 'Take a seat. I'll see if he's available.'

There was a row of fold-out chairs along the wall. I sat down and grasped my knees with my hands, still rattled and shaken by my conversation with Hannah, already feeling as though the whole thing were a bad dream.

A door swung open, and Leeson stepped out into the reception area. With his crisp blue uniform and – more importantly – his sidearm, he looked somehow bigger. He stood over me, backlit by the strobing light.

'I told you to text when you got here,' he whispered. He checked over his shoulder, made sure the desk was still clear and then glared at me. Then, in a hushed, urgent tone, he said, 'We shouldn't be seen together.'

Leeson might have been right, but at this point, I didn't care. Hannah had been scared of me at the ledge. *Scared of me.* Scared of what I had done, who I was in that deep soul-place strictly reserved for those we love the most.

I had let her in, and I had lost her anyway.

'What's the development?' I asked.

Leeson's eyes lit like fire. He quickly checked over his shoulder again, moving his hand instinctively to his hip, as if he meant to shoot me if I didn't do as he asked. Here was a man used to getting what he wanted.

'Jesus, keep your voice down. How's it going to look if—'

'Everything okay out here, Geoff?'

Detective Eckman had appeared in the reception area as if by magic. She wasn't wearing any shoes and was instead padding around in socks. That's probably why we didn't hear her approach. She'd shed her puffer jacket since this morning and was now in a plain white T-shirt, tucked in. She had a Pepsi in one hand and a manila folder in the other. A label on the folder read: *LAB RESULTS*. Was that the development Leeson had mentioned or was Eckman trying to get in my head?

'Yep, everything's fine, Bobbi,' Leeson called over. 'We're just making dinner plans and I guess we got caught up talking.'

'Dinner plans,' Eckman echoed. 'You two know each other?'

Leeson shrugged. 'We went to the same high school.'

Eckman chugged her Pepsi and smiled in my direction. 'Long time no see.' Then to Leeson, 'I spent five minutes in his motel room this morning, but it's not as sordid as it sounds.' Gesturing to the Band-Aid on my head, she added, 'How's the ouchie?'

'Fine,' I said.

Leeson looked hard at me. As casually as he could muster, he said, 'You and Bobbi have met?'

Eckman didn't give me a chance to answer. 'Are you excited about tonight?' she asked.

'Tonight?'

'The thing at the bookshop.'

'Oh, right,' I said. 'Yeah. Sure.'

'Me too. I've never been to a book signing before.' Smiling and sucking down Pepsi, Eckman watched me. She drained the can, tossed it into the yellow recycle bin beneath the front counter, and then gave the manila folder a satisfied tap. 'Enjoy your dinner.' To Leeson, she added, 'Both of you.'

Then she was gone, padding away silently like a cat.

Leeson lowered his voice. 'Outside,' he said. 'Now.'

When the automated doors rattled open and I stepped out of the police station into the wind, big hands grabbed the back of my parka and swung me sideways. I'd stuffed my hands into the pockets of my jeans to ward off the cold and I didn't get them out fast enough to break my fall. I hit the wet grass with a ringing thud. The gash on my head flared, and my teeth rattled.

'Get up,' Leeson snapped.

It seemed like a strange thing to say – he was the reason I was on the ground in the first place. I planted my hands beneath me and stumbled to my feet, half expecting to see Detective Eckman coming at me with handcuffs, her side-arm drawn in one hand and her manila folder in the other, shouting, 'You have the right to remain silent!' The cops didn't say that in this country, but it had been the mother of all long days and my mind was still catching up to my body.

Leeson came around again, looking wild and savage – a guard dog off the leash. There was a frightening, crazed expression on his face. He must have been crazed to attack me like this in front of the police station. I scanned the area. He moved on me again, picked me up by the scruff of my neck and slammed me against the bough of a gum tree.

'Get the fuck off me, man,' I snapped. 'What the hell are you doing?'

'What did you tell her?' he hissed at me.

Was he talking about Hannah?

'What did you tell the detective?' he said.

'Nothing, I swear—'

'What was she doing at your motel?'

'Scott attacked me, all right? Then he turned himself in and sent Eckman after me. But I didn't tell her anything. I promise.'

Leeson looked around as if suddenly remembering where he was. He ran a hand through his hair to calm himself. A deep crease appeared between his eyes, like a mathematician running lines of complex equations in his head.

'Scott attacked you?'

'Knocked me out cold,' I said.

'Why?'

'Why do you think?'

Leeson sighed and gave a small nod.

'I spoke to Faye,' I said. 'We have nothing to worry about with her.' I hesitated. 'She said you bullied her.'

Leeson's nostrils flared. 'I didn't bully her.'

'I told you I'd take care of it.'

'I had a few too many last night after getting back from Chen's place,' he admitted. 'You know how it gets when it's late, and you're by yourself and you just can't help but pick the scab.'

I did.

'But I meant what I told her,' Leeson said. 'I know you two have history, but if she starts running her mouth—'

'She won't.'

'All I'm saying is, there's no line I won't cross.' He frowned.

If he was still talking about Faye, why did that last part feel directed at me?

I thought about Hannah.

'What's the development you called about?' I asked.

'Not here,' he said.

He led me to his car, and I got in.

We started driving towards Old West Haven.

22

SATURDAY 6 / SUNDAY 7 FEBRUARY 1999

Shit shit FUCKING SHIT it's all fucked *I'm fucked* breathe, Justin keep going just breathe keep going keep writing get it down on the page out of my head breathe …

I left the house at 11.30 in my wedding pants, and wait.

There was a telephone call before that.

Around 8.30. Scott picked it up, then called out that it was for me. I went into the kitchen. Mum was already in bed. Scott went back to the couch and spread out. He was drinking Coke from a two-litre bottle.

'Who is it?' I asked on my way past.

'A girl,' he said.

I figured it must be Benita. I don't really know any other girls.

It wasn't Benita.

'Hi, Justin.' I didn't recognise the voice right away. 'It's Faye.'

'Oh,' I said. 'Hi.'

'I hope you don't mind, but I got your number from the book,' she said. 'I had to try four different Smiths before I got you. I guess that's not too bad, considering how common *Smith* is.'

'Why are you calling?' I asked. I didn't mean to sound rude but I didn't exactly mean to sound un-rude, either.

'Have you talked to Aaron?' she said.

I didn't know what to tell her, so I kept my mouth shut.

Sensing something in the silence, she said, 'Thought so. He's mad at me, isn't he? For what I told you about his stepdad. I tried calling his place last night and this morning and again tonight, but he hasn't called me back. I broke his trust, Justin. When I told you all that stuff. Now I feel sick about it.'

'Faye, have you told anyone else about' – I lowered my voice – 'Devin?'

'Of course not.'

That gave me a little relief. Just a little.

'Good,' I said. 'Listen, Aaron isn't mad at you. He just needs a bit of space.'

'Thanks, Justin. I'm pretty sure you're only trying to make me feel better, but I hope you're right.' She paused. 'You're pretty wise, you know. Has anyone ever told you that?'

'Never,' I said. 'I should go.'

'Can I ask a favour?'

I waited.

'Now that I have your number, can I call you sometime?' she asked.

I felt a flush of heat in my cheeks. 'Sure,' I said.

'Good.'

'Faye?'

'Yeah?'

'I have to go.'

'Okay,' she said. 'Hey, Justin?'

'Yeah?'

'When you see Aaron next, put in a good word for me.'

Something hung unsaid between us, but I didn't know what it was.

'I will,' I said. Then I hung up.

At eleven, I got dressed quietly, watched the clock until it reached half past, and then tiptoed out into the hall. Halfway across the pitch-black living room, as I paused to fumble my sneakers on in the dark, the lamp in the corner flicked on. It was Scott. He was lounging in the armchair with our dad's dusty old guitar on his lap. He wasn't strumming it. He was just holding it.

'Why are you sitting in the dark like a creep?' I asked.

He scoffed. 'I'm waiting for the kettle to boil. Making Milo. You want some?'

'No thanks.'

'Where are you sneaking off to?'

'I'm not sneaking off. I'm just ...' I looked down at myself, dressed all in black, bike helmet in one hand, backpack in the other. 'Don't tell Mum, okay?'

'What's her name?'

'Who?'

'The girl you're meeting up with.' If only. 'Was it the one who called you before?'

I saw my chance and took it. 'Yeah,' I said. 'Are you going to tell Mum?'

'Not if you don't want me to.'

I nodded and went for the door.

Scott picked gently at the guitar strings. 'By the way, what happened on Bowman Street?'

I froze.

'There's an address written down on the note next to the phone,' he said. 'Is that from when Aaron called?'

The kettle whistled in the kitchen. Scott set the guitar down on the coffee table and rose to make his Milo. I made sure I was gone before he came back.

The streets of West Haven were deserted. It was still T-shirt weather, even that late, but a cool breeze cut through the night. I cruised past darkened shop windows and locked shutters, past the backlit life-size cardboard cut-out of the *Terminator* in the door of West Haven Video Hire. Past the looming CFA building and the Scout hall, past the public swimming pool, moonlight reflecting on the black surface of the water.

I realised then it wasn't just my bedroom that felt small. It was the whole town.

Aaron was waiting at the corner of Castle Creek Hill Road and Elm Street. He was dressed all in black, camouflaged in the shadow of a gum tree. His ten-speed was resting against the little brick wall nearby. He had something shiny in his hand that caught the light. As I got closer, I saw it was a hip flask.

'Hey, man,' I said. 'Chen isn't here yet?'

Aaron checked his watch. 'Not yet.'

Nearby, the storm drain loomed like a big yawning mouth. I pictured a pale, eyeless sewer monster inside, then decided that was less scary than what we were all about to do.

'Is there any news?' I asked. 'What did your mum say when Devin didn't come home?'

'Not much,' Aaron said. 'She's freaking out but she's freaking out quietly. She's so desperate not to upset me.'

'Do you think she'll call the cops?'

'Not for a while.' He took a drink.

'What's with the flask?' I asked.

'You want a sip?'

I took it from him and sniffed it. It stank of whisky. I jiggled the flask. There wasn't much left. There was an inscription on the side. I angled it towards the dull light of a streetlamp and read, *Happy 40th D, you old bastard! With love, Lucy.*

'This is Devin's,' I said.

'Yeah, well, he doesn't need it anymore, does he?' Aaron took back the flask and had another sip.

'How much of that have you had?' I asked.

'Not enough,' Aaron said.

We heard the clinking of bike spokes and turned to look up Elm Street. A silhouette on a bike appeared over the crest of the hill. Then another.

'Here's Chen,' I said.

'There's someone with him.' Aaron pointed. 'It's Leeson.'

The boys pulled up.

'What are you doing here, Leese?' Aaron asked.

Leeson shrugged. 'I figured you guys would need the extra help. Besides, you'd do it for me.'

'Let's not test that, shall we?' Chen said. 'I mean, your dad's a dick, Leeson, but one body is enough to deal with.'

Fucking Chen.

Leeson and I remained stone-faced. But Aaron laughed. He *actually* laughed. Then he took another hit from the flask.

'Can I get in on that?' Chen asked.

'Sorry, mate, I tapped it.' Aaron shook the flask. It was empty now. He wiped his mouth with the back of his hand, and then headed for the bikes.

'Aaron,' I said. 'You're supposed to drive the ute.'

'Yeah. So?'

'So you're drunk,' I said.

'Just chill, Justin.' He picked up his ten-speed and straddled it.

Leeson said, 'I'll drive.'

'Are you sure?' I asked.

Nodding, he said, 'My cousin gave me a go of his paddock bomb when I went to visit over Christmas. I pretty much got the hang of it.'

It was better than nothing.

'I'm glad you came back, Leeson,' I said.

He offered a small, strange little smile, then got back on his bike. And the four of us rode off to dispose of a body.

★

On the ride to Bowman Street, we broke off into groups of two: Chen and Leeson up front, riding handlebar to handlebar on the wide open road, Aaron and I bringing up the rear. Old West Haven was just as lifeless as it had been in the middle of the day. There was nobody around for miles, nothing but old empty houses, barbed wire and shaggy vacant blocks.

'Dude,' I said, out of earshot of the others.

'What?' Aaron said.

'Me, Chen and Leeson. We're risking a lot tonight. We're risking everything. You'll be no help to us drunk.'

'Give me a break, Justin,' he said. 'I just need to be numb for this part.'

'Give *you* a break? Seriously?'

'You don't know how it feels.'

'We're doing this for you, man.'

'That's not exactly true now, is it?'

'What does that mean?' I asked.

Backlit by the moon, Aaron's face was dark, without features. I couldn't see his mouth moving, so when he spoke his voice seemed to be drifting in through a portal to somewhere else. He said, 'You're doing this to protect yourself as much as me. You helped me clean the crime scene, Justin. You wrapped his body in plastic. You're *in* this. Maybe not as deep as me, but pretty fucking deep.'

Pretty fucking deep.

He was right.

And we were all about to go deeper.

Chen made a sound, a gasp and a whimper combined. He stepped back hard against his pedal brake. The BMX skidded. The back tyre spun out in a wide arc, nearly taking him off the road. Leeson rolled to a more elegant stop. Aaron and I pulled in close behind them, seeing now what they already had. A big, glowing blossom of red and blue police lights.

The house on Bowman Street was crawling with cops.

23

NOW

Bowman Street was gone now. In its place was a pristine housing estate, a series of curved, maze-like roads, all named after Australian native flowers: Banksia Drive, Eucalyptus Way, Lilly Pilly Avenue. Big houses lined the road. Every yard was well manicured. Every other driveway had a four-wheel drive parked out front.

'I can't believe we're in Old West Haven,' I said.

'Actually, it's West Haven Rise now,' Leeson told me.

He slowed down for a speed bump. It was the third one we'd thumped over since pulling into the estate.

'How long have you lived here?' I asked.

'Shelley and I bought here in 2011,' he said. 'The idea was, this would get us into the housing market and then we'd save up for something on a bit of land. But I don't know. Life happened.' He watched the road. The day was wet and grey. 'She moved to Flockhart after the divorce, and I paid her through the nose to keep this place.'

We pulled onto a spotless concrete driveway. Leeson's house was a grey-rendered cube at the end of a line of grey-rendered cubes. He hit a button on the dash and the garage door rolled open. He pulled in, hit the button again, and waited for the door to close all the way before killing the engine.

He led me into the house. It was a sad picture. The walls were full of photos of his kids and a glossy portrait of him and Shelley Hutchinson hung above the mantlepiece, her striking red hair draped over one slender shoulder. But the rest of the place was mostly empty. There was a single armchair in front of the TV, no rugs and no books. The barest of essentials.

Leeson noticed me looking at the picture of Shelley. 'She had a crush on you when we were kids,' Leeson said.

'Bullshit,' I told him.

'Seriously,' he said. 'She confessed it on our second or third date. She said she liked you because you were shy, which made it seem like there was a lot going on in your head.' He turned to me. 'I set her straight on that.'

'I bet you did.'

'You want something to drink? I bought a slab on my way home from Chen's last night, and there should be a six-pack left.'

I did the math and was quietly alarmed. 'No thanks,' I said. 'Do you know when Chen is getting here?'

'He said he'd come as soon as possible.'

I was eager to hear about the development in the case. Not that it mattered a whole lot. Hannah was probably sitting down with Detective Eckman right now. I should have warned Leeson. I owed him that much. But I was also scared of him, scared of what he was capable of, scared that there was *no line he would not cross*.

Leeson got a beer from the fridge and gestured to the back door. I followed him out onto the deck. It was icy out there, but I guess the view made it worth the cold. Leeson's place backed onto West Haven State Forest. It rose like a wave, lapping at the feet of the mountains.

'Can I ask you something, Leese?' I said.

'You want to know how I live so close to where it happened?'

'Exactly.'

'That house was torn down not long before we moved in. It's a playground now.' He sighed. 'I don't know. It feels right, somehow.'

'It feels like you're punishing yourself.' Off his raised eyebrows, I clarified. 'You became a cop and moved into the same neighbourhood where Devin ... you know.'

'Maybe I am punishing myself,' he said, and drank. 'Maybe living shouldn't be easy.' He drank again. 'Not for us.'

The thought of that filled me with a sick, heavy sadness. 'Do you think we deserve to get caught?' I asked.

Leeson glanced at me cautiously. 'Do I need to check you for a wire again?' I made a show of opening my parka. 'Objectively, yes. I spend my career trying to catch guys like us. But subjectively, well, that depends on what day of the week you ask me.'

The sky darkened.

'Do you think what we did was unforgivable?' I asked. Hannah's words were still ringing in my head.

'I don't think that's for us to decide,' he said. 'Not long after it happened, I thought about turning myself in, you know. I felt like I had to tell. Like if I didn't, the only other way out was to take a walk off the ledge. Then later, right about when my marriage was eating shit, I looked at my life and thought, *is it worth it?*'

'Is what worth it?'

'Carrying the load.' He turned his palm up to show me the scar there. 'All of us go free or none of us do, remember? I don't know about you, mate, but I haven't felt free in a long time.'

'What stopped you from turning yourself in?'

He shrugged. 'Sometimes I'd think about my kids, picture them seeing my face on the front page of the newspaper. Other times I'd think about you and Chen. Confessing wouldn't mean just blowing up my life, it would mean blowing up yours.'

I felt a strong stirring of guilt in my chest. Earlier, as I'd poured my heart and soul at Hannah's feet, I hadn't thought about Leeson at all. Now I could see concentric circles rippling outward, could see all the lives I was about to wreck by telling Hannah.

I checked my phone. There were no missed calls. I wondered if it was too late. If I called Hannah now and begged her to reconsider going to the police, would she listen?

We heard a car pull up out front and went back inside. I saw Chen climbing out of a little white mud-speckled Toyota through a picture window in the living room. He was practically swimming inside a big woollen cardigan, buttoned once in the middle. He gave us a cautious wave, his face etched with concern.

Leeson met him at the door.

'Thanks for coming, Chen,' he said.

'Well, you made it sound pretty urgent on the phone. I spent the whole drive over shitting myself.' He came inside and noticed me. 'Do you know what this is about?'

I shook my head.

Chen started pacing. 'Okay, Leeson, you got us both here. Now what's this news?'

Leeson drew in a deep breath and was silent for a long moment. Just how bad *was* this news?

'We need a drink first,' he said.

That bad.

While Leeson took a bottle of whisky down from the cupboard above the fridge and fetched three tumblers, I looked out into the street, trying to see the playground that was once the dreaded house on Bowman Street. I didn't spot it.

Chen joined me and said, 'How'd you get that cut on your head?'

I lightly fingered the Band-Aid and said, 'I bumped into Scott.'

'Oh, shit.'

'Yeah.' I hesitated. 'Have you heard much about him?'

'Like what?'

'Like how he's doing?'

Chen shrugged. 'Whenever I see him around town, I cross the street to avoid him.'

'That bad, huh?'

'He's into some pretty hard stuff,' Chen said.

'Drugs?'

'I don't want to speak out of turn.' Then, 'Scott's not a whole person, you know what I mean?'

I did.

Leeson set three glasses down on the island bench in the kitchen and poured us each a finger of whisky, then a second finger. He passed around the drinks, and performed a heavy, theatrical sigh.

'Are you going to put us out of our misery now or what?' Chen said.

Leeson looked hard at Chen, then harder at me … and then he smiled. It was a wide, toothy smile, one I'd not seen since we were kids, before the dark times, when our lives were simple and peaceful and funny, when we were into girls and ghosts and not much else.

'Are you having a stroke right now?' Chen asked.

'I'm smiling,' Leeson said. 'This is not a commiseration drink. Don't get me wrong, it's not a celebratory drink either, because that would be much too macabre. Let's just call it a toast.'

Chen and I exchanged a grim, baffled look.

'What are we toasting?' Chen asked.

'The lab results came back from Melbourne,' he said. 'The cause of death was inconclusive. Without a cause of death, there's not a whole lot to investigate, much less prove. The remains were found below the ledge. For all anyone knows, he could have slipped and fallen from the cliff or—' He caught himself. 'He could have jumped.'

'What does this mean, exactly?' I asked.

'I think we're free,' Leeson said.

'Free?' Chen had to set the drink down so he wouldn't drop it. 'Don't fuck with us, man.'

Leeson said, 'Detective Eckman is already starting to wrap things up here. The case will then be handed over to the West Haven Crime Investigation Unit, and with no new information and no evidence to suggest foul play, it'll sit in a file and go cold.'

'Jesus Christ,' Chen said. He ran a hand through his hair and exhaled. 'Is it over?'

'That depends,' Leeson said.

'On what?'

He stared a warning at both of us. 'We can't give anyone a reason to keep digging.' To me, he said, 'I went off on you before because I was worried you'd given Eckman some ammunition. But as long as we stay quiet and honour the oath … it's over.'

Chen grinned, his face awash with relief. I said nothing but offered a small noncommittal nod. I'd already broken the oath.

'You all right, mate?' Chen asked. 'This is good news.'

'Yeah,' I said. 'I know.'

'Tell that to your face.'

If Steffi was here, she'd probably call my expression *scrunchy*.

Steffi.

Damn.

I had to find Hannah. I had to contain this. It wasn't too late.

'I'm fine,' I said. 'I think I'm just, you know, processing it all.'

Chris and Leeson exchanged a look. It was the same loaded, telepathic gaze they used to give each other as kids. Leeson asked, 'Is there something you're not telling us?'

'No,' I lied. 'But I need to get back to town. Will one of you give me a ride?'

24

SUNDAY 7 FEBRUARY 1999

I woke up wearing the clothes I'd worn last night. Black hoodie and wedding pants, clinging to me with sweat. Six in the morning and it was already too hot. The sun fell into my bedroom, made everything look sick and yellow. My brain felt fried. Still does. My bones felt weak. Still do. Because the fucking walls are closing in, folks. The sky is falling.

Yet somehow I managed to lift my head and swing my feet out of bed this morning. Mum was already awake. I could hear the whistle of the kettle, the *glug-glug* of coffee being poured and the familiar *scratch-thud-scratch-thud* of my mother's ancient pink slippers against the lino. I peeled off my clothes, went across the hall into the bathroom and had a lukewarm shower. I sank down to the floor, put my back against the cold tiles and listened to the pipes scream in the walls.

Afterwards, I dried myself, pulled on a pair of shorts, and went into the kitchen. Mum had set a fresh cup of coffee down beside the stove and was leaning over the counter to read a *Cleo* magazine. I stood in the doorway and watched her for a couple of seconds without letting her know I was there. Like everything else in this house, she seemed smaller.

'Hi,' I said. As if everything was fine. Normal. Hunky-fucking-dory.

She turned and wiped sleep from her eyes. With her arms crossed, she looked at me, waiting for an apology after last night. I wanted to give it to her. I still felt shitty about what I'd said to her. But in that moment, I just didn't have the energy. Mum must have seen that, I think, because after a few seconds, she said, 'You want some eggs?'

'Yeah,' I told her. 'That'd be nice.'

I sat down at the table while she cracked and whisked and poured, then poked at the eggs in the pan with a wooden spatula. After my cool shower, the sunlight falling in through the window above the sink felt warm and good and healthy. It made my mother look beautiful and angelic, like a character in a stained-glass window.

If she ever finds out

(I can't bring myself to finish that sentence.)

There's nothing about Devin on the news yet.

I've been thinking a lot about this diary. I have to destroy it. It's evidence. I'm not a total idiot. I've deleted the file from my PC. It's now stored on a floppy disk I'm meant to be using for school, with *JUSTIN SMITH, 9F, COMPUTER STUDIES* printed on the label, in case anyone decides to snoop.

But why am I still writing if I'm just going to get rid of it?

Good question.

I don't know, exactly. It's not like I want to. It's more of a need now. If I don't put all this stuff somewhere, it'll build up inside me, and I don't know how much I can hold before I split at the seams and spill everything, and then my whole life is over and my

Sorry. Aaron just called.

He wants to meet up.

'At the usual spot?' I asked.

'No,' Aaron said. He was talking really quietly, almost in a whisper. 'That's not private enough. Let's meet at the ledge. Can you call the others? Things are getting weird here.'

'Weird how?' I asked.

'The ledge,' he said again. Then he hung up.

Gotta go.

More soon.

Chen and Leeson were waiting for me outside the train station. Chen looked how I felt, fiery and panicky. He kept looking over his shoulder as if a fully armed SWAT team might swarm us at any minute. Leeson was quiet. As in, real quiet. He mumbled a greeting when he saw me, but that was about it.

When the 11.42 train pulled away from the platform, the guys and I hopped down onto the tracks and headed into the forest. Sunlight filtered in through the canopy of trees overhead, casting a spider-web pattern over the tracks.

For a while, none of us talked. We just walked single file along the tracks. But soon the sound of us *not talking* became unbearable, and I blurted, 'What the fuck happened last night?'

'Someone must have tipped off the cops,' Chen said. 'I'm telling you, man, someone knows something and it's freaking me the fuck out.'

'Nobody knows anything,' Leeson said. 'If they did, we would have been arrested by now.' He was ahead of me on the tracks. He turned around and said, 'Right, Justin?'

'I guess,' I said.

Chen said, 'We must have left all sorts of skin cells and junk in that place.'

'I thought you said you scrubbed it,' Leeson snapped.

'I scrubbed it raw, but there's stuff, like, on a microscopic level. What if they take sniffer dogs through there and they pick up on our scent? We are *so* fucked. This is all *so* fucked. And fuck Aaron for this, right? I mean, I love him like a brother, and what that fucking monster did to Benita was about as far away from okay as you can get, but come on.'

'It was our choice to help him, Chen,' I said. 'Aaron didn't hold a gun to any of our heads.'

Chen shook his head and spat into the valley.

Leeson paused, went down to his knees and put his hand on one of the train tracks.

'You feel anything?' I asked.

'I thought I heard something,' he said. But then he shook it off, rose to his feet and kept walking. 'I keep trying to, like, mentally prepare myself, you know. Like, if we get caught, I want to be ready for it.'

Funny. I'd spent all morning trying *not* to think about it.

'Getting pulled in and questioned and arrested is one thing,' Leeson said. 'But the thing I can't get out of my head is, it's not just me that's going to be affected. It's my family — my dad, my brothers.'

I thought about Mum and Scott. Even Dad, wherever he was.

'Which takes us neatly back around to *fuck Aaron*,' Chen said.

'There it is,' Leeson said. '*X* marks the spot.'

One at a time, we slipped onto the narrow path behind the *X*-shaped stone, then followed the maze of turns to the embankment. I'd climbed this wall three times in as many days. I was starting to know where all the best footholds were.

The sun was high, but a cool breeze swept up from the valley.

Aaron was waiting for us in the clearing, sitting cross-legged near the foot of the ledge, looking off over the sun-bathed mountains. His old boy-scout pocketknife was on a stone before him, a retro piece with gold and brown trim, blade retracted. I looked at Leeson and Chen. I think we were all thinking the same thing. *Why did Aaron bring a knife?*

'Az,' I said. 'You okay?'

He turned around, shrugged, and then turned back to look at the mountains. 'Take a seat.'

We did as we were asked. None of us mentioned the pocketknife.

'Someone phoned the house at 5am,' Aaron said. 'Mum took the call. I listened from my bedroom. I heard her burst into tears and then, ten seconds later, I heard her car pulling out of the driveway. It must have been the cops. They must have asked her down to the station or maybe made her, like, identify the body.'

'You don't know?' Chen asked.

'She hasn't come home yet,' Aaron told us.

'How did the police know, Aaron?'

'I don't know.'

'Did you tell anyone?'

Aaron glared at Chen and said, 'Like who?'

Then, because I didn't like the way he was looking at Chen, I said, 'What about Faye?'

Aaron turned his glare on me. 'What *about* Faye?'

'Did you talk to her last night? She said she'd been trying to call you.'

'I didn't tell another soul,' he hissed. 'Leeson was the one who disappeared for half the day.'

'What's that supposed to mean?' Leeson snapped back.

Aaron took a deep breath in, then deflated. He raised his palms in surrender.

'It doesn't mean anything,' he said. 'I'm sorry, Leese. I'm just tired and paranoid, and I don't know what else. Look, I asked you all here because there's only one way I see out of this thing, and that's if we stick together. We stay quiet. We tell no one. We carry this shit between us. But see, here's the thing. A promise isn't good enough. Not for something like this. We need something stronger. A vow.' He took up the pocketknife and extended the blade. 'A blood oath.'

In one smooth, quick motion, Aaron drew the blade of the pocketknife over the palm of his hand. Skin split open like a peeled banana. Blood gurgled out in time with his heartbeat.

'Jesus,' Leeson cried. 'What the fuck?'

Chen leapt to his feet and took two big steps back.

'You're already my brothers, but now you'll be my blood brothers,' Aaron said. 'We all go free or no one does.' He handed the blood-smeared pocketknife to Leeson. 'Your turn, Leese,' he said. 'We all have to do it.'

Leeson stared down at the blade in dull, dumb wonder. 'I can't, Aaron,' he said.

'This is the only way,' Aaron said. 'If you're not with us, then you're against us.'

'Give me the knife,' Chen said.

Leeson hesitated. 'Wait, Chen ...'

'Aaron's right,' he said. 'We all go free or no one does, Leese.' Chen pressed the blade against his palm and closed his hand around it. 'We all go free or no one does.' He tightened his grip on the handle and yanked it out. He screamed at the pain. Then he handed the knife to Leeson.

Leeson closed his eyes, tilted his face up to the sun and gritted his teeth. He repeated the chant. 'We all go free or no one does.' Then he cut himself.

Blood dripped against the rocks. I'm not sure whose it was.

Finally, the knife made its way to me.

Aaron, Chen and Leeson waited, watching, each nursing his own bloody wound. I looked at the blade. It was already wet with the blood of my friends.

'We all go free,' I said, 'or no one does.' I put the blade into the palm of my hand and dragged it across my skin.

When I got home, Scott was waiting in my bedroom with Dad's guitar, gently strumming a Nirvana song. He'd drawn the curtain and was sitting in the dark.

What's with my brother sitting in dark rooms lately?

'What are you doing in here?' I asked.

I banged on the light switch and moved to my desk, trying to act casual, trying not to look suspicious. Inside, though, I was quietly panicking because what if Scott had found my diary? Like an idiot, I'd left the floppy disk with *JUSTIN SMITH, 9F, COMPUTER STUDIES* in the drive. I put my good hand on the monitor. It was cool, which meant nobody had booted it up in the last hour or so. I figured that put me in the clear. Besides, Scott knows next to nothing about computers.

Even so, if I'm going to honour this crazy blood oath and get through this, I need to be smarter.

'What happened to your hand?' Scott asked.

I'd washed the blood off with the tap outside, then stopped by the bathroom on the way here. I didn't want it to get infected, so I soaked it in that stinky brown liquid Mum used to put on our scraped knees as kids, then bandaged it with a strip of gauze I found in the cupboard behind the mirror.

'I came off my bike,' I said.

'Where have you been?'

'Nowhere,' I said.

'Have you talked to Aaron?'

I went with a lie and shook my head. I leaned on my desk and poked at my bandaged hand. It stung like a motherfucker. Then I asked, 'What are you doing in my room, Scott?'

Scott had been leaning back on my bed. Now he put the guitar aside and sat forward, hands flat on his bare knees. He said, 'Bronwyn called before.'

'Who's Bronwyn?' I asked.

'The girl I told you about,' he said. 'The one I've been hanging out with in Flockhart. She knows Aaron's sister, Benita.'

I thought about that. 'Are you talking about Bronwyn Ross?'

Scott nodded.

Bron Ross is in year twelve at West Haven Secondary. She hangs out with Benita. Her, Regina Thofna and Else-Marie Darnton. Bron is cute in an unwashed sort of way. She has a streak of green in her hair and is always wearing headphones. She keeps the volume on her Discman way up so you can hear it whenever you pass her in the corridors. She's always listening to punk.

'Why didn't you tell me you were going out with Bron Ross?' I asked.

'We're not *going* out, we're just *hanging* out,' Scott said. 'And I don't know, it's sort of embarrassing hanging out with a high school girl.'

I didn't really get that. Scott finished high-school last year. As in, a few months ago. But I let it go. He still hadn't told me why he was in my room, but if he'd talked to Bron and Bron had talked to Benita, I was pretty sure what was coming next.

'Mate, Aaron and Benita's stepdad died last night,' he said.

I didn't know how to act, what to say, what to do with my hands. I thought about how people reacted to news like this in the movies, but I wasn't about to scream and howl and fall on the ground crying. Scott would see right through me. There's a reason I got an E in Drama.

'What are you talking about?' I asked.

And the Academy Award goes to …

'He was killed, Justin,' Scott said.

I just stood there, trying to keep myself from trembling.

'Aren't you going to ask me how?' Scott said.

'What?'

'Aren't you going to ask me how he was killed?' Scott sounded annoyed all of a sudden.

I didn't know what to say, so I said, 'How was he killed?'

'He was murdered,' Scott said. Then, 'On a worksite.' Then, '*On Bowman Street.*'

I held my breath.

Scott had seen the address Aaron had given me. I left it on the notepad beside the phone because I am the world's biggest fucking idiot.

My hand was still stinging. I checked it. Blood was seeping out around the edges of the bandage.

'That's terrible,' I said. But the words were useless and hollow and entirely fucking pointless.

'Aaron asked you to go to Bowman Street yesterday,' Scott said.

'Scott.'

'Tell me you don't know anything about this, Justin.'

'I don't know anything about this,' I said. But I was crying now.

'Where did you go last night?' he said.

I could hardly talk. I managed, 'Scott.'

'Talk to me, Justin. Let me help you.'

'You can't.'

My brother stepped off the bed and took hold of my shoulders. There were tears in his eyes. He said, 'An innocent person is dead, Justin. If you know something ...'

Then I whispered, 'What if he wasn't innocent?'

'What?'

'What if it was self-defence?'

'What are you telling me, Justin?'

I squeezed my hand shut. The pain helped. I stopped crying and shook it off. 'I'm not saying anything, Scott,' I told him. 'I don't know. Maybe I'm in shock.'

Scott frowned at me, then took a few steps back, like we were camping, and he'd just heard a scary noise in the bushes. He said, 'Devin was hit in the back of the head. The cops said there were no defensive wounds or signs of a struggle.'

'What does that mean?' I asked.

'It means it wasn't self-defence,' Scott said. 'It was murder.'

25

NOW

Chen drove me back into town. He dropped me off outside the cafe that had been West Haven Video Hire, once upon a time. It was late afternoon and already getting dark. The sun had dipped behind the mountains, casting long yawning shadows over the town strip. I yanked off my seatbelt and slung open the passenger-side door. I couldn't wait to get out of the car. My head was buzzing, and Chen's little Toyota felt claustrophobic.

'Thanks for the lift,' I said. 'I'll be in touch.'

'Don't be,' Chen said.

I paused. 'Chen?'

'I don't want this to come out the wrong way,' he said. 'But I don't ever want to see you again.'

'How could I possibly take that the wrong way?'

Chen, the so-called comedian of the group, didn't even crack a smile. 'If Leeson is right, and I hope to the god I don't believe in that he is, we might finally be free. This was the worst-case scenario, and we survived. But that's all out here, you know—' He spread his hands to indicate the outside world. Then, pointing to his head, 'In here, it's a different story.'

'I get it.'

'I love you, man,' Chen said. 'I mean that. I really do. But if I'm going to make it through the rest of my life, if I'm going to be able to give Pete what he needs and give myself what *I* need, I have to forget. Seeing you makes that harder. It makes it impossible.'

'I get it,' I told him.

And I did. The tragic part was this: in order to purge the bad stuff, you had to purge the good stuff too. Childhood, friendship. Laughter, love. You had to let it all go. It was a package deal.

'So I guess this is goodbye,' I said.

'I guess it is.'

A handshake seemed too informal, so we hugged.

'Bye, Chen,' I said. 'Take care of yourself.'

'One more thing,' he said.

'Yeah?'

He looked me hard in the eyes. 'Fix it.'

'Fix what?' I asked, playing dumb.

'You told someone,' Chen said. 'I saw it on your face back at Leeson's house. I didn't want to press you on it in front of him, because honestly, I couldn't trust him not to do something crazy.'

'Chen, I—'

'I get it, mate. In a way that nobody outside our group does or ever will. I've wanted to tell Pete over the years, but we made an oath.'

We all go free or no one does.

My mouth was dry.

'Are you going to tell Leeson?' I asked.

'If you can fix it, no.'

'And if I can't?'

He turned away from me to look through the windscreen.

Message received.

Without another word, I got out of the car and watched Chen drive away.

I whipped out my mobile and tried calling Hannah. It didn't even ring. Straight to voicemail. She'd probably switched off her phone.

I walked briskly in the direction of Westlake Drive. My car was still parked outside Scott's house. I wasn't sure what I was going to do when I reached it, but it felt like the next logical move. As I walked, I tried calling Hannah. Again and again, over and over, feeling helpless.

Shops were closing all around me and lights were coming on inside homes. I drifted past the general store and Woolies, past the big brick CFA building and the ugly brown Scout hall, past the West Haven public swimming pool and the visitor centre. It was funny how all the things you didn't want to change did. And vice versa.

I tried calling Hannah again.

Again, there was no answer.

Then my phone buzzed. It was an unknown number. I answered it. 'Hannah?'

There was a pause. 'It's Lisa.'

Lisa Wu. From the bookshop.

'Oh no.'

'What?'

'You forgot, didn't you?'

Yes.

'No.'

I was starting to feel like my own worst enemy. But there was no choice. I had to cancel. I reached for the easiest lie there was – feeling sick – and said, 'I'm sorry, Lisa, I didn't forget. But—'

'Phew,' Lisa said. 'Well, we're all here and ready to get started when you are. We got a pretty good turnout, especially on such short notice. Even the detective is here.'

'The detective …'

'The one who's in town investigating the body,' Lisa said. 'Apparently, she's a big fan.'

I hesitated.

What choice did I have?'

'I'll be there in ten minutes.'

Hidden Books was brightly lit, at the end of the cobblestone laneway. To one side, the Italian restaurant was buzzing with young families eating loaded pizzas, laughing and smiling and being wonderfully normal. As I neared the bookshop, I took a peek through the window. Beyond the stacks of books and my dumpy, generic headshot, I saw a packed house. Lisa hadn't been kidding about the turnout. There looked to be thirty seats arranged around a table in the middle of the shop, and every one of those seats had someone in it. More people stood at the back, and more still sat on the front counter with their feet dangling over the edge.

Under normal circumstances, seeing this type of crowd might have done wonders for my ego, but Lisa had told me why I was famous in West Haven. They weren't here for my books.

'Admiring the view?' A voice from my right. Detective Eckman was wrapped up tight in her winter parka, smoking. Holding up her cigarette, she said, 'If you tell my wife about this, I'll kill you.'

'I should get in there,' I said.

'I didn't realise you were so popular. You just about packed that place out. I got here early to get a good seat,' Eckman paused to drag on her cigarette. 'It gave me a chance to chat to the bookseller too. Lisa Wu. Nice lady. She thinks very highly of you, by the way.'

'Lisa's great,' I said. 'I guess I'll see you in there.' I moved for the door.

'She said something funny,' Eckman said.

I paused. 'Oh?'

'Lisa told me that she came up with the idea for this event when you popped into the shop, which is a bit weird because you told me that's why you came to town in the first place.'

'Did I?'

'You did.'

'I guess I misspoke.'

'Lisa also told me that you declined her offer. Only to call back and change your mind later.'

I gritted my teeth.

'Have you thought any more about what we talked about?'

'I don't mean to be rude, Detective, but there are people waiting for me inside.'

She stepped closer. 'It's getting pretty warm in that pot, isn't it?'

Had she already talked to Hannah?

'I have no idea what you're talking about,' I said. 'But this is starting to feel like harassment.' Everyone knows not to kick a hornet's nest. But I couldn't help myself. I was angry. I was scared. Besides, the lab results had come back with nothing. No cause of death meant there was nothing more to investigate. Why was this bitch still riding me? 'I don't have to talk to you.'

'Yet here we are, talking.'

'Just leave me alone, all right?'

'Nah,' Eckman said. 'I think I'll hang around for a while. I'm like a bad fart that way.'

'Why are you even here?'

'To hear where you get your ideas from,' she said. She gestured towards the shop. 'Shall we?'

'Why are you still in West Haven?' I blurted. 'You've hit a dead end, Detective. There's nothing left to investigate.'

Eckman cocked her head at a curious angle and asked, 'What do you mean by that?'

Damn. 'Nothing.'

'You and Geoffrey have been talking.'

'No—' I started. But then I thought: *Fuck it*. 'It doesn't matter where I got my information from. The bones are too far gone to determine the cause of death or a positive ID. I had nothing to do with what happened. And if I did …'

'Go on.'

'You couldn't prove it anyway.' I opened the door to Hidden Books and went inside.

People were talking in huddled groups, but they all fell silent when I entered, like I'd just wandered into a dangerous saloon in the Wild West. Lisa, who was sitting in one of two armchairs that had been placed at the front of the crowd, stood up and smiled with relief.

'Finally, I can stop vamping,' she said. 'Here's the man of the hour.'

There was applause and gentle laughter as I moved inside.

A small hand grabbed me. I turned around.

Whispering now, Eckman said, 'You're right about the lab results. No cause of death. No positive ID. But the shape of the pelvic bone and the development and growth in the teeth gave an indication of gender and age.'

Lisa frowned at us from across the room. I held up a trembling finger to her as if to say *one second*.

'The results indicated the body was an adolescent male, approximately sixteen years old,' Eckman said. 'I can't *prove* it's him, but we both know it is. I can't prove you had anything to do with it either. But we both know that's not true.'

I pulled away.

'Either way, you have to live with it,' Eckman said after me, her voice quiet but venomous. 'You either killed your best friend or know who did.'

26

SUNDAY 7 FEBRUARY 1999

I left the house around 8.30pm. It was still light out, but by the time I'd climbed Stricklin Avenue on the Mongoose, it was fully dark. The wall of trees that lined the edge of Aaron's property was black, and so was everything else, now that I think about it. The house was dark too. The outside light was off, and there didn't seem to be any movement inside. I wondered if everyone was out, but then I saw Aaron's mum's car in the carport and Aaron's ten-speed parked alongside it.

I left the Mongoose at the bottom of the steps, then rang the doorbell. The porch chair on the veranda was empty. There was a little glass ashtray beside it, practically overflowing with cigarettes. Benita is the only one in the Wynn family who smokes.

Nobody answered the door, so I rang the bell again.

Again, nothing.

I tested the handle. It was unlocked. I nudged open the door and called out, 'Hello?'

'Who's that?' came a voice from inside. Benita.

'It's Justin,' I said.

'Come in.'

I stepped inside. The house felt different. All the lights were off and the air con wasn't running. It was stuffy and hot. There was just enough light to navigate without bumping into stuff. I went into the kitchen. Benita was cooking something in a pot over the gas stove.

'Is your power out?' I asked.

Benita turned around but, in the dark, she was just a silhouette in baggy jeans and a singlet. She said, 'Huh?' Then she shook her head, crossed to the wall and turned on the lights.

'I didn't notice it had got dark,' she said.

Something boiled over on the stove. Water spilled out and hissed against the burners. Benita ran back to it and pulled the pot off the stove.

'Fuck,' she said. 'All I want to do is cook some fucking pasta, and I can't even do that.'

'Just turn the heat down,' I told her. 'Here.' I dialled back the gas and set the pot of pasta back down.

Benita put her face in her hands and sighed. Now that the lights were on and I was closer, I saw that her eyes were red and raw from crying.

'Are you okay?' I asked.

'What the fuck do you think, Justin?'

She was right. It was a stupid question.

'I'm sorry,' I said.

'Justin.'

'Yeah.'

'Can you do me a favour right now?'

'Of course,' I said.

'Can you just fucking hold me?'

I stared at her like a stunned dummy for a second, then I put my arms around her. She collapsed into my chest and began to sob. She put her hands on my back and pulled the fabric of my T-shirt into fists. I held her tight. I wanted to tell her she was safe now. Devin wouldn't be able to hurt her anymore. But instead I just said, 'You're okay, you're okay,' over and over again like a little mantra. I think I was talking to myself as much as Benita.

I don't know how long I held her like that, but by the time I let her go, the pasta was cooked. As Benita dropped it into the strainer and stirred through a jar of Paul Newman's, she said, 'Nobody in this house is going to eat this, but I just feel like I have to be doing something, you know?'

'I get it,' I said. 'Where's your mum?'

'She hasn't come out of her room in hours,' Benita said, turning to gaze through the arched doorway and into the dark corridor beyond. 'I've never seen her like this. She's so broken. We all are. With Devin gone — fuck, I still can't believe this is happening — but with him gone, we're not a family anymore.'

'It'll be okay,' I said, because that's what people say.

'When Dad left, we were a fucking mess,' she said. 'Devin saved us, Justin. He was the glue, you know?'

I blinked, and with all the tact of a dog with four broken legs, I said, 'You liked him?'

Benita glared at me. 'What kind of question is that?' she said. 'I fucking loved him, Justin. Devin was more a dad to me than my actual dad will ever be, and, Jesus, why didn't I tell him that while I could?' She put her head over the sink and started crying again. Her tears fell into the pasta.

I put my hand on her back, but this time she shrugged me away.

'Is Aaron in his room?' I asked.

'He's outside.'

'Outside?'

I found him at the far edge of his block. He was sitting outside on a lawn chair, a beer in one hand and more in an esky beside him.

He handed me a can when I reached him. 'Devin left a whole slab in the fridge,' he said.

I took the beer, but didn't open it. There was a pile of empties beside his chair, I noticed.

'How many have you had?' I asked.

'Not enough,' he said.

He chugged the rest of the can, dropped it into the pile with the empties, and then plucked another from the esky. He looked over at the house, then lowered his voice. 'The cops were over before,' he said. 'They separated me and Benita, asked us both a load of questions about Devin. What he was like, who his friends were, how his relationship was with us and Mum.'

'Who found him?' I asked. 'How did the cops know he was there?'

'A plumber,' Aaron said. 'Devin had arranged to meet him there yesterday to get a quote on a bathroom fit-out. I didn't know that. I just thought he was trying to get a head start on next week. You know what the really weird thing is, though?'

'What?'

'That plumber was supposed to give him the quote yesterday, but he had to cancel because his daughter-in-law went into labour. If that woman had had the baby one day later, none of this would have happened. Makes you wonder, right?'

'Wonder about what?'

'Like, maybe he was supposed to be found. Maybe the world was supposed to know he was dead.' He burped again. 'Or maybe I'm just too drunk to think straight.'

That part was right. He was starting to slur his words.

'Did the police say anything about evidence?' I asked.

'Evidence?'

'Like, did they find any fingerprints or hairs or—'

Aaron burped and shook his head. 'They don't have a clue what happened.'

'What did you tell them when they asked about Devin?'

He tilted his head back and looked at the sky. There were no stars tonight. He said, 'I told them he was a great guy, a wonderful human, the best stepdad you could ever have.'

'You lied.'

'Of course I lied, Justin. I had to throw them off the scent.' He took another swig of beer but missed his mouth. It spilled down the front of his shirt. He sat forward, cursed, shook his head and then chuckled. He must have been drunk. 'The cops asked about my dad. Like, maybe they think he had something to do with it.'

'Why would they think that?'

'They always blame the ex,' Aaron said. 'Good. Let him go to prison for it. That would be, like, perfect karma for him abandoning us.'

'You don't mean that,' I said.

'Don't I?'

My hand hurt. I rolled the cold can of beer against it, then cracked it open. Because fuck it, a little liquid courage might help me say what I came here to say. I chugged the can, winced at the taste (why do adults like this stuff?), then chugged some more.

'Have the cops come to see you?' Aaron asked.

'Why would they do that?'

'They probably won't,' he said. 'But I told them I was with you. You know. When it happened. It's not like I'm a suspect or anything, but Mum and Benita know I wasn't here at home, and I had to tell them something.'

It was another lie in the growing list of lies I had to tell for Aaron.

'What exactly did you tell them?' I asked.

He shrugged and said, 'I told them I was hanging out at yours.'

'At my house?'

'Yeah. So?'

'So Mum and Scott will know you weren't there.'

'Keep your voice down, dude,' he said. 'Look, I doubt the cops will even ask.'

'But what if they do, Az?'

'Tell them we met at your house and then we went out for a hike. It doesn't matter, Justin. If they don't have a reason to suspect us, they won't need to check our alibi.'

Suspect *us*.

Our alibi.

Aaron was making me nervous.

'Bron Ross talked to my brother about it,' I said.

'Why is Bron Ross talking to your brother about anything?'

'It doesn't matter. Benita told her that Devin was hit in the back of the head. She said that there were no ... defensive wounds or whatever.'

I waited.

Aaron said nothing.

'Is that true?' I asked.

But he just sat there drinking beer, looking off into the trees.

'What really happened in that house?' I asked.

'Monsters get slain, dude,' he said. His voice was cold all of a sudden. No, it wasn't just cold. It sounded like someone else's voice.

'What does that mean?' I asked.

He finished his beer, crushed the can, and opened another one. 'I got to the worksite early,' he said. 'I knew where it was because he drove the whole family past there when he got the job. We parked out front so he could point out all the things he was going to do, and which parts of the house would stay and which parts would have to come down.'

'Why did you get there early?' I asked.

'To hide,' he said. 'To stalk my prey.'

'You told us it was self-defence.'

'It was,' he said. 'And it wasn't. When I heard him get to the worksite, when I heard those big ugly workboots moving along the floorboards, I thought about all the times he'd crept out into the hall in the middle of the night. The wicked are supposed to be punished. Monsters get slain.'

'Are you saying you planned to kill him before you got there?' I asked.

'I'm saying the universe put us both there in that moment for a reason,' he said. 'It put the hammer in my hand. All I had to do was swing it.'

Maybe that shouldn't have rattled me as much as it did. The other night, Aaron had joked about killing Devin. But there's a big difference between a person saying a thing and doing a thing. Especially if that person is your best friend.

'What happened next, Aaron?' I asked. But I didn't want to know.

'I took my shoes off so he wouldn't hear me coming.' Another drink. 'I learned that trick from him. Think about that for a second.' Another drink. 'I only had to hit him once. I thought it would be harder.'

'Jesus, Aaron.' I dropped my half-empty can of beer onto the lawn and stepped away.

'Where are you going?' he asked.

'Home,' I said. 'I want to go home.'

'Don't do anything stupid, Justin.'

'You killed a person, Aaron.'

'And you helped me clean up the crime scene,' he said. 'You wrapped him in plastic and got rid of the murder weapon. You, Chen and Leeson. You're my accomplices.' He looked at me. His eyes were black. 'We all go free or no one does. Remember?'

'You didn't have to do it,' I said.

'If I didn't, he would have kept on doing what he did.'

'You could have told your mum,' I said. 'Benita could have given a statement to the police and—'

'Benita doesn't know what he was.'

I took another step back.

'It wasn't her door he stopped outside,' Aaron said. 'It was mine.'

27

NOW

The decades-old scar on the palm of my hand started to ache as I sat before a crowd in Hidden Books. Countless faces stared in my direction. I recognised some of them from the old days, but it was hard to tell. Everyone got old, including me. Lisa Wu sat in a matching armchair, angled slightly so that we were facing each other without closing off our body language to the audience.

'Welcome to Hidden Books,' she said. 'Thank you for coming.'

Detective Eckman was sitting in the front row. She wasn't kidding when she said she'd got here early to get a good seat. She watched me, smiling in a way that suggested she knew all my deepest, darkest secrets.

I dug deep and summoned my own smile. 'Right, yes, thanks for having me,' I said, stumbling over every second word. Then, as an afterthought, 'Better late than never.'

There was some polite laughter from the audience.

My phone buzzed. Lisa fixed me with a please-for-the-love-of-God-don't-answer-that-phone look, but it might have been Hannah calling. I slipped it out to look at the screen. *Leeson.*

Had Chen told him about Hannah?

Had Hannah told the cops about me?

'Looks like someone missed the announcement to turn their phones off,' Lisa said.

There was more laughter from the audience, but it was stilted and awkward. This was not going well. Eckman went on staring and smiling.

Jesus. How the hell was I going to get through this?

'Sorry,' I said.

My phone buzzed again. I looked at Lisa, at Eckman. If I wanted to survive, I'd have to compartmentalise. One thing at a time. Get through this. Find Hannah. Convince Leeson she wouldn't talk. Easy, right?

I pulled out my phone and flicked on the Do Not Disturb button. Lisa nodded in appreciation.

'We're lucky to have our favourite local author back in West Haven,' Lisa said, spreading her hands and projecting to the audience. Then, back to me, she said, 'It's just a shame about the timing. This town has seen a lot of excitement over the past few days for all the wrong reasons. Those of us with long memories can recall in vivid, traumatic detail a gruesome murder that took place here around the turn of the century.'

There were sad murmurs of agreement around the room. My throat turned dry. Lisa folded her hands in her lap, looked at me, and waited.

'Is there a question there?' I asked.

'You lived in West Haven in 1999,' she said.

'Yes.'

'You knew the victim.'

'I did.'

'Devin Frohiki,' Lisa said.

I tried not to flinch at the mention of his name.

'He was brutally murdered,' Lisa continued. 'And now you write about brutal murders.'

'I still don't hear a question.'

'But I bet you can guess where I'm going with this.'

'I think so,' I admitted.

'Did the fact you lived through that dark time in this town's history define you as a writer?'

I crossed my legs and took a deep breath. 'The short answer is, I don't know,' I said.

'We're here for an hour,' Lisa said. 'What's the long answer?'

More laughter in the audience.

Eckman was watching me. Everyone was watching me.

Get through this. Find Hannah. Convince her not to talk. Then convince Leeson that she won't talk. *Get through this.*

'I wouldn't say it defined me as a writer,' I said.

'Can you expand on that?' Lisa asked.

Another deep breath. Another quick glance at the detective.

'Imagine your life is a big bucket of sand,' I said, drawing on my vast collection of pre-prepared soundbites. 'Finding an idea is a little like sifting through it, looking for flecks of colour. Personal experiences, fears, trauma. The trick is turning them into something positive.'

Lisa nodded along with my answer. I had her on the hook. Now all I had to do was broaden the subject, and then we could move on. I loaded another soundbite into the chamber.

'There are two ways to look at crime fiction,' I said. 'The uncharitable way is it turns misery into entertainment. Which is true, of course. But the more charitable way to look at it is, crime fiction offers catharsis in a world where catharsis is in desperately short supply. In books, mysteries are solved, our characters get closure, justice is served. In real life, we don't usually get that lucky.'

'In real life,' Lisa said, 'killers don't get caught.'

'Not always,' I said. 'But in my books, you can count on it.'

'That's a wonderful sentiment, and I agree,' Lisa said. 'But I noticed you didn't actually answer my question.'

Why was she pushing me so hard?

'Ha,' I said. 'Maybe you should repeat it.'

'Did the events of '99 draw you to darker subject material?'

'I thought we were here to talk about my books.'

'I thought that's what we were doing.'

The audience grew silent. Wide eyes looked at me. People shifted forward in their seats. Lisa waited. Eckman waited. Someone's mobile phone went off. A woman, somewhere in the middle, scrambled through her handbag to shut it off, making embarrassed little *tsk* sounds. I recognised the ringtone. Jerry Butler's 'Moon River'. The hairs on my arms stood up.

'I was a teenager when Devin was murdered,' I said. 'As you pointed out, I knew him. I knew him well. He was a big figure in my childhood, in my adolescence. My own father wasn't around much. There weren't many grown men in my life that I could look up to.'

'Did you look up to him?' Lisa asked.

Carefully choosing my words, I said, 'If there was one word to describe Devin, it was *strong*. He was, for better or worse, a *man*. I thought he was invincible. When he died, it reminded me that nobody was safe. Not even the strong. Not even the invincible.' I scanned the crowd, then looked through them, into the middle distance. 'So, yes, his murder and everything that happened after it had a big effect on my childhood.' I hesitated. 'It darkened me.'

Stained me was closer to the truth.

'It darkened you,' Lisa echoed, nodding.

She leaned back in her chair and took me in.

The truth was – and I wasn't about to admit this in front of Lisa Wu and Detective Eckman and everyone else in town – I didn't have a choice but to write about it. If I didn't write about it, it would consume me. A monster followed me out of this town. I tamed it. I used it to write a handful of bestsellers. If I hadn't, it would have torn me in two.

'Was it Mark Twain who said, *Write what you know*?' I said.

Lisa smiled at me, narrowing her eyes.

'Who do you think killed him?' Lisa asked.

'I'm not a detective, Lisa. I just write about them.'

'There were a lot of rumours going around back in the day,' she said. 'Like, maybe he had ties to the underworld, or got in over his head with a gambling debt, or maybe he was killed by a jealous mistress.'

'Small towns and rumours are like peas and carrots,' I said.

'Do you think the fact that your best friend went missing just days after Devin's murder has anything to do with what happened?'

The bookshop was silent. I glared at Lisa and felt Eckman glaring at me.

'I'd rather not go into that, Lisa,' I said.

'I get that,' she said. 'But you don't really think it was a coincidence, do you?'

My vision began to blur. I put my hands flat on my knees and dug my fingernails into my jeans.

'He was a good kid,' Lisa said.

'You don't have to tell me he was a good kid.'

'He came in here sometimes.'

'I came in here with him,' I said. 'We'd go halves on the latest Stephen King and take it in turns reading the chapters. But, respectfully, it's not an area I want to go into.'

'Some people think you know what happened to him.'

'People think a lot of things, and like I said—'

'Other people think you had something to do with what happened.'

I threw her a severe look. Ecksman or not, I didn't have to sit there and let this woman lay into me. 'Move on, Lisa.'

'Do you think the remains in the forest are him?'

'I said *move on*.'

'Do you think he's been out there all this time, alone in the forest, waiting to be found? Waiting for justice?'

'Why are you coming at me so hard?' I snapped.

Lisa held my gaze. 'Because this town never got closure, and I think you could give it to us.'

I looked up. A familiar face stood at the back of the crowd, just inside the door. Hannah. Eckman shifted in her seat to see who I was staring at. Lisa followed my line of sight and asked, 'Is everything all right?'

I stood up. Hannah turned and disappeared into the night. Eckman wasn't smiling anymore. The faces of countless eager locals were staring at me. I was blazing towards the exit. The faces in the audience blurred together. Even Eckman's. Then I was pressing through the doors. Then I was out in the cold dark night, under blinking fairy lights. Then I was in the alleyway. A Journey song was playing in the Italian restaurant. There were no other sounds. Hannah was gone.

'Hannah?' I called.

No answer.

I checked my phone. There were four missed calls from Leeson and zero from Hannah. I didn't want to turn around and see the people watching me from inside the bookshop, so I started towards Main Road without looking back. I had no clear direction in mind. I just knew I needed to be away from here. It was cold out and getting colder. West Haven might even get snow, I thought. The sky was clear and crisp. A big blanket of stars was rolling out. There was a whole universe out there and all the evidence pointed to its being completely indifferent.

When I stepped out into the strip of shops, I called her name again.

'Hannah.'

Nothing.

'Hannah!'

'I'm right here,' she said.

I spun around. She was huddled beneath the awnings outside the West Haven newsagency, crossing her arms against the cold. The shop behind her was dark, the shutters closed and locked.

'How did you know where I was?' I asked.

She held up her phone. The Family Tracker app.

Why hadn't I thought of that?

'I tried calling,' I said.

'I blocked your number.'

'Why did you come back, Hannah?' I asked.

She took a small step out of the shadows.

'Because I'm ready to let you go,' she said. 'But there's some stuff we need to talk about first. Is there somewhere we can speak in private?'

28

SUNDAY 7 FEBRUARY 1999

Chen's house was lit up like a Christmas tree against the night. It was closing in on 10pm, my unofficial curfew. My official curfew was 9.30, but Mum gives me a grace period. This side of ten, I'm safe. That side of ten, she starts to worry. Tonight, I'd be pushing it to get home, but this couldn't wait until tomorrow.

I stashed the Mongoose behind the hedge outside the house, then skulked around it in the dark, sticking as close to the shadows as I could. Chen's place is a huge, double-storey thing, with pillars and posts and awnings, so getting around without being seen wasn't too much hard work.

At one point I paused to peer into the living room. Chen's parents — Jun and Mei — were sitting on the couch watching a repeat of *The Simpsons*. It would have aired hours earlier but Mei tapes everything so she can fast-forward the ads. Chen's mum hates ads more than anyone I've ever met. For her, they're less like something you have to sit through and more like something that happens to you, aggressively. Jun is always teasing her about it.

This'll sound weird, but I could have watched them for hours. I did for a while. Too long, probably. But there was something nice about the way they laughed along with the show, drinking tea, eating chips, holding hands. Sometimes I think Chen doesn't know how lucky he is. He's the only one in the group whose parents are not only still together but are also still in love.

They're also the only parents I know who haven't let their kids down. Leeson's mum only wants to see him every second weekend. My mum does her best, but Dad treats me and Scott like a bag of dog turd in search of a bin. Aaron's dad left too, creating a vacuum for Devin to creep into. Aaron's mum should have protected him. Maybe she had no idea what was going on — I hope to God she didn't — but at the end of the day that doesn't matter. It happened.

I left Jun and Mei with Homer and Marge and cut around the side of the house. Chen's room was on the second floor. A light was on in the room. The window was shut. Chen's place has air con in every room so there's never any need to open one. I looked around for a stone or rock or a bit of bark to toss at his window but the yard was perfectly manicured. Jun has a green thumb and is probably also anal retentive.

I shimmied halfway up a nearby tree, hoping to get Chen's attention, but I stepped down too hard on a branch and the whole thig snapped off. Luckily, it was long enough that if I stood directly below Chen's window and went up on my tiptoes, I could just manage to scrape it against the glass. From inside the room, it must have looked terrifying: gnarled, narrow fingers rapping against the glass.

It worked. The window slid open and Chen's head appeared above me.

'Justin?'

'Can I come up?' I whispered. A second head appeared. 'Leeson?' I was glad to see him. I'd planned on asking Chen to relay everything to Leeson, but this was better.

'What are you doing here, Justin?' he asked.

'We need to talk,' I said, keeping my voice as soft as I could. 'It's about Aaron.'

Chen and Leeson turned to look at each other. Then Chen looked back down and said, 'Meet me at the back door and I'll let you up.'

Chen's bedroom was a mess, as usual. There were little nests of clothes strewn across the carpet and dirty glasses on the windowsill. His poster of Christy Turlington had come off the wall in two places and was folding over itself, but Chen hadn't bothered to fix it. Chen gets away with keeping his room a pigsty because he's an only child. Besides, Jun and Mei hardly ever come upstairs.

The N64 was in the middle of the floor, cords snaking back to the TV. Chen and Leeson had been playing *Mario Kart* when I came in and paused it halfway through Banshee Boardwalk. It seemed weird they'd be playing video games after everything that had happened, but in another way, it wasn't weird at all. I remembered the way Aaron played with his G.I. Joes when he'd come back from the forest.

The three of us sat in a circle: Leeson and I on the floor, Chen in his beanbag. They listened quietly as I told them about my trip to

Aaron's place and everything I'd learned there.

When I was finished, Chen said, 'No offence, Justin, but I wish you hadn't told us any of that.'

'What do you mean?'

'I mean, that is beyond fucked up on so many levels, but — and hear me out — it doesn't actually change anything.'

'How can you say that? This changes *everything*. There's a big difference between covering up an accident and covering up a murder.'

Leeson said, 'What Chen means is, Devin's still dead. If anything, it's more important than ever that nobody finds out.' He lowered his voice. 'You haven't told anyone else about this, have you?'

'No,' I said. 'But I'm going to.'

Leeson glared at me. Chen clamped down on the N64 controller so hard I heard something crack.

'Justin ...'

'It's the only way,' I said. 'If we come clean and explain everything—'

'Our lives will be over,' Chen said.

'Maybe,' I said. 'But if we don't, and it comes out anyway, then we're fucked.'

Chen turned to Leeson and said, 'Can you talk some fucking sense into him?'

Leeson ran a hand through his hair. Grabbed a clump and tugged on it. 'Justin's right,' he said.

'Jesus,' Chen snapped.

'Hear me out, Chen—'

'No,' he said. 'Just no. We promised. We made an oath. If we don't stick to the plan ... you don't understand ... my parents would fucking disown me. They'd ...' He started to cry. Leeson put a hand on his shoulder. Chen sagged under his touch. That's when I knew I'd convinced them both. Where Leeson goes, Chen goes.

'What about Aaron?' Chen asked, so quietly I almost didn't hear him. 'If we confess, maybe — *maybe* — people will get why we did what we did. But Aaron fucking killed a guy. He won't come back from this.'

They both looked at me.

'This'll sound way harsher than I mean it,' I said. 'But that's not our problem. It can't be. Aaron is my best friend and I love him. What Devin did to him is fucked up and unfair and tragic. He shouldn't have done what he did. But neither should Aaron. Now he's asking us to keep a secret that's way too big for any of us to keep, but it's *his* secret, not *ours*. He's asking us to give up our lives.' I started crying now too, because I was scared of what had happened and scared of what came next. 'There needs to be rules.'

What I meant was that without right and wrong, everything unravels and becomes meaningless. I couldn't say that to the guys because I didn't know how. It's so much easier to write about your feelings than talk about them. It is for me, anyway.

Maybe I really will be a writer one day.

At least now I have something to write about.

What I did manage to say out loud was this: 'If we get caught, our lives are over. The lives of our families are over. If we get caught, we'll never get to give our side of the story.' I squeezed my bandaged hand shut. The pain woke me up. 'But if we tell ...'

'We have a chance,' Chen said.

'It's not much, but it's something,' I said.

'When?' Leeson asked.

'Tomorrow,' I said. 'I want to tell Mum first, before I go to the police. You guys should do the same. Tell your people. But first, we need to tell Aaron.'

'To warn him,' Chen said.

'No,' I said. 'We're going to convince him that the only way out of this is to come clean. Then all four of us can do this together.'

'What if he doesn't listen?' Leeson asked.

'Then we'll make him,' I said.

29

NOW

I still had my room at the Golden Fern Motor Inn, so we went there. I offered to take Hannah's jacket. She shook her head and hovered by the door, shifting her weight from one foot to the other as if, at any moment, she might make a break for it. I ached to see her like this: the mother of my child, the love of my life, scared to be around me.

'You can sit down if you like,' I said.

She stood by the door. 'I won't be staying long.'

'I thought you'd be back in Melbourne by now.'

She looked at me almost longingly. 'I've been driving around all day. I drove halfway back to Carlton before I realised I wasn't ready to take this home yet. So I turned around and came right back. I didn't want to stop. Like, if I just keep driving, maybe it won't catch up.' She hesitated. 'I guess that's how you've felt for the last twenty-four years.'

'Have you told anyone, Hannah?' I asked.

There was a pause – heavily pregnant – before she shook her head. I felt a surge of relief so strong that if I hadn't been sitting down on the bed, I might have fallen over. I was getting ahead of myself, of course, but there was still time to fix this.

'Let me be clear,' Hannah said. 'Just because I haven't yet doesn't mean I won't.'

'I understand.'

'Oh, you understand. Good. Thanks.' She turned as if to leave, then planted her feet.

'I shouldn't have told you,' I said. 'If I could take it back …'

She shivered.

'Shit, sorry, I'll put the heat on,' I said.

There was a space heater below the window. I moved to turn it on, but Hannah waved at me to stop.

'Don't,' she said. 'The cold is helping. It hurts, like when you pinch yourself to make sure you're not dreaming.'

'Han, I spoke to Leeson. He thinks we're okay. All the tests came back from the remains, and the cause of death was inconclusive. This could be over.'

Hannah made a sound, something like a sigh or a growl. It was loaded with something. Maybe relief, maybe anger. Probably both. She said, 'And all I have to do is keep my mouth shut.'

I didn't reply. To put it bluntly, she was right on the money.

'Two deaths go unpunished,' she said. 'But you'll go free.'

We all go free or no one does.

'I know it's a lot to ask,' I said.

'It's not *a lot*,' she said. 'It's *everything*.' She looked down at her feet. I waited. 'I'm not going to tell,' she said finally.

I just looked at her.

'I'll keep your secret.'

'Hannah—'

'Don't you dare thank me,' she said. 'I'm not doing it for you. I'm doing it for our daughter. I don't want her to grow up without a father.'

I spread my hands out on the bed for balance. Tears welled in my eyes. A primal scream of relief rose in my throat, but I swallowed it.

This was over.

This was finally, blissfully, wonderfully over.

She'd asked me not to, but I wanted to thank her, knowing those two little words wouldn't be enough. No words in the English language – or any language, for that matter – could convey what she meant to me in that moment. 'Can I hug you?' I asked, feeling childish.

'No,' Hannah said. Her tone was firm and colder than the air. 'You'll never touch me again. You gave me Steffi. But I wish I'd never met you.'

She opened the door. A rush of cold air swept into the room, reminding us both this wasn't a dream. She left without another word, closing the door gently behind her. I went to the window and drew back the curtain. I watched her climb behind the wheel of her RAV4 and drive away.

She didn't look back.

Not even once.

When she was gone, I took out my phone. In the time I'd been talking to Hannah, Leeson had tried calling me three more times. I called him back. He answered on the first ring.

'Why weren't you answering your phone?' he snapped. 'Where the fuck have you been?'

'Chen told you,' I said.

'What the hell were you thinking?'

'I talked to her.'

He was quiet for a beat. Then he said, 'And?'

'Hannah's not going to tell the police,' I said.

'Not right now, maybe,' Leeson said. 'But after she digests it, after she carries it around for a while – Jesus Christ.'

'You have to trust someone, sometimes,' I said.

'Like I trusted you?'

I squeezed the phone. 'I took care of it. It's done. It's over.'

Leeson sighed. 'What if she breaks?'

'She won't.' It was true. I was sure of it. 'Everything's going to be all right, Leeson.'

'We can't take that chance,' he said.

'What does that mean?' Silence. 'What are you saying, Leeson?'

He didn't answer. He wouldn't, not over the phone.

I remembered what Faye had said about him, when she'd called him a desperado. *Only the goddess knows what people like that are capable of.*

'Stay away from Hannah,' I warned.

Another long, heavy silence. Then, 'Or what?'

'Or I'll kill you,' I told him, and meant it.

I ended the call, grabbed my parka and hurried out into the cold.

Without a car, I had to walk. I cut through the World War I memorial gardens, moving at a fast pace. The chill in the air had sharp teeth.

With hands firmly in the pockets of my parka, I started a long steep climb up Castle Creek Hill Road. This hill was, and always had been, a bitch. In the old days, the guys and I would ride up this thing on our bikes, standing up on the pedals, lungs in overdrive. Right now, I was struggling just to walk it. After a few minutes, I no longer felt the cold. My thighs were burning, my neck was starting to sweat. But I didn't stop. I didn't slow down, even. I didn't think I could have if I tried.

I soon found myself at the intersection of Castle Creek Hill Road and Elm Street. Our gang's old meeting place. The same chipped footpath passing underfoot. Running down the side of Elm was the same old concrete channel flushing rainwater to the same gaping storm drain. I looked up the street, half expecting the guys to come riding down towards me. Wouldn't that be something?

There was a big concrete block of flats on the corner. I hit the buzzer for Flat 7, and waited.

I'd told Leeson Hannah wouldn't break and I'd meant it. It had broken me, but she was stronger. No, it wouldn't break her. But it might just ruin her life.

Out on the ledge, she'd told me that telling the truth was the right thing to do, but I'd confessed to the wrong person. It took me all day to understand what she had meant. Now I understood. And now, for the first time in a long time, I was about to do something right.

The buzzer hissed with static. Then a voice said, 'Hello?'

'Hi, Benita,' I said. 'Can I come up?'

The steel gate buzzed open. As I made my way to the front door, a sudden, frightening force built up inside me. I was a long way past the threshold. Beyond the point of no return. The horse had already bolted. The toothpaste was out of the tube. You could pick whichever clichéd metaphor you liked best because they all worked. I had little choice left but to do the right thing.

For Hannah.

And because there had to be rules.

Benita's front door stood out from the rest in the row because it was cluttered with potted plants and a big welcome mat with the words WELCOME: WE HOPE YOU BOUGHT WINE AND DOG TREATS. Benita's dog, a lumpy fox terrier called Spud, had died earlier that year, at the ripe old age of sixteen, so the *dog treats* part wasn't quite accurate anymore. But my guess was she'd get a new dog before getting rid of the mat.

The door opened as I reached it. Benita stepped out to greet me with a warm smile and a glass of red wine. Her red glasses were folded into the collar of her jumper.

'I was wondering when you were going to grace me with your presence,' she said, offering me a one-armed hug so she didn't spill her wine. 'I saw your event listed on Lisa's Instagram so I knew you were in town.'

'I'm surprised I didn't see you there,' I said.

'Technically, I wasn't invited.'

'That didn't stop you crashing my event in Melbourne.'

'Touché,' she said. 'Get inside out of the cold, and excuse the mess, it's my weekend with the boys.'

The boys – Adam, thirteen, Josh, nine – had apparently taken over the flat. Josh was in the middle of creating an elaborate Ikea train set that wrapped around one leg of the dining table before snaking off into one of the bedrooms. Adam, meanwhile, was sitting on the couch in front of the TV, second-screening on his phone.

'Wow,' I told them. 'You two have grown. Adam, are you taller than your mum now?'

'That'll never happen,' Benita said.

'Face it, Mum, it already happened,' Adam said. His voice had broken since I saw him last, which was, to be fair, years ago. He went to his mother and, towering over her, said, 'See?'

'I really need to get some of that anti-growth medication that evil stage mums feed their child stars,' Benita said. Then, turning to her youngest, 'Josh has promised me he's never going to grow up, haven't you, honey?'

Josh didn't look up.

Benita told me, 'He has mastered the art of selective hearing, especially when he's playing with his trains.' Louder, to Josh, she said, 'Haven't you?'

Josh finally noticed her. 'Huh?'

'Go hang out in your rooms so the grown-ups can talk about grown-up things.'

Begrudgingly, the boys did as they were told.

When we were alone, Benita poured me a glass of wine without asking if I wanted one – but let's face it, I would have said yes if she had – and we sat down at the table together.

'They're good kids,' I said.

'They really are.' Benita smiled and looked at their shut doors. Then, turning back, she said, 'What's it like being back in West Haven?'

'Weird,' I said. 'I saw Faye yesterday.'

'Jesus. Crazy Faye. Why?'

'I thought you liked her.'

'I pretended I did when you two started going out,' she said. 'But she was never good enough for you.'

'She was a lot,' I said. 'Still is.'

'She's more than *a lot*, she's too much.' Benita leaned back and sipped her wine. 'But to be fair, I think I was just jealous.'

'Jealous?'

'I was jealous of everyone that took your attention away from me,' she admitted. 'What can I say, I was a weirdo.'

'*Was?*'

'Shut up,' Benita said. 'Did Faye give you that?'

She pointed to the Band-Aid on my head.

'Scott,' I told her.

'Seriously?'

'It could have been worse,' I said. 'He brought a tyre iron but used his fist instead.'

'Want me to beat him up for you?' Benita asked.

'Nah,' I said. 'I deserved it.'

Benita frowned and took my hand. 'No, you didn't.'

I moved my hand away from hers. I didn't want comfort right now.

'I talked to the detective running the case,' I said. 'They ran tests on the remains. They couldn't figure out how he died, but they were able to confirm the body was that of a teenage boy.'

Benita had no reaction. 'You seem surprised,' she said. 'I didn't need to wait for the lab results. I already knew it was him. Didn't you?'

I nodded. 'I knew up here,' I said, pointing to my head. Then, pointing to my heart, 'But in here, I think maybe I was in denial.'

She looked at my wine and asked, 'Do you want something harder?'

I nodded.

She got up, opened the cupboard above the fridge, and brought down two shot glasses and an unopened bottle of tequila. She poured us each a glass. I threw mine back, wincing at the taste but welcoming the warmth. Benita poured me another.

'I love you,' she said. 'But you're not a pop-in kind of guy. You came here for a reason. What is it?'

I took another shot and gestured for another.

'Are you sure?' Benita asked.

I nodded. She poured me another shot. This time I just looked at it.

'You're right,' I told her. 'I did come here for a reason.'

That sudden, frightening force rose in me again. But this time, I couldn't contain it. I burst into tears. It was as if a valve had broken, rupturing the wall of a dam. Benita looked shocked for a moment, then slid her chair around the table to be closer to me.

'Hey, hey, hey,' she whispered. 'What's going on?' She put her hand on my back.

I said, 'I'm sorry, Benita, I—'

One of the bedroom doors opened. Adam peered out with a concerned expression. He must have heard me crying. Benita gave him a cautious smile and said, 'Everything's fine, honey. We just need a little privacy. Go be with your brother, okay?'

Adam stepped out of his bedroom and into the next one along, closing the door quickly behind him. Benita turned her attention back to me.

'Shit, I'm sorry,' I muttered, dabbing at my eyes. 'I didn't mean to come here and do this. This wasn't the plan.'

'Hey, I get it,' she said. 'You still miss him.'

'It's not that,' I said, feeling foggy and dreamlike and wildly unstable. 'Benita, listen, I need to tell you something. When you hear it, everything will change.' I put my hands on the table to steady myself. The world seemed to be tilting beneath my feet. 'You'll never look at me the same way, but you need to know. You *deserve* to know.'

My lips quivered.

More tears came.

Benita took my hand again. She held it more firmly this time. Then she said three little words that rocked me to the core.

'I already know.'

I stared at her.

'What did you say?' I asked. Because I couldn't have heard her right. Right?

'I figured it out a long time ago,' she said. There was no ice in her tone. There was only warmth. 'Or maybe I always knew.'

'Benita …'

'It took me a while to understand it, and there are still parts I don't,' she said. 'It took me longer to come to terms with it.' She squeezed my hand and looked me in the eyes. Then, 'It took me longer still to forgive you.'

For a moment, I couldn't breathe.

I had expected Benita to call me a monster.

I'd never felt love like this before.

When I could breathe again, I said, 'How?'

'How what?'

'How could you possibly ever forgive me for what I did?'

Benita was crying now as well. 'Because it's my job to forgive you, Aaron,' she said. 'What are sisters for?'

30

MONDAY 8 FEBRUARY 1999

It's a school day. Yeah, remember school? I'd practically forgotten it existed. It all seems so pointless now, the stuff I used to worry about and long for and be scared of. I still haven't got around to writing that essay for Mr Wilson's media class about the differences between *The Age* and the *Herald Sun*. Dave Biller is still out for revenge but honestly who even cares anymore? All of these things seemed so important last week. Now they mean nothing.

For those reasons and a million others, I'm not going to school today. Neither are Chen and Leeson. I called Aaron's house late last night after I got home. I told Aaron that we all wanted to meet up to talk about something important. I'd suggested midday at the corner of Castle Creek Hill Road and Elm Street. Aaron said we should meet at the ledge instead. That seems to be our new spot and

★

Sorry. Mum just came in for the fiftieth time this morning. She's worried about me. She knows about Devin's death. Scott told her. Everyone will know soon. Small-town gossip moves faster than a bullet train, and it's only a matter of time before it's on the news. Mum saw a Channel 7 news van parked outside the bakery on Main Road this morning when she nipped out to get bread. Nobody knows the full story yet. But they will soon.

'Are you sure you're okay, honey?' Mum asked. 'I can call in to work and stay home with you instead.'

'I'm fine, Mum,' I told her. But as she started out the door in her smelly West Haven Meats polo, I called after her, 'Mum?'

She turned.

'I said some horrible things to you the other night,' I told her.

'You're forgiven,' she told me.

'Just like that?'

'Just like that,' she said. 'We're all entitled to be arseholes from time to time, Justin. The trick is not making a habit out of it, so when you're my age, you can look back and see you were a good person more than you were a bad one.'

Will I be able to say that when I'm forty?

'All that stuff I said about me not being a kid anymore was true,' I said. 'But the other part, the part about me not needing you …'

She smiled and said, 'Good.'

I smiled back.

Mum reminded me I could call her at work if I needed anything and asked if I was okay at least six more times. Then she left. I sat in the still, hot quiet of my bedroom for a few minutes, then plucked up enough courage to walk across the hall to my brother's door.

I knocked.

'Come in,' Scott called.

I nudged open the door. Scott was sitting up in his bed, reading a book. The windows were wide open, letting in a breeze that was only slightly cooler than the air.

'What are you reading?' I asked.

He held it up. It was *On the Road*, by Jack Kerouac.

'Any good?' I asked.

'It's okay,' he said.

'I don't think I've ever seen you read a book before.'

'It's Bron's favourite,' he said.

I nodded and drifted in. I wasn't sure what to do with my hands, so I put them in the pockets of my shorts. 'So,' I said. 'How are things going with her?'

Scott marked his page, closed the book, and looked at me as if I'd just stolen one of his vital organs. 'We can't do this, Justin.'

'Do what?'

'Talk to each other like nothing happened.'

He was right.

'I'm heading out for a while,' I said. I hesitated. Then added, 'But when I get back, can we talk?'

Scott just looked at me.

'I'm going to need my big brother, Scott,' I said.

He nodded. 'I'm ready when you are.'

Then I told him, 'I love you.'

I'd never told him that before. It's not something you tell your brother. It's not something one guy says to another. You feel it. You know it. But you don't say it. I wonder why.

'I love you too, Justin,' he said.

I smiled at him. 'Pussy,' I said.

'Dickhead,' he told me.

Then I closed his bedroom door and left him to his book.

It's time to go and meet Aaron and the others now. I'm not sure when I'll write in this diary again, but I get the feeling it might not be for a while. My life is about to get pretty hectic. When I leave this desk, I'll be walking into a dark tunnel. But I think there will be a light at the end. That's how tunnels work, right?

Maybe I'll find my way back here. Maybe I won't need to. Maybe if I let it out, I won't have to write it down.

I'm stalling.

I really have to go now.

Wish me luck.

Signing off, Justin Smith.

31

NOW

It was a long walk back to Westlake Drive, but I didn't mind. For the first time in a long time, I had a clear mind. My sister's love had filled me up. Benita and I had never been particularly close as adults. I'd kept my distance from her for the same reason I'd kept my distance from everyone. But she had known the real me for years and loved me anyway. That meant a lot. That meant everything.

There was only one thing left to do.

Confess to the right person.

Impulsively, I flexed my hand as I walked. The one with the scar. I still remembered how the cold blade had felt when I dragged it across the soft part of my hand. I remembered the hot blood spilling out of the opening like a gutted fish and the metallic smell that hit the air. It had meant the world when I was a kid. But now I saw the blood oath for what it was – the actions of a few scared kids.

My car was still parked where I'd left it that morning, across the street from Scott's house. *Scott's house.* That still didn't feel right. I guess it would always be *Justin's house* to me. Scott's Subaru Forester was still in the driveway. The outside light was off, but a pencil-thin sliver of yellow snuck out through a crack in the curtain. Scott was home.

I walked up the path, trotted up the three concrete steps to the front door, and paused. I was sixteen the last time I'd stepped foot in this house. In those days, there was a strict no-knock-necessary policy. But I was pretty sure that if I tried to let myself in now, I wouldn't be leaving alive.

I knocked.

A hunched, skinny shape answered the door, a distorted silhouette behind the flyscreen. Scott stared at me for a long moment, his face mostly hidden in the dark of the interior hallway.

'Hi, Scott,' I said.

'What's wrong with you, Aaron?' he asked.

'Huh?'

'I told you to leave West Haven and never come back. Twice. Instead, you show up at our house. There must be something wrong with you.'

Our house, Scott had said. From what I could tell, he lived alone, but he must have still thought of it as the family home.

'I just want to talk,' I said. 'It won't take long.'

After a long, contemplative moment, Scott reached forward. I flinched, but he was just opening the flyscreen. He stepped aside to let me through.

The exterior of Justin's little L-shaped cottage might have been the same, but it was a different story on the inside. The living room had been stripped back. There was hardly any furniture and no television. All the photos had been removed except for one, standing on the coffee table between a stack of empty pizza boxes and a Dell laptop.

I went to the picture and picked it up. It showed Justin, Scott and their mother smiling for the camera, caught in an eternally happy moment. It looked to have been taken one Christmas morning in this same lounge room.

'I still miss him,' I admitted.

'The only reason you're in my house is because I came at you when you weren't ready,' Scott said. 'Be ready, Aaron. Because if you talk about my brother again …'

'Have you talked to Detective Eckman?' I asked.

Scott nodded cautiously. 'She stopped by on her way out of town,' he said. 'To tell me the case of my brother's murder is unofficially closed. You must be pretty relieved about that.'

I said nothing.

'Do you know what I've been doing for the past twenty-four years, Aaron?' Scott said. 'I've been looking for my little brother. I put posters up. I called hospitals, visited homeless shelters. I followed kidnapping cases and child killings on the internet. Every day for me is the same. Not knowing. That's my life.'

Scott took a step towards me. I held my ground. If he moved to hit me, I'd let him. As if I really had a choice at this stage.

'When the body was found, I thought maybe – *maybe* – I could start to move on,' he said. 'People have been telling me to move on for my entire adult life. Therapists, drug counsellors, strangers in support groups. But when you don't know, you're stuck. When the detective knocked on my door today, I thought I was about to know. But instead, on it goes. On and on and on.'

He looked at his feet and shook his head. His eyes looked hollow. They were the eyes of a broken man.

'Go home, Aaron,' he said. 'Be with your kid, write another bestseller, remarry, travel, live. But know that I'm still here. And know that if I can ever prove you had something to do with Justin's disappearance—'

'I came here to tell you everything, Scott,' I said. 'It's time you knew what happened to your brother.'

32

THEN

I got to the ledge before Justin.

He had called me late the night before, saying we needed to talk, and that we couldn't do it over the phone, sounding secretive and conspiratorial. I was drunk, in that wonderful numb sort of fog that beer put you in, but his tone sobered me up. I agreed to meet.

Then, not two seconds after putting the phone down, it rang again. It was Chen and Leeson. They handed the phone back and forth, talking at me in hushed, urgent whispers. When one talked, I could hear the other in the background, chipping in.

'Slow down,' I said. 'What's going on?'

'Justin came over to my joint tonight,' Chen said. 'He wants to go to the cops.'

If Justin's tone hadn't sobered me up, the part about Justin going to the police certainly would have. I leaned forward and gripped the phone between both hands. The cord it was attached to was the extra-long springy type, so I took it with me all the way into the adjoining laundry and slid the door shut behind me.

'What exactly did he say?' I asked.

They filled me in. He wanted us all to confess together. But he wanted me to agree most of all. That's what our meeting was about. He was panicking. That made sense. I was confident I could talk him down from the ledge (so to speak) but my heart felt like a rock in the pit of my chest.

Mum was still in her bedroom, shifting between crying and unconsciousness and occasionally overlapping the two. Meanwhile, bizarrely, Benita was taking care of every chore in the house. After making a dinner nobody ate, she washed up, scrubbed the stove, cleaned out the oven and was halfway through her third load of laundry. I guess everyone handles grief differently.

For me, I was oscillating between a crippling fear of getting caught and the wonderful relief that Devin was gone. Never again would he stop outside my door in the night. Never again would he pad into my room in Explorer socks, close the door gently behind him, and drift towards me like a vampire. He was a monster. And monsters got slain.

After hanging up with the guys, I thought about calling Faye. I missed her. I didn't know much, but I knew enough to know that meant something. But I also knew that tonight it would be a mistake. In time, maybe Faye and I would make a real go of it, I thought. I turned out to be right about that. But, for now, I found another one of Devin's beers in the fridge and smashed it down.

The next day, I climbed to the ledge alone with a pounding hangover. Justin arrived right on midday, emerging from the tree line puffed from the climb up, red-faced and covered in sweat, flanked by Chen and Leeson.

'Hi, Justin,' I said.

'Hey, Aaron.'

'Dude, I'm sorry about last night,' I told him. 'I was already plastered when you got to my place and I was saying some shit I shouldn't have. To be honest, I can't remember a whole lot about it.'

'You told me the truth,' Justin said. 'Which is sort of what we want to talk to you about. Maybe you should sit down.'

I stayed standing.

'Actually, Justin,' I said, 'maybe *you* should sit down.'

It took him a beat to get it. He watched Leeson and Chen move from his side to mine, which was about as obvious and symbolic as you could imagine. Then, as he realised he hadn't brought me out here to talk but it was in fact the other way around, he deflated. There was a look of deep and pure heartbreak on his face. It killed me. I just wanted things to go back to how they were. Back then, I saw the world through the lens of twisted puberty. Through that lens, we *could* get back to normal. Now, with the benefit of years under my belt, I can see how naive I was.

'What is this, like, an ambush?' Justin said.

'Of course not,' Leeson said.

'A decision like this would have to be, like, anonymous,' Chen said.

'He means *unanimous*,' Leeson said. 'We'd all have to agree, and we don't. We all go free or no one does, remember?'

'But last night you said—'

'Last night we were scared,' Leeson said. 'We were worried that if we disagreed with you, you'd do it anyway.'

Justin shrank. He chewed his lip. His eyes darted between everyone, close to tears.

'Maybe you're right,' he said. 'Maybe we shouldn't turn ourselves in.' He turned to me. 'Maybe you should.'

My damn hangover was killing me. Sunlight belted down on us like little darts of pure agony. Chen and Leeson looked at each other. Was Justin turning them against me? I made a steeple with my hands and pointed it in their direction.

'Look,' I said. 'I know I fucked up. I fucked up bad. But it was a mistake. Devin *hurt* me. But please. I need you. I need all of you. If this gets out my life is over.'

'You're asking us to give up our lives to save yours,' Justin told me.

'You guys are my family,' I said, pleading.

Justin held firm.

My best friend, my enemy.

'No, we're not,' he said. 'We're friends. *Kids.* We're not equipped to deal with this.' He chewed his lip again. He seemed to be choking back tears. He puffed out his chest and turned to the others. A hot wind swept up from the valley, dancing his mop of dark hair around his face.

'I'm going home now,' he said. 'I'm going to tell them everything. My brother, my mum, the police. You can come with me. It'll be better if you do, for everyone. But you should know my mind is made up. I want to do it together, but I'll do it alone if I have to.'

He waited. Leeson hovered anxiously but made no move to follow him. Chen saw that Leeson had made his choice, which made it easier for him to make the same one.

Justin asked them, 'Are you sure?'

Leeson said nothing.

Chen said nothing.

Justin turned his back on us and started towards the trail that would take him down the mountain. He was right. That's what killed me. He was right about everything. But we were a long way beyond right and wrong now.

'I'll say you were in on it,' I said.

Justin stopped just before the tree line.

'I'll say you were there from the start,' I told him. 'I'll say you helped plan the whole thing out. You were in the room when it happened. I'll say you distracted Devin while I did it, that you kept him busy while I snuck up behind him with the hammer.'

Chen and Leeson watched and waited.

'Tell them whatever you want,' Justin said. His eyes were dry now. 'I'm going home.' Then, 'Goodbye.'

'Justin,' I said, taking slow steps towards him. 'I'm sorry.' Another step forward. 'Just … know that much, okay?'

'I know, Az,' he told me.

'No,' I said. 'I mean I'm sorry I can't let you go.'

Justin blinked against the sun. He seemed confused at first. Then he saw the pocketknife in my hand, the one we'd used to cut our palms to perform the blood oath. *We all go free or no one does.* There was a glint of recognition on his face. He knew I wasn't bluffing.

'I wrote everything down in my diary,' he said, his eyes full and fearful now. 'Every detail.' He looked over my shoulder. 'About each of us.' Then back to me, back to the knife, he said, 'If I don't come home my big brother will find it and read it and—'

I pressed the blade into his belly.

Droplets of blood dripped onto the stones underfoot. Perfect little circles of red against the earth. Chen and Leeson began to shout and scream and cry but nothing they were saying made sense to me. It was like they were speaking another language. I looked back at their shocked, gaping expressions.

They looked young. I guess we all did.

Overhead, a flock of cockatoos took flight, drifting over and away from the ledge and over the valley.

Justin didn't look scared or shocked. Surprised, maybe. But more like he was disappointed in me. Not betrayed or outraged or angry. Just disappointed.

'I'm sorry,' I whispered. 'I'm so sorry.'

I fixed him with a regretful but determined look.

Then I stuck the knife in deeper.

Chen and Leeson went on shouting, but neither moved to stop me. Neither did they protest when I grabbed Justin by the shoulders and spun him, forcing him backwards towards the cliff edge. He clutched at my hand, the one holding the knife, clawing and groping at me weakly, but there was no fight left in him. He didn't seem to be in any pain.

A strange warmth radiated out from his body, as if his soul was passing over mine, like ripples on the surface of the West Haven public swimming pool.

I backed him up and out onto the ledge.

He looked at me helplessly, then past me, through me. 'Shh,' he said. 'Do you hear that?'

I didn't hear anything. All the sounds on the mountain had faded, as if the world was waiting to see what happened next, as if the universe was not as indifferent as Faye thought, and as if some mystical hand — *the same hand that passed me the hammer?* — had hit the mute button. 'It's the Oz Factor,' Justin managed. Then, 'That sounds about right.'

I closed my eyes.

Then I let him go.

I kept my eyes closed for a long time, with the heat on my face, with hot blood on my hands. I kept them closed until the cosmic volume came back up. I didn't see him hit the valley floor. But for years after it happened, I had a recurring nightmare. A quiet forest. Still. No wind. The drone of insects. Bird calls. Hot, filtered sunlight. Then, a body falls through the canopy of trees with a series of sharp, frightening snaps. It dangles momentarily — snagged on the jagged branch of a mountain ash — then slips into the greenery below. A whisper-quiet thump against damp earth as the body is swallowed up by ferns.

Then, after a while, the birds start to sing again.

I wonder what Justin's dream book would make of that.

33

NOW

I told Scott most of it, but not everything. I didn't tell him about Justin's diary. I knew he had been keeping one. We'd both agreed to write a journal after reading King's *On Writing* because we both wanted to be writers, but I hadn't held up my end of the deal. If he had lived, he would have made an amazing author, much better than me.

After that day on the ledge, after Justin was reported missing and before everyone in town thought I had something to do with it, I came by the house. I lied my way up to Justin's room. It was easy. I asked his mum if I could go into his room for a while, and she didn't hesitate to let me in. She probably thought I wanted to be around his things, to smell him, to remember him. If so, she would have been partially right.

Scott had been out, spending time with Bronwyn Ross, probably. They became a big item there for a while until they broke up a year or so later. Benita told me Bron had wanted to move away for uni and asked Scott to come with her. But Scott refused to leave West Haven. He wanted to be there in case his brother ever came back.

The floppy disk had been hiding on Justin's desk in plain sight. It was the one marked *JUSTIN SMITH, 9F, COMPUTER STUDIES*. I was his partner in that class. Sitting next to him during one of Mr Paisley's laborious lectures, I'd doodled a drawing of an alien on the label with almond-shaped eyes, flashing the peace sign. I swiped the disk and spent the next twenty-four years trying to get rid of it. But I hadn't been able to bring myself to do it. I couldn't let Justin go. It had been consigned instead to a packing box marked *MISC*.

The other thing I didn't tell Scott was that Chen and Leeson had anything to do with it. A little revisionist history was the least I could do for them. It felt like the tiniest of gestures and decades too late – Justin was right, I had asked them to give up their lives to save mine – but it was the only gift I had to give them. Out of respect for them, I omitted their names. Out of respect for Justin, I told the rest exactly as it happened.

Scott listened to everything. He must have had questions, but he remained silent, absorbing everything. When I had finished, he blinked rapidly as if waking from a decades-long nightmare. Something fell to the carpet with a dull *thud*. A kitchen knife. I hadn't even realised Scott was holding one, nor did I know what he'd intended to do with it. I waited for him to attack me. I even wondered if he might kill me. But he reached out absently for the armchair and then collapsed into it. His face was ghost-white, his eyes dark and red and prickling with tears.

'Why did you tell me?' he asked.

'You deserved to know,' I said.

'I've *deserved* to know for twenty-four years, Aaron.' He wiped his eyes with the back of his hands. 'Why now?'

I thought about that.

Because the truth will set you free.

I know that's a cliché and a writer should know better, but it's a cliché for a reason. This was the only way any of us could be free. Chen, Leeson, Hannah, Scott. Even me. Yes, there were likely concrete walls and steel bars in my future, but I'd been living in a prison for all of my adult life.

'Because there have to be rules,' I said.

Scott didn't bother wiping his tears now. He let them flow. 'I knew,' he said. 'I always knew. I thought about killing you, you know.'

'Why didn't you?'

'Because then your suffering would stop,' he said. 'And I do hope you suffer, Aaron. I hope you never sleep again.'

I was crying too, now.

'How did you know?' I asked.

A lot of people in West Haven turned on me after Justin disappeared. It was too much that my stepdad was murdered and my best friend went missing in the span of a few days. The rumours were inevitable, but as time went on they quietened. Scott never let it go, though.

'Because Justin was keeping a secret,' Scott told me. 'And the only other person he'd keep a secret for, besides me and my mum, was you.' Then, 'You were his family too, Aaron.' Then, 'You were as much his brother as I was.'

His words were a gunshot to the chest.

'What now?' I asked.

'Now,' Scott said. 'I'm going to call the police.'

I nodded. 'If it's okay with you,' I said, 'I'll wait for them outside.'

The weather on Westlake Drive had cleared, and a big blanket of stars had rolled out. The air was still freezing, but that was good. The cold reminded me that this was real. The pinch to know you weren't dreaming. I unlocked the Prius and took something out of my overnight bag. Then I sat down in the gutter outside Justin's house, turned on my phone and made a call.

Tim answered on the fourth ring. He sounded surprised to hear from me. 'Aaron?'

'Hi, Tim,' I said. 'I know it's late, but I need to talk to Steffi.'

'She's just hopped into bed, mate. Can it wait until tomorrow?'

'No, it can't,' I said. 'It'll only take a second, Tim.' I hesitated. 'Please.'

Tim sighed and said, 'Yeah, of course, I'll give her the phone.'

Steffi was on the line a few seconds later. 'Hi, Dad,' she said.

'Hey, sweetie, how are you?'

'I'm okay. Are *you* okay? Because your voice is all wobbly.'

I smiled. 'God, it's good to hear your voice.'

'Did you talk to Mummy?'

'Mummy's fine,' I said. 'She's coming home. I bet she'll be there when you wake up in the morning. Speaking of' – I checked my watch – 'it's past your bedtime.'

'I'm not tired.'

There were sirens in the distance. The police would be here soon. Leeson might be among them. Detective Eckman was probably pulling a U-turn and on her way back to West Haven.

I looked at the long-faded scar on the palm of my hand, then at the floppy disk I was holding. It was the only thing connecting Chen and Leeson to everything, but it was also all I had left of Justin.

I dropped it into the mouth of a drain. It disappeared in a torrent of rainwater. It had been raining on and off in West Haven since I got here. The gutters were swollen with water, moving rapidly like a tiny, wild river. A small yellow ping-pong ball glided down the gutter on the opposite side of the street, turning over and over in the baby rapids. I wondered where it had come from. It was the same colour as the moon.

'Huh,' I said to nobody. 'Moon River.'

Maybe Faye wasn't as crazy as I thought.

'Hey, Daddy?' Steffi said.

'Yeah, honey?'

'Will you help me get to sleep?'

'Sure,' I said. 'Want me to sing you a night-night song?'

'Yeah,' Steffi said. Then added, 'If you want.'

It was the only thing I wanted in the world, so as the police sirens grew louder and closer, I sang my daughter a lullaby. I looked at the mountain – a dark looming shape now. I thought about the ledge, about the endless blanket of green that rolled out beneath it, and how your stomach lurched when you climbed to the edge to look over. I thought about my childhood, about everything I'd lost and everything I'd taken away. I never really came back down from the ledge. Until tonight.

AUTHOR'S NOTE

It's been a long time. Too long. *Wild Place* came out in '21 and we're now approaching the pointy end of '24. But I have not been resting on my laurels. Between books, I've written two films and a handful of television shows, and co-authored another novella with my wife. And eclipsing all that other stuff is this: I'm a dad now!

To say I've had my hands full is an understatement. That's why I'm a little behind on replying to your emails. If you've sent me a message and haven't heard back yet, please know that I read and cherish each and every one ... except for the mean ones.

While you're here, I'd like to tell you a little bit about the inspiration behind this book. But first, a confession: when I'm writing a novel, I usually have no idea what it's about. *None*. I know what happens, I understand the characters, and the twists are pretty fleshed out in my head, but I don't understand what the story is actually about until the manuscript is finished. I'm too lazy to consider *themes* and *meaning* while I'm working. I let that stuff bubble up naturally. I'm less a *writer* and more a *courier*, delivering a package from the back of my mind to the front of your eyeballs without getting a really good look at what's inside.

But with *The Ledge*, things were a little different. This is the most personal book I've ever written, and not just because the protagonist is an author in his forties who writes thrillers. The writing process was more organic this time around. It felt like I was finding a story that was already there rather than making one up. And I actually knew what I *wanted* it to be about this time. A crime thriller about the inevitable death of childhood!

Cool, right?

And don't get me wrong – this book *is* that – but it's about a lot of other stuff, too. That stuff caught me by surprise. I hadn't got such a good look inside the package, after all.

See, originally, there was no modern-day storyline in this book. It was just about four boys going through the hell of puberty, a love letter to two of the greatest books of all time: William Golding's *Lord of the Flies* and Stephen King's *It*. It was never about *my* childhood exactly, but I drew from it. When I was Justin Smith's age, I was a weird kid. I dressed in black, dyed my hair crazy colours, and carried my books around in an old bowling ball bag. All of that made me a pretty easy target for bullies. I survived with the help of a small – and equally weird – band of friends. I thought a lot about those friends when I started writing and realised how tragic it was that I hadn't talked to any of them in years (aside from Angie, who I saw at a Morrissey concert). How can someone mean everything to you when you're a kid, yet somehow become a stranger when you turn into a grown-up? I thought about the four friends at the heart of this story and wondered if they'd still be friends when they were my age (those who survived, I mean). Then I sat down and wrote what would become the first chapter of this book.

See, I knew I was writing a story about boys.

I didn't know I was writing a story about *men*.

That's it for now. Thank you for reading this far. Thank you for your reading at all. One of the single greatest things about being a writer is connecting with you, so if you have questions or comments or just want to say hi, you can contact me through my website, christian-white.com (I don't use social media anymore). I couldn't do what I do without you. From the bottom of my heart, thank you for reading this book. I'll try not to make you wait so long for the next one.

ACKNOWLEDGEMENTS

I couldn't have written this book without the help of many wonderful people: Martin Hughes, Keiran Rogers, Ruby Ashby-Orr, Laura Franks and all the other amazing people at Affirm Press; Jenn Naughton and Candice Thom and the rest of the crew at RGM; all the incredible booksellers around the country who sell the shit out of my books; and Adam Waddell, who gave me the title for this one. Big thanks to my dear friends and family, and my second mum, Chris DeRoche.

Huge thanks also to my mum and dad, Keera and Ivan White. As far as parents go, I hit the jackpot. But today I'm going to single out my old man. Since becoming a father, I've thought a lot about my own. William Makepeace Thackeray said 'mother' is the name for God on the lips and hearts of all children, but 'father' is a close second. Ivan White is the model of a perfect dad. He continues to show me what it is to be a good man.

Speaking of dad stuff, my life changed the moment Zaleese joined our family. Parenthood makes everything more complicated, but it also makes everything really simple. The complicated part is keeping a human being alive while maintaining a career and relationships and still making time to read the latest Stephen King. The simple part is this: when you view life through the lens of your kid's wellbeing, everything is clear. Who cares about a bad review if you can make your daughter laugh with a dumb joke? Why worry about a bad note from a producer when you can put your phone away and watch *Dragon Riders* together?

Thank you for that, Zaleese. And for everything else.

Last but not least, I want to thank my wife. What can I say, Sum? You don't just make my books better; you make *me* better. One of the greatest joys of the last few years has been seeing you grow as a writer, a mother and a human being.

Now for the sad part. Between this book and the last, we lost our beautiful greyhound, Issy. Saying goodbye to you was the single hardest moment of my life. You were my best friend and constant companion. Writing just isn't the same without you beside my desk. To anyone reading this who has a pet, go and give them a pat from me. To Issy, if you're out there somewhere – and I think you are – *good girl, good girl.*

BOOK CLUB QUESTIONS

1. Do you think that the four boys' friendship would have lasted if not for the events of February 1999?
2. "'That's the kind of quiet West Haven is,' he said. 'The kind that makes people do crazy things.'" How does the author use the setting of the story to build atmosphere and feed the plot?
3. Does this novel have a hero, and if so, who is it?
4. Consider how the author has used both a modern narrative and an old diary to tell this story. Do you think these two narratives give us the full picture?
5. What do you think of the parental figures in the novel? How are they depicted, and how responsible is each for what happens to their sons?
6. Arguably, this is a story about trauma. What kinds of trauma do we see at play in this novel, and how do they impact the story?
7. Is Aaron's behavior in any way justified by his experiences?
8. 'He'd make me take my medicine eventually, but right there and then, I enjoyed the feeling of sticking it to him. It felt, I'm guessing, like how it must feel to be a man.' Considering the events of the book as a whole, what do you think the author is suggesting about masculinity and the experience of growing into a man?
9. Did your feelings about the characters change in the final chapters? If so, how?
10. Did you find the ending tragic, or happy? (Or both?)

READ THE PROLOGUE OF

WILD PLACE

PROLOGUE

Friday

8 December 1989

'The existence of Satan is a matter of belief, but the existence of Satanism is undeniable. Darkness lurks behind the lyrics of your child's favourite song, on the shelves of your local video store, in the homes, schools and parks of every small town across the country. In tonight's Special Look, *we'll be diving deep into the dangerous and troubling world of devil worship. It's an epidemic and spreading fast. Nobody is safe. Especially not your—'*

Nancy Reed muted the TV. It didn't make much difference. There was still plenty of noise in her head. She was doing the two things guaranteed to bum a person out on a Friday night: drinking alone and reflecting on her life.

Somewhere along the way, something had gone wrong. She was forty-one, unemployed, and staring down the barrel of a divorce. But when she looked back, performing a kind of post-mortem on her life, there were no obvious signs of trouble. There was just a series of wrong turns and bad decisions. The cause of death, it seemed, was life.

It was coming up on 11pm. That was late, for suburbia. Her daughter was sleeping over at a friend's house and her husband – *ex*, she reminded herself – was in a budget room at the Camp Hill Motor Inn, where he'd moved while they finalised the divorce. Nancy was alone, free to fall into a pit of despair and self-pity.

On the coffee table in front of her lay *The Camp Hill Leader*, open to the employment section. Her yellow highlighter sat beside it. She hadn't even needed to take the cap off. The only jobs she seemed qualified for were night filler, check-out chick and flipper of burgers, and she wasn't that desperate. Yet. The problem with being a stay-at-home mother was that none of her skills translated to the workplace. Seventeen years of child rearing should have qualified her for a job as a hostage negotiator or an upper-management position in a psychiatric hospital.

It was Owen's fault. He had insisted Nancy stop work. He was old-fashioned that way. Or maybe he just needed something to excuse his bad behaviour. Maybe he knew that when someone depends on you for everything, it's harder for them to leave.

Feeling bitter, she drank more.

Creak.

The noise came from somewhere behind her. She spun around to look over the armchair. Most of the lights in the house were off – she'd be paying the electricity bills herself soon and wanted to get used to keeping costs down. The TV cast wavering shadows across the walls. There was nobody there. At least nobody she could see.

Nancy stood in the dark and listened. There it was again: a soft metallic *click*, a long, slow *creak*. A window in one of the other rooms was being slid open from the outside. She crept through the kitchen and stood in the mouth of the hallway.

Silence.

Before creeping down to the end of the house to investigate, she went right past the rack of hefty frying pans and the block of Ginsu kitchen knives, which were sharp enough to slice through a leather shoe – *but wait, there's more!* – and armed herself with the *Yellow Pages*.

A gun would work better. There was one in the house, a rifle Owen used to hunt rabbits when he visited his cousins – they lived up north, directly in the middle of arse-fuck and nowhere – but the gun was at the other end of the house, on the top shelf of her wardrobe, in a locked case. The key was in the pocket of her ex-husband's jeans, which were now, no doubt, slung over a chair in a room at the motor inn.

Nancy briefly considered calling him, but decided she'd rather be dismembered and left in a shallow grave than give him the satisfaction. As much as she hated to admit it – and never would, out loud – Nancy missed having a man around at times like this. She was getting the hang of being a single mother, but sometimes wished it came with an add-on option. A male she could send blindly ahead of her, into danger.

She reached into the dark and flicked on the light, relieved to find there was no psycho killer waiting there for her. She held the phone book aloft and moved steadily down the hall. Halfway, she heard movement. A light blinked on somewhere. A pencil-thin sliver glowed beneath one of the doors. Tracie's bedroom. Two more steps, then the sound of drawers being opened and rifled through. If they – whoever *they* were – had been ransacking any of the other rooms, Nancy might have snuck to a neighbour's house to call triple zero.

But they were in her daughter's room. Common sense abandoned her and white-hot rage swept in. She raised the phone book high with her right hand. With her left, she took hold of the knob and swung the door open.

In the middle of the room stood a small, slight woman with a striking sweep of blonde hair, bleached so recently that Nancy could smell the chemicals wafting off her.

'Tracie?'

Nancy's daughter let out a court-room gasp, scrambled backwards so fast she knocked a stack of cassettes off her side table, then sighed with relief. 'Jesus, Mum, you scared me.'

'*I* scared *you*? I thought you were an intruder.'

'And you were planning on calling him a taxi?'

Nancy exhaled, smirked and lowered the phone book. 'What happened to your hair?'

When Tracie had left earlier that evening, she'd been a brunette. A pretty, effortlessly natural brunette. She'd come home looking like Debbie Harry. 'I felt like a change. Like a statement. Do you like it?'

'I do.' She didn't. 'You know, most kids sneak *out* of their bedroom window. Not the other way around.'

'I forgot my key and didn't want to wake you.'

'I thought you were spending the night at Cassie's.'

'We had a fight.' Tracie stepped out of her sneakers. 'How's the job hunt going?'

'It isn't.'

'Good,' Tracie said. 'You don't need to find a job; you need to find a man.'

'I'd rather blow my own brains out, but thanks anyway.'

'Come on, Mum. You're still pretty and funny and young. *Ish.*'

'Your dad's side of the bed is still warm.'

'But I won't be around forever,' Tracie said.

That stung in a way Nancy hadn't been expecting. It was true, of course. Tracie had just finished high school. She was off to university next year, and then there would be work and boyfriends and weddings and children, and Nancy would eventually die alone.

But that's not what bothered her. Correction: that's not what was bothering her in that moment. It was something in Tracie's tone. *I won't be around forever.* It was the kind of thing a parent said to a child, not the other way around. Since the separation, Tracie had aged. That was a strange thing to say about a seventeen-year-old, but it was true. Her eyes had darkened.

'Your father and I will be fine,' she said. 'You don't have to worry about us.'

'I'm not worried about Dad. Not in that way, at least. He'll marry the first bimbo he meets.'

'He's not like that.'

'He's a survivor, Mum.'

'If he's a survivor, what does that make me?' Nancy asked.

Tracie shook her head. 'I just hate to think of you living in this big house all by yourself.'

Nancy sighed, then sat down on the bed and helped Tracie under the covers. A whisper of warm air drifted in through the open window.

'So,' Nancy said. 'Talk to me about the hair.'

'What about it?'

'Usually when a woman does something this dramatic, it's because she's lost control of something major in her life and this is her way of taking back that control. Oh no, you did that because of the divorce, didn't you?'

Tracie raised a smile but it fell away fast. 'It has nothing to do with you, Mum. This'll probably sound crazy, but I wanted to look like someone else. I ... I think someone's been following me.'

Nancy sat forward.

'A few nights ago, someone called the house,' Tracie explained. 'When I picked up, whoever was on the other end of the line didn't say anything, but I could hear them breathing. And since then I've just had this feeling, you know, like I was being watched. The other day, at the roller rink. And then again tonight at the movies.'

Nancy waited. Then she asked, 'Is that it?'

'*Is that it?*'

'Did you actually see anyone?'

Tracie glared at her. 'Not exactly.'

'Is it possible all your spying has made you a little paranoid?'

'I don't *spy*, Mum. I capture truth. That's like, journalism 101.'

'I'm sorry, honey, but you often do this.'

'Do what?'

'Last month you were convinced someone was outside your window, scratching on the glass, but the noise magically went away when I pruned the lemon tree. The month before that, you thought a poltergeist was moving things around the house, until we discovered the window in the spare bedroom had been left open. You have a rich imagination, Trace. It's one of the things that makes you unique. But it also makes you ...' Nancy chose her next word wisely. 'Reactive.'

'You sound like Cassie. She says it's because I'm an only child and we need more attention.'

'I hate to say it—'

'Then don't.'

'—but Cassie might have a point.'

'I hate you.'

'I love you too. Is that what you and Cassie fought about?'

'Actually, the fight was about you and Dad.' Tracie's expression hardened. 'Mum, I'm going to ask you a question now and I want you to tell me the truth. Don't sugar-coat it, don't placate, and don't give me some vague, rambling non-answer like you and Dad usually do.'

'I'm not even sure I know what *placate* means.'

'Mum. I'm serious.'

She meant it. Nancy could see that, and it made her nervous.

'It's about the divorce,' Tracie said. 'Did Dad ... Was he ...' She paused to compose herself. 'Was there someone else?'

Tracie Reed went missing the next day.

ALSO AVAILABLE BY CHRISTIAN WHITE

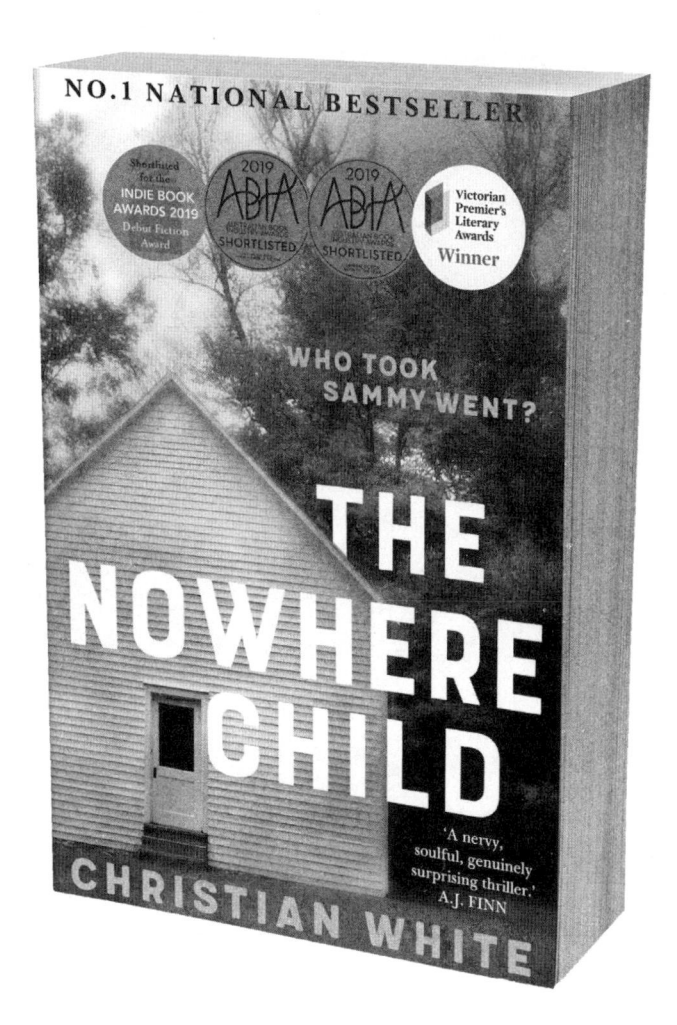

'Her name is Sammy Went. This photo was taken on her second birthday. Three days later she was gone.' *The Nowhere Child* is a combustible tale of trauma, cult, conspiracy and memory.

ALSO AVAILABLE BY CHRISTIAN WHITE

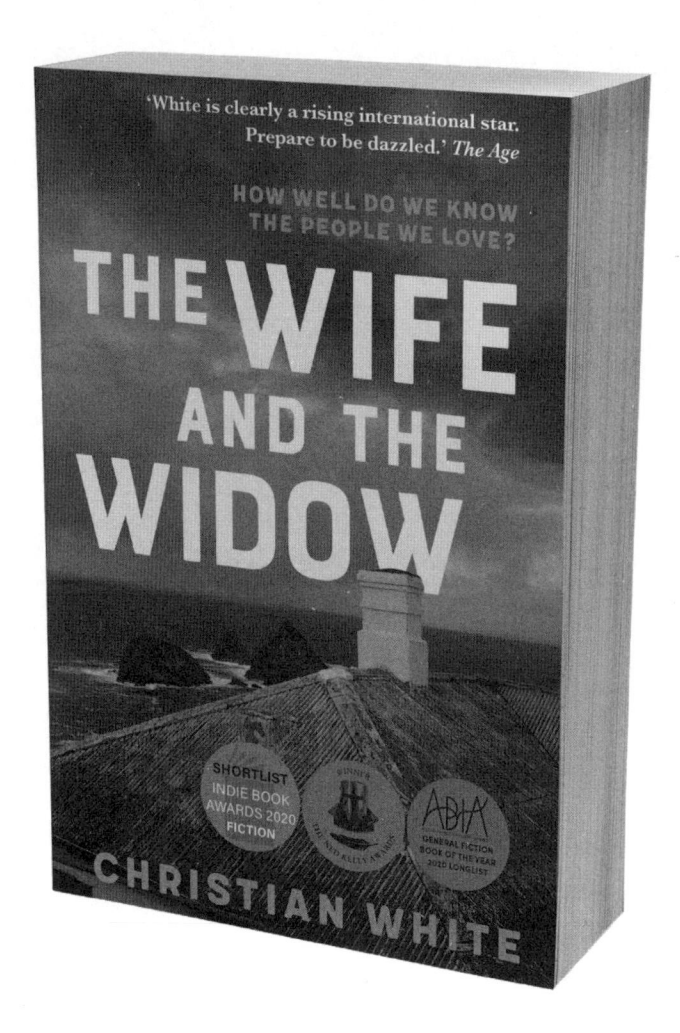

Set against the backdrop of an eerie island town in the dead of winter, *The Wife and the Widow* takes you to a cliff edge and asks the question: how well do we really know the people we love?

ALSO AVAILABLE BY CHRISTIAN WHITE

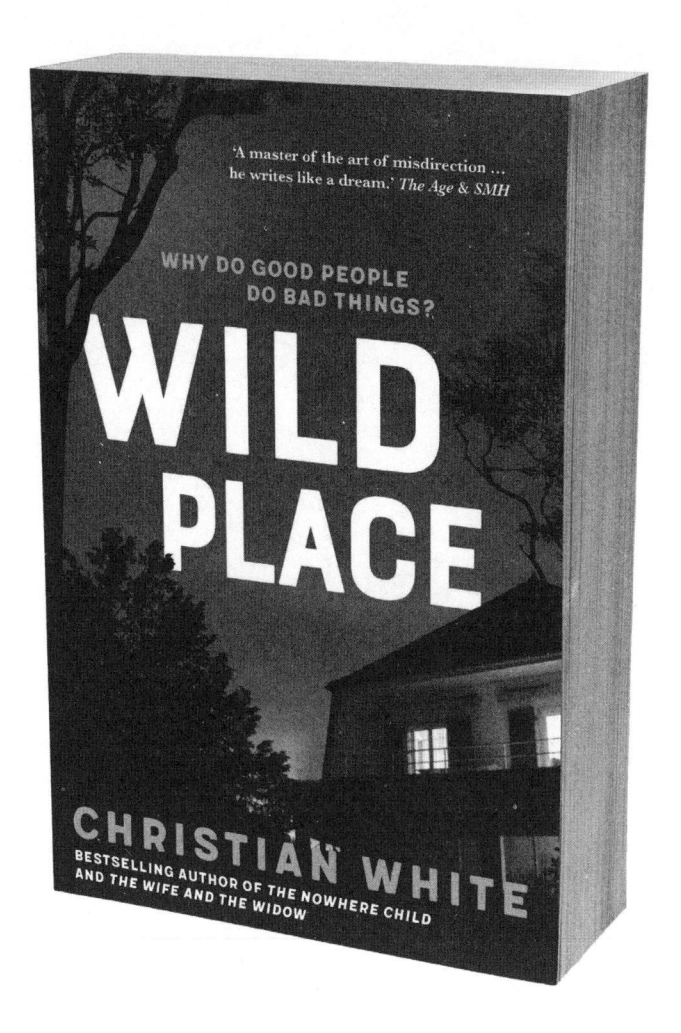

In the era of Satanic panic, a local teen goes missing from the idyllic suburb of Camp Hill in Australia. *Wild Place* peels back the layers of suburbia, exposing guilt, desperation and violence, and attempts to answer the question: why do good people do bad things?